PACT OF SEDUCTION

Stacey Kennedy

LooseId.

ISBN 13: 978-1-62300-463-7
PACT OF SEDUCTION
Copyright © 2014 by Stacey Kennedy

Cover Art by Valerie Tibbs
Cover Layout and Design by April Martinez

Publisher acknowledges the author and copyright holder of the individual works, as follows:
BIND ME
Copyright © October 2011 by Stacey Kennedy
BEG FOR IT
Copyright © May 2012 by Stacey Kennedy
BET ON ECSTASY
Copyright © September 2013 by Stacey Kennedy

Printed in the U.S.A. by
Lightning Source, Inc.
1246 Heil Quaker Blvd
La Vergne TN 37086
www.lightningsource.com

Contents

BIND ME

DEDICATION

For Christy and Crystal, who welcomed me to a new family and made me feel at home.

CHAPTER ONE

Aching feet, too many martinis, and dancing the night away at a club located in the heart of Baltimore led Marley to this moment—her twenty-fifth birthday celebration, to be exact. She plopped down on one of the pillows along the floor, surrounded by her three best friends. The two-story colonial-style house located in the quiet eastern neighborhood of the city had been home to all of them since college.

"Okay, girls, I have an idea," Bella said.

Sadie's large breasts—thanks to Dr. Lee—bounced as she squirmed on her pillow. "Oh...do tell."

"I can hardly wait to hear what you've come up with now." Kyra snorted, flipping her black silky hair over her shoulder.

As usual, Marley didn't know what Bella was up to. She always attempted to make their lives interesting. "Okay, spill it. What trouble have you planned for us now?"

"Well." Bella's crystal blue eyes sparkled with wicked intentions. "Life has been boring lately, right?"

"Mm hm," Marley responded. That was an understatement. Not saying her job at the elementary school didn't fulfill her. Heck, she'd worked hard to get the full-time position as a sixth-grade teacher. Yet her life held no spunk. Same routine. Normal hours. Nothing ever changed.

Sure, Marley had had a few boyfriends, but none of them made her feel anything but friendship, and she grew tired of searching for Mr. Right when they all ended up being Mr. Wrong. She'd given up dating altogether a year ago.

"Let's make a pact of seduction," Bella said.

Sadie spit out her wine, and it sprayed on Marley's face. "Oh shit, Marls. I'm so sorry."

Marley groaned as the warm liquid dripped off her nose. She wiped her face, annoyed, yes, but too stuck on what Bella had said to care. "What do you mean a pact of seduction?"

"Exactly what you think I mean. We each have to fulfill our hottest fantasy. You know, the one you've always wanted to do but never thought possible. You've got to make it far past what you think you are capable of, something only imaginable in your dreams."

"You can't be serious!" Kyra exclaimed.

Bella frowned. "Of course I'm serious. Come on, let's ruffle things up a bit. We're all single. Marls is twenty-five now, and the rest of us are all approaching our birthdays too. In a few years we'll likely be married with kids. All settled down with a life more *normal* than the one we live now. Let's do something crazy, fulfill our ultimate fantasy while we still have the chance." She paused.

Marley blinked.

Bella continued. "Two rules: the first, no judging. We're here to help each other find our fantasy, not laugh at it. The second, whoever commits cannot back out. Friends' oath."

Marley looked to Sadie, who shrugged, but her eyes showed undeniable interest. Kyra nibbled her bottom lip. What to do? Could Marley make such a pact? Their friends' oath was solid and unyielding. The exact reason their friendship held so tight. They'd never broken a vow to each other, and Marley did have a fantasy.

She spent her days guiding youths to do right, and had always been the one in control—she wanted to give that all up. She wanted a man to show her how to behave properly, and punish her for her disobedience. A man who had a body she could drool over, maybe even smoldering eyes, and one who could lift her tall frame with little effort. Add sex into the equation and heat exploded into every molecule of her body.

Before she agreed to anything, Marley needed to see if this had been just another thought passing through Bella's busy mind or if she meant what she said. "Exactly how do we decide who goes first?"

"We draw straws." Bella grinned.

"Draw straws to get *it* on." Kyra laughed.

"Yes, exactly," Bella retorted. "Tell me you're not a little interested. We'd never fulfill our fantasy alone, or be brave enough to do it. So let's make a pact. I don't know about you all, but I'm bored as hell. I need something to spice up my life. Don't you?"

Marley considered this. If she made the pact with her best friends, there would be no escape. Did she have the strength to make good on her word? She glanced around to her friends, and excitement showed on their faces, even Kyra's. Marley would let her hesitations go too.

This was her chance to do something she'd never do if not forced. Maybe this could be a turning point for her. A way to break this boring cloud that had settled over her life, and maybe she could meet a man who could stir something more than friendship-level feelings. She drained the rest of her chardonnay, wiped her mouth, and smiled. "I'm in. What do we do next?"

Bella took a pad of paper and a pen off the end table and handed each of the women a sticky note. "We write our fantasies down; then we'll share them." She lowered her head, and Marley did the same.

By the time it was Marley's turn to read her fantasy, she had discovered Kyra wanted two men, Sadie wanted a firefighter, and Bella had an interest in being with a woman.

When all eyes focused on her, Marley cringed. She had a hard enough time thinking these thoughts, let alone voicing them. "I can't read this to y'all."

"Oh, it's gotta be good." Bella snatched up the paper and read the note. "Our Marley here wants to be dominated."

"You do?" Sadie asked.

"Like bondage, sadomasochism, that type of stuff?" Kyra interjected before Marley could respond to Sadie.

"Well..." Marley suspected her cheeks burned red. "I'm not sure what I want because I don't know much about BDSM, but I like the idea of being told what to do and having someone else in control of my pleasure."

All heads nodded, and in unison they said, "Sexy."

Bella jumped up, then ran into the kitchen. A moment later, she returned holding four straws. "The shortest straw goes first, and so on. Here, Kyra, you're up."

Kyra pulled one that could be the tallest, but at this point, it was only guessing.

Bella held the straws out for Marley. "You next, Marls."

Marley took a straw and grumbled at the small size, barely measured up to her pinky finger. Okay, she'd agreed; however, she didn't want to go first. She didn't think her friends would bail out, and she didn't plan to either, but she wanted to go somewhere in the middle. A comfortable place to be.

Sadie took her straw, measuring the size of her index finger. Then Bella raised hers. "Hold 'em up, ladies."

Marley looked from straw to straw, then realized she'd picked the wrong damn straw. Bella was next, then Sadie, with Kyra picking the largest straw. Smiling faces looked at Marley, and she groaned. "Oh no."

"Oh yes." Bella beamed. "You're up, buttercup." She practically ran over to the computer desk, only to return with her laptop a moment later. "And I've got the perfect place in mind."

"What place?" Marley scooted toward her as Bella clicked away on the keyboard. "And how long have you been planning this?"

"Oh, not long, just a week or so," Bella replied. "When I did some research on fantasies, I discovered this place in Bowleys Quarters."

On the small screen, a Web site with a castle decorating the background and big, black, bold letters on the top read, *Castle Dolce Vita.* "What is it?"

"A sex club."

Kyra's eyes went huge. "A what?"

"Don't get your granny panties all in a bunch." Bella shushed her with a flip of her hand. "They have forums where you can contact people who have similar interests as you do"—she wiggled her eyebrows—"sexually."

"Ew." Kyra groaned. "This sounds really dirty."

Bella ignored her as she usually did when Kyra protested one of her plans. "I was reading here. The rules are: all participants must sign a waiver form to insure privacy will be kept while at the castle. No cameras allowed and no videotaping permitted. All participants must provide a clear STD and AIDS test and a background check to the members they're involved with before they are allowed to engage in sexual acts. And lastly, when members are involved in club life, they're not allowed to engage sexually with anyone outside of the castle."

Bella stopped reading and glanced to Marley. "Sounds safe to me."

Marley looked to Kyra, waiting for her to disagree, but she only shrugged. "It sounds safer than if you went to a bar and slept with some random guy."

"Oh God." Marley grumbled, dropping her head into her hands, realizing the inevitable had fallen upon her.

"Ha." Sadie giggled. "Let's just hope you'll be saying that when you're with the guy."

The others laughed. Marley didn't. She raised her head, full of apprehension. "Do I have to go first? Can't one of you?"

Bella scowled. "Fate decided, and you've got to listen. Follow the rules, remember."

"Yeah, yeah, I remember."

Sadie squirmed closer to Bella to look at the computer screen. "So what do we do to become members of the castle?"

"The rules say it's by invitation only," Bella replied. "We have to join the forum, write a letter from Marley describing who she is and what she wants, then wait for someone to call to discuss the possibility of an encounter."

Kyra snatched the laptop from Bella and settled it onto her lap. "Let me write the letter. We want to make you sound sexy but smart. We don't need some lunatic responding to you." She rubbed her hands together. "Now then, let's make this good."

Stone walls didn't give the air of a warm room, nor did the cold cement on the floor, but it set the mood perfectly for the BDSM scene. Reed circled his submissive as she stood atop a wooden box in the center of the bare room.

Zoie was good and obedient. The nipple clamps pinched her areolae hard, just as Reed wanted. He tugged on one to induce a mild amount of pain, and Zoie whimpered, yet not in a way that made him hesitate—she sounded too desperate. Reed had enough confidence to know she needed more than he could give her.

Not every sub Reed played with could tolerate the pain Zoie managed. He enjoyed pushing her limits because she could take the overload. He added two weights to the chain that connected the nipple clamps. Zoie's gaze burned with desire as she hissed.

"I think I'll leave you waiting for a while." Reed strode toward the other side of the room. He grabbed the plastic bottle off the metal tray containing the sex toys, and drank the lukewarm water as his gaze scanned the small space. The old American country estate, Castle Dolce Vita, catered not only to BDSM but to all desires.

By day he was a criminal lawyer, but on evenings and weekends, the BDSM floor had become his home since his lifestyle submissive, Samantha, left him two years ago. He'd loved; he'd lost. He wouldn't make the same mistake again.

Just as he placed the bottle back on the tray, the door to the room opened. "You were looking for me."

Reed glanced over his shoulder to find his good friend and roommate Kole drenched in sweat and running a hand through his blond hair to wipe off the perspiration. Kole punished harder than Reed. Reed used floggers and crops, among other toys, but he refused to make the sub bleed or leave bruises, while Kole delighted in granting such pleasures.

Kole took a quick glance at Zoie before he looked back to Reed with curiosity in his eyes. "What did you want?"

Reed understood his friend's inquisitiveness—it wasn't often he called Kole into a scene. "She's outgrown me, and I think you'd be better suited to her."

"Sounds interesting." Kole all but purred. "Tell me about her."

"She's got a high tolerance for pain, and I can tell she needs, craves more, but you know it's not my thing."

"But it's mine." Kole grinned.

Reed held no jealousy, mainly because he'd never had the connection with Zoie to warrant it. If he needed to put his submissive with another dom to satisfy her, he would. No questions asked.

"Well, well. Let's go have a look, shall we." Kole stepped over to Zoie. Her breathing hitched when he ran his hand over her hip. He gave her ass a light slap, and Zoie squealed.

Reed settled near her, expected her to focus on him. When she didn't, he issued a demand. "Zoie, look at me." He grasped her jaw and squeezed firmly. "Tonight was our last night together."

She shook her head. He tightened his grip, putting a stop to her disobedience. "Kole will take you on. You're safe with him. I would not give you to just anyone."

Zoie's gaze flickered over to Kole, and excitement lit her eyes. Reed squeezed her jaw again, drawing her attention back to him. "You've been a good girl, and I've enjoyed my time with you. I offer you Kole as a reward for how much you've pleased me." He kissed her cheek. "Be a good girl for Kole too."

"I will, Sir," Zoie responded.

Reed stepped away just as Kole slapped Zoie's ass with another light hit. Her eyes closed, and she moaned. The reaction from her confirmed Reed had done the right thing. He grinned at Kole, and Kole smiled back.

He turned on his heels and proceeded to leave the room. As he opened the door, he heard Zoie's screams echo against the stone walls. Kole laughed. "I'm going to enjoy you, sweet Zoie."

The door closed behind Reed, and silence fell around him as he made his way toward the restaurant. He was satisfied he'd done right by Zoie. However, a thought stayed in his mind: what now, and more importantly...who?

He passed through the dining room in the castle, entered the restaurant, and emptiness greeted him. At this late hour, the only other person here was the barkeep. He took a seat on the stool in front of the black marble countertop where the laptop was located, and the bartender handed him his usual choice of beverage, a cold beer.

Reed took a long swig before he clicked the mouse on the laptop to venture into the BDSM forum. He scrolled down the messages and was not surprised at what he found. *Woman looking for dom. Slave ready and willing.*

Minutes drew on as he read through them, one by one, and nothing jumped out as an interest. Frustrated, he raised his beer to his mouth again, and as the liquid filled his throat, his gaze landed on something that spiked his curiosity.

The seduction pact! Indulge my fantasy!

He placed his beer back on the bar and clicked on the message. First he saw the words but didn't pay the note any attention because the picture of the woman captured him and stirred his cock.

Her green eyes stood out against the dark, wavy curls of hair surrounding her face. He glanced over to her stats. Five-eight. His cock grew heavier. Reed stood at six-one. He was always looking down on women at an uncomfortable angle. If this woman had heels on, she'd be close to eye level with him, and the thought aroused him.

He scrolled back up to her message to see what the sexy woman had to say.

One woman needing a dom to fulfill her desires of BDSM. Limits unknown but will try new things to discover herself and satisfy the man who controls her.

Reed's heart pounded. He wanted to be the one to introduce her to BDSM. His reaction surprised him.

He clicked the *claimed* button at the top of the screen to indicate she had been contacted by a dom and was now off limits. Then he reached into his pocket to grab his cell phone, and after he entered the last number, he placed the phone to his ear.

It rang twice, and then a string of curse words followed by shuffling filled his ear. Reed had expected to receive voice mail. He had not anticipated someone would answer at this late hour. "Hello?

More rustling sounded before a trembling voice answered, "Hello."

In the background, Reed could hear a couple of women giggling, and he wondered if he had the right telephone number. "I'm looking to speak with Marley Adams. Is she around?"

"Um...er..." The woman cleared her throat. "This is her."

"I'm Reed Matheson. I've seen your profile on the castle's forum and am interested in arranging a night with you."

He was met with silence and pulled the receiver away to look at the screen, curious if she had hung up, but the lit screen indicated she hadn't. He returned the phone to his ear. "Are you still there?"

"Yes."

Reed waited a good thirty seconds before he concluded something was amiss and wondered if maybe this was a joke. "I'm not in the mood to be trifled with. I'd recommend the next time you ladies want to play a game, you choose another method to do it. Good night."

"No, don't go."

The desperation in her voice stopped him. Clearly something else was going on here. If this wasn't women being drunk and playing around, what could be Marley's hesitation? Then it dawned on him. "Is the problem because you're not alone?"

"Yes."

Another round of hushed giggles sounded. "Right. Then I take it you don't want to discuss this with your friends there?"

"Exactly." Marley sighed.

That sigh of hers sent a rush of blood straight to his cock. Her voice held a wonderful sensual tone that appealed to him and confirmed he had made the right decision to contact her.

His reaction intrigued him. When had he been so interested in a submissive? Not since his ex-girlfriend and that knowledge sent a ping of pain to his heart, which he flatly ignored.

He wanted to be the one to guide Marley. Something about her made his stomach clench, and the thought of not having her maddened him.

Now understanding that she'd paused because she craved privacy, Reed took another approach. He scrolled back up to Marley's information, clicked on her e-mail address to open a new message, and attached his profile. "We'll keep this short then. I've sent my details to the e-mail address you've provided on the forum. Have a look, and we'll go from there."

He heard shuffling again, some whispered arguing, before Marley gasped. "Oh...um...you're..."

Reed chuckled. He didn't mind that his looks left her speechless. Hell, hers had done the same to him. "Do you approve?"

"He's gorgeous," a woman said, not Marley.

The sound of a slap followed by Marley's grumble informed him she'd just issued someone a punishment for speaking so loud. "I'm interested," was all she said.

That was enough for him. "Read through the castle's rules and follow them accordingly. It'll take you around twelve days to get all the documentation you require, so let's meet two weeks from tonight. Come to the restaurant at the Castle Dolce Vita at seven p.m. When you arrive, you will ask for and always address me as Master Reed. Understood?"

"Mm hmm."

Her response made him tighten his jaw. "You will answer me with words, not sounds."

"Okay...sorry. I'll be there."

He would rid her of that behavior. He preferred that his submissives to speak forthrightly and for their responses to be clear. "Very well. I look forward to seeing you then."

A long pause followed before Marley whispered, "Me too."

Reed waited for her to hang up first, and as her friends in the background laughed, he heard Marley exhale, long and deep. Nervous? Excited?

He could only be pleased he'd gotten to her first. Many Castle Dolce Vita doms would want her, but he'd snagged her. His throbbing cock reminded him he'd gotten lucky tonight.

CHAPTER TWO

Marley—or rather her friends—decided on her attire. She wore skintight jeans, a low-cut black silk halter top, and knee-high black leather boots with four-inch heels. She'd been dressed in everything from skirts to all leather to a bikini top with jeans. But this outfit made her most comfortable. Still sexy, yet casual.

They had all agreed the pact hadn't been made in a drunken state. But Marley still held reservations. Not that the idea didn't appeal to her; it did, especially after the short conversation with Reed. The man had a voice that traveled like liquid heat through her body, and she couldn't deny the tingles that erupted between her thighs at the idea of meeting him, but she was still nervous, really nervous.

Marley had obtained her police check and clear test results. Now the time had come to meet Reed.

After half an hour of palm-sweating, gripping-the-steering-wheel hell, the castle in Bowleys Quarters came into view. The photos online hadn't done the building justice. The castle was stunning, surrounded by evergreens all dusted with snow. She pulled into the parking lot to the right, which was stuffed full of cars, then put the car in park and sat for a while.

You made a promise. Finally realizing that if she stayed any longer, she'd drive away, she undid her seat belt, grabbed her purse—documents included—from the passenger seat, and exited the car. Her heels clicked against the stone path that had been cleared of snow. A thin walkway of sorts led to a big wooden door. She tried to open the door handle, but it didn't budge, so she knocked twice. A small peephole opened, and a blue eye stared back at her.

"Name?" the man behind the eyeball asked.

"Ah..." *What have I gotten myself into?* "I'm here to see Master Reed." The term felt awkward: she never thought she'd call anyone *Master*. "My name is Marley Adams."

The door jiggled, then opened. "You've been authorized to enter." The man wore black plants with a matching T-shirt that had Castle Dolce Vita written in bold white letters across his chest. All muscles—all business.

The outside of the building was castlelike in appearance, but the inside was the exact opposite. She stood in a large foyer. The ceiling soared thirty feet high above her. Wooden balconies wrapped the foyer, showing off four different floors, all lined with doors leading to who knew where.

The bouncer led her to the back of the castle, gestured for her to enter the restaurant area, then returned to his post at the front door. Marley stepped into the room to find a typical restaurant, simple in design. Rich cream fabric lay over tables with intimate place settings. Candles were spread out around the space, giving a relaxing glow to the atmosphere.

"May I help you find your table?" a soft voice asked.

Marley glanced over her shoulder to see a small woman, twenty-two or so, standing next to her with a beaming smile. "Has Master Reed arrived?"

"Oh yes, he's here and waiting for you. Please follow me."

The server strode by Marley, and she forced her feet to work. She'd never been bold, brave, and she'd certainly never done anything like this before. She passed by the row of tables and noticed the customers were dressed in everything from business attire to sexy clothing, which did include leather outfits. Some couples were talking, some eating, and some staring adoringly at each other.

The server rounded a corner, and Marley spotted Reed sitting at a table against the back wall. He spun a bottle of beer in his hand, not looking at Marley, but when her heel scuffed against the floor because she stumbled and bumped into the waitress, he glanced up. His deep blue eyes swept across her body, which caused heat to rise and spiral straight to her center. Her breath quickened, but as Reed stood, her lungs froze. Broad shoulders led to a wide chest, and with his inviting lips and stylish dirty blond hair, he charmed her.

Then the sexy man spoke. "Marley." His voice rumbled—it was somewhere between a gravelly tone and a deep growl, one that made her tingle between her thighs.

She managed to find her voice. "Master Reed." He grinned and nodded. He pulled out her chair and gestured for her to join him. Marley sat, unable to take her gaze off him. The way his mouth turned up so slightly when he smiled didn't make him look soft, but made him appear more confident.

"Would you like to order now, or do you need a few minutes?" a woman asked.

Marley glanced to the gal beside her, surprised the hostess had left and the waitress had taken her place. She'd been so caught up in Reed all she could do was laugh. "No food for me, thanks. A glass of wine will do just fine."

"No alcohol," Reed said. "I prefer you not to have any in your system before I take you into a scene."

"Oh, um…a glass of water then."

The waitress glanced at Reed. He shook his head, and the server left to fetch Marley's drink. Reed looked at Marley then, his gaze intent and focused on hers, yet he said nothing.

Was he waiting for her to say something? If so, what was she supposed to say?

REED'S INTENT WAS purposeful. He needed to see Marley unraveled. Her reactions to his silence would show him what kind of woman she truly was.

"I'm not sure why you're not saying anything, but I want to go through with this, you know."

He hid his smile. "I suspect you *do* want to continue with our night, since you're still here." He'd seen a flash of the strong woman within her, and he planned to draw that part of her out.

She raised her head, and uncertainty filled her expression. "Why then are we just sitting here not saying anything?"

"I demand my subs start the conversation, especially with you since you appear to have some hesitation in that regard. You apparently have nothing to say."

Her green eyes lit up as she laughed, her dark hair fell over her shoulder to trail along her breast, and her lips captured his gaze—it all stirred his cock. "Okay, well then, you should have said you wanted me to go first, because I have a few questions."

Yes, he could clearly see she did. Her inquisitive eyes screamed a thousand questions at him. "You may ask anything you'd like."

Marley sighed, and her gaze lifted to the ceiling as she clearly processed her thoughts. She glanced back to him with a serious expression. "Well, I suppose my first question is, you're not married or dating anyone, right?"

Reed found her question sweet, and it showed him her morals, ones he approved of. "No, I'm not involved, but you should know penetration play normally does not happen in the scenes I create—if that is a concern of yours."

"Oh, I thought we'd be…"

His response obviously disappointed her, and he took note of the little pout that formed on her mouth. He'd rectify her disapproval. "But that's not to say you won't orgasm."

"Oh." Marley's cheeks burned red. She glanced down to her hands, fiddled with her fingers before she looked up and the blush vanished. "So do you live a *normal* life?"

"What's normal?"

"You know, everyday job and such." She exhaled deeply. "I guess what I mean is, are you the dom persona outside of the castle?"

"Yes, I have a typical life outside of the castle walls, but my personality isn't different. I am who you see now. The scene created for you is more about you than me, anyway. I'm merely there to bring pleasures into your life you've never experienced."

She nodded, appearing content with his response. "I suspected as much from what I've read about BDSM."

It'd been so long since a woman intrigued him enough to ask questions outside of the usual ones to discover her limits and safe word, but he couldn't stop himself now. "You've never dabbled in the lifestyle?"

Marley shrugged. "I've never had anyone to do it with."

"Tell me then, why have you searched this out now?"

"My friends and I made a pact. We're each going to fulfill our ultimate fantasies, things we'd never do before but something we've always dreamed of doing."

Now he understood the telephone call two weeks ago, and who the others were. He leaned forward in interest. Her answer was a first for him. He'd heard many reasons that drew a woman to this lifestyle, but the thought that he'd be her fantasy aroused him, and he needed to hear her reasoning behind her choices. "Why did you agree to such a pact?" He ran his finger along her inner wrist and felt her quiver.

"Be-be-because." She steadied herself, then spoke in an even tone. "I'm a teacher, always disciplining and being in control. The idea of being on the other end intrigues me—I want to be the one to obey. The idea of adding pleasure into the mix makes me hot."

All things he'd give her, and it pleased him she spoke so frankly. Her skin beneath his finger felt inviting, only causing him to wonder where he'd find other soft skin on her body. "Are you willing then to give yourself over to me completely, trust me enough to take you to a place you've never been, and fulfill your fantasy?"

"Yes," she whispered. "I've come here to do that."

Resolved to do right by her, he drew his hand away. He wasn't surprised to hear her gasp at the loss of contact. He left her heated gaze and nodded to the server. She hurried to their table with documents in her hands.

Reed took the papers and pen and waited for her to leave before he spoke next. "We need to get the details handled before we arrange anything between us." Marley stared at the papers wide-eyed. Reed chuckled. "Having a change of heart?"

"No. It's just seems so serious, but I guess the rules are in place for a reason." She reached into her purse. "Here's my background check and test results."

He took the papers from her, scanned them—both were fine—and then he responded to her earlier remark. "There are things to go over before I take you into a scene, and rules the castle has set in place that must be followed." He waited for Marley to respond, but she only nodded, which he did not find acceptable. "As I told you last night on the telephone, I prefer to be answered with words."

"Oh, sorry…er…I'm okay with what you've said so far."

The woman who spoke forthrightly appealed to him much more than the nervous, shy one she hid behind. "You need to sign the consent." He handed her the waiver. "Read over it, and you'll see the rules of privacy. What happens here, stays here."

Marley read over the paper, then peeked up at him through heavy lashes. "The privacy bit I like."

"Most do." Reed laughed.

"Not you, though?"

"I am who I am, Marley. I've made no attempt to hide what I enjoy sexually, but of course I do not speak freely of the lifestyle in my day-to-day life. If I were confronted, I would not deny I am a dom." Time to show her the challenge she made couldn't hold up. "Would you deny you have an interest in the lifestyle?"

She stared at him for a moment, blinked, then signed the waiver. "What's next?"

He'd let her cop out for now, but the defensive technique wouldn't last long once he got her in the scene. "We need to discuss your limits. What you'll do and what you won't do." He arched his eyebrow. "Have you thought about your limits?"

"Of course, a thousand times," she said it, and immediately her mouth formed an O, indicating she hadn't meant to be so bold.

He could hardly wait to free her of this behavior. From being around her so far, he imagined discussing what she would do might make her feel uncomfortable, so he took another approach. "Tell me what you won't do."

"Ménage, anything anal, and no clamps."

None of her answers surprised him, nor did the fact that she had a hard time holding eye contact with him, looking everywhere but at his gaze. "Flogging?"

"I-I…" She inhaled sharply and lifted her chin. "I wouldn't mind flogging as long as it doesn't leave me bleeding."

Not in *his* limits either, but he'd definitely add color to her skin and enjoy every damn minute of it. "How do you feel about being bound, gagged?"

"Bound, yes. Gagged no."

"So vaginal play only?"

Reed thought he'd seen her blush before, but he hadn't seen anything yet compared to the color her skin could turn; her cheeks burned crimson. "I—we—you..." She chuckled nervously before she straightened her shoulders. "Yes, only that."

He wrote down her list of limits. "Look over what you've told me; if you agree, sign your name at the bottom and put your address on the top for legal purposes. As I stated, your information will not be shared or seen by anyone other than myself and the legal department here at the castle."

"It feels as if I'm signing my life away," Marley said.

Reed stood, approached the side of her table, and tucked his finger under her chin to bring her gaze to his. "No, you're signing to discover the life you've missed out on." He brushed his lips across hers merely as an introduction.

Marley leaned in to take more of his mouth, and here she'd get her first lesson. He backed away from her and tightened his hand on her jaw. "You don't take. I will give you what you need, always. Staying in line and being disciplined will bring you pleasure. Be sure to remember that tonight." She stared doe-eyed at him. "I need to bring the documents to the office. Go back to the doorman, and he will locate Raven for you. She'll help you prepare for the scene."

Reed stroked her jaw lightly. Marley sighed as her eyelids fluttered. He dropped his hand and then headed for the door. He'd been given a treat tonight, and damn would he savor her.

CHAPTER THREE

Marley watched Reed walk away from the table; she was slightly confused as to what to do next. He'd said something to her, but being the fool she was, she didn't hear a word. She'd been too focused on his soft lips. Was she to follow him?

Instead of sitting there looking as ridiculous as she felt, she hurried to find him. In the main foyer, Marley scanned the room, but Reed was nowhere in sight. The only other person was the doorman, who approached her.

"You have to wait here," he said as he walked by her and headed toward a door to the left of the restaurant.

Butterflies flew in Marley's stomach, but she clamped down on them; she couldn't lose her nerve now. As she exhaled to smooth her anxiety, the bouncer returned, and with him was a woman dressed in a sexy leopard-spotted minidress.

He strode past Marley and resumed his place at the door, while the woman waved her toward the staircase. Who was she? Marley hadn't expected to be introduced to a woman and couldn't quite figure out what her involvement was here.

She pushed her reservations aside and followed the woman up the large staircase to the left. She trotted up the stairs, then approached a door with the words DRAGON'S LAIR written in bold gold letters on the mahogany wood.

"My name is Raven. Master Reed has requested that I prepare you."

"Um...er...nice to meet you." Marley was glad she remembered her manners, but she needed some answers. "Not to be rude or anything, but what exactly are you helping me prepare for?" She thought it was all simple—drop her clothes and wait for Reed.

Raven stepped through the door, motioned for Marley to enter, and when she did, closed it behind her. "I've lived the lifestyle for some time now. Since you've never been in a scene before, I can help you get ready for your master. He's left orders of how he wants you presented, and trust me, you won't be able to do it alone."

"Oh." Marley's surprise wasn't only from what Raven said, but also in regard to the view before her. A black wooden box was in the center of the room, the castle walls were bare, and candles gave off a dim light.

A series of racy images formed in Marley's mind as she fantasized about what Reed planned for her tonight. Heat burned between her thighs, and wetness formed there.

"Master Reed has picked your attire for the evening," Raven said as she walked toward an open door at the back of the room. "But first you need to shower."

Marley gave her head a little shake, trying to snap herself out of the scenes playing in her mind, and she followed Raven into the other room, clearly a bathroom.

Raven approached a bench against the wall and sat down. "You only have fifteen minutes to be ready for him. I'd suggest you not make him wait—he won't be happy."

Right, the last thing Marley needed to do was piss him off. She understood enough of the rules of BDSM to know if she defied him, she'd be punished. The thought sent a tickle through her body, causing her already swollen clit to throb—what if she wanted him to punish her?

Marley left Raven behind and moved around the corner to enter the shower area.

"Put the shower cap on," Raven called out. "Master Reed doesn't want your hair wet—he wants you to wear it down."

"Okay." So many thoughts kept her mind busy as she hurried through her shower. What did Reed plan for her to wear? What did he intend to do to her? Her excitement made her rush to find out.

Marley grabbed a towel from a hook and dried off, then returned to Raven in the change room to find her holding clothing.

Leather. Marley's heart raced. Oh yes, her fantasies included leather clothing, and the knowledge that she'd wear it for Reed only increased her already overdriven arousal.

"Now so you know, this is a job for me." Raven smiled. "Just like a nurse or a doctor. I have seen hundreds of pussies, and yours is no different. So you don't have to be shy or worried. To me your goodies mean nothing, just a day at work."

"Do you say the same line to everyone?" Marley laughed.

"Yes." Raven shrugged and laughed with her before her expression firmed up. "Now drop the towel, and I'll help you into this."

"What's *this*, exactly?"

Raven held up a corset in one hand and gripped a long piece of ribbon in the other. "Reed picked the corset for you tonight." Raven gestured toward the towel. "Drop it."

Marley let the towel pool at her feet. She wanted—no, needed—to feel the cool leather against her skin. She'd never considered herself a sex kitten, yet wearing a leather corset demanded she be seen as such, and she had never been so eager to get into a piece of clothing before.

Raven put the ribbon over her shoulder and placed the front of the corset against Marley's chest. "Hold it in place, please."

Marley held the front tight while Raven began to tie the corset together with the ribbon. She glanced down at the black leather against her pale skin. The material seemed like a cool body pressed against her, and it felt perfectly right, undeniably sexy.

Within ten minutes, the corset sat snug against Marley, creating cleavage she didn't know possible with her small breasts. Raven wandered back over to the bench and held up a garter belt—leather, of course. She placed it around Marley's hips, settling it into place, then fastened it. Next Raven handed her thigh-high stockings and helped her attach them to the garters.

Raven gave her a once-over and smiled. "Master Reed will be happy. You look beautiful." She took Marley's hand and pulled her toward a mirror. "Take a look for yourself."

Marley gasped. She'd seen images like this before, but on models, never on her body. She did a spin to examine the *new* her and spotted two round steel loops attached to the sides of the fabric.

Before she had a chance to figure out the purpose of the loops, Raven handed her sleek black heels. "The finishing touches."

Marley put them on and stabilized herself to get used to the steep angle. In no time, she found her balance. So many emotions rushed through her, but she surprised herself by not feeling nerves ping-ponging in her body—more so, her pussy throbbed with excitement. "Okay, I'm ready."

Raven nodded, left the bathroom, and Marley followed. At the center of the room, Raven pointed to the ground. "Master Reed wants you here."

Marley looked to the spot she gestured to before glancing back at Raven to clarify. "Standing there?"

She shook her head. "Master Reed prefers a submissive to kneel when she's presented to him. Here, I'll help you get the position right." Once Marley knelt, Raven used her feet to nudge at Marley's knees. "You want to display yourself for your master. Show off your body to him. You want to entice him so he rewards you."

Marley scooted out her thighs until the air swept along her pussy, indicating she now held herself wide open. The position amplified her arousal. Waiting. Wanton. Being shown off like this, totally exposed, did more for her arousal than any amount of foreplay she'd ever had before.

Raven took a step back, her gaze drifting between Marley's thighs before she nodded, then glanced back up to Marley. "Yes, that's good." She grabbed Marley's shoulders and pulled to arch her back. "Bring your arms behind you, hold on to your hands, and push out your chest."

Marley complied.

"Now lift your head. You've got a beautiful long neck—show it off to him."

Again Marley listened. Not a comfortable position, yet she assumed Raven knew what Reed wanted. Besides, a sense of calm washed over her while she knelt and waited. All her nerves, the butterflies whipping about, settled.

Raven fiddled with her hair, getting the waves perfectly displayed, before she gave Marley a final look. "Yes, that'll do." She walked to the door, opened it, then glanced over her shoulder. "Oh and, Marley, don't look at him until he directs you otherwise, and always end your responses with 'Sir.' This is his space now, and I suggest you don't forget that fact."

Easier said than done!

<hr/>

The restaurant had been busy when Reed entered and only seemed to fill up more as time went by. He drank the glass of water to replenish his fluids before he met with Marley. From the moment he sat on the stool, he felt impatient, and as the minutes drew on, it only intensified and he found himself fidgeting.

"Marley is ready for you, Master Reed."

Reed spun around to see Raven grinning from ear to ear. "What's with the look?"

"If I didn't know you better, I'd say you appear anxious."

Reed snorted. "But you do know me well." Raven had always been the woman to prepare Reed's subs, and over the years, they'd formed a solid friendship.

Her eyes sparkled as she laughed. "Right. Well, you better get going unless you're making her wait on purpose."

Reed drank the rest of his water and then approached Raven. He rested his hand on her shoulder. "Like I said, you do know me well." He wanted to test Marley. Would she hold her position?

He couldn't deny it excited him to see if this would be a natural role for her to fall into, or if it would take some teaching on his part. Either way he would enjoy discovering his answer.

"Enjoy yourself tonight," Raven said.

"I imagine I will." He patted her shoulder. "Thank you for preparing her."

Raven winked. "It's my pleasure."

Reed left Raven behind and made his way toward the dungeon. He ventured up the stairs and noticed the tray of toys he'd requested waiting for him at the door. After a quick look to ensure the items were all there, he took the folded black sheet off the side and covered the tray. He grabbed the door handle and entered the room.

The image Marley presented sent blood rushing straight to his cock. She also hadn't looked to him in curiosity, just as he'd instructed Raven to tell her.

Impressive.

Reed strode farther into the room, pushed the cart, and placed it against the wall. He approached her then and stopped in front of her. She never looked up, never wavered in her position, even though he could see her tremble. "You may stand."

Marley stood in an awkward way, which didn't surprise him since she was new to BDSM. He knew he couldn't fault her, as a smooth transition needed to be learned. Besides, he had been too busy staring at *her* to really care. The corset had been a perfect choice, and Reed held back his groan. The woman could leave him flustered if he hadn't possessed the control he did.

"You may look at me, and if I ask you a question, you are to answer."

She looked to him, and the burn in her gaze indicated that nerves played no part there. Clearly the trembling of her body had been due to her arousal. He suspected her pussy would be slick with need, which only made his cock harder.

Reed glanced along the length of her body, admiring her. The corset stopped just at her hips, where the garter belt sat lower and stretched over her tight ass, leaving her creamy skin exposed in the places he planned to pay attention to later. He circled behind her and gazed upon those fabulous long legs of hers. Then he trailed his finger along her thigh. "Your legs are sexy, and they please me very much." She murmured a thank-you, sounding more breathy than anything else.

Yes, she had been perfectly presented to him as he requested, and she stunned him. He instructed most of his subs to alter their appearance to his liking. He demanded some grow their hair longer since short hair did nothing for him, stop tanning since he enjoyed creamy, untouched skin, and wax their pussy instead of shave because it left a smoother feel, but Marley did all these things. Already she had done everything right without even knowing it.

Her mouth was slightly parted as if she couldn't pass enough air through her nose. Reed knelt and nudged her thighs open. Her pussy was bare except for the thin line pointing the way to her clit, just how he liked it. "You've got a pretty pussy." He raised his hand and cupped her, then squeezed the heated skin. "Always keep it like this."

Marley moaned. Reed moved his fingers back slightly and felt the wet warmth beneath his touch. Her sensitive skin was already damp, and he hadn't even shown her anything. Oh, how she teased him. "You've done very well."

"Thank you, Sir."

Reed rejoiced to hear her address him as she should, and he'd also commend Raven for how well she'd prepared Marley. "You will need to choose a word that will be your safe word. If things go out of your comfort zone, you can say this word and I will stop."

"Stop the scene completely, Sir?"

He shook his head. "I will move on to something else. This is how we will build trust. You will have a way out if you need it, but I warn you not to use it unless necessary. Believe that I know what you can manage and I would not do anything I don't think you can handle."

She paused, clearly considered her word, then grinned. "Pact, Sir. That's the word I'll use."

Reed nodded, finding her safe word sweet and appropriate. "Very well." He pressed his palm against her clit. She moaned. "My rules are not hard to follow. Whenever you please me, I will pleasure you in return. If you don't, I will force you to earn your reward." He circled his palm to roll her clit beneath his hand, and her eyes fluttered closed. "Ah, beautiful…" He withdrew. "You have not earned that much pleasure yet."

He left her and strode toward the cart. There he removed the linen to reveal ropes, his flogger, and a crop. He took the smaller of the two crimson ropes, which he'd picked because he knew the color would be a stunning contrast against the black leather corset, her dark hair, and her pale skin.

Marley glanced at the rope before her molten eyes returned to his.

"Hold your hands out in front of you," Reed said.

She responded instantly.

He took one end of the rope and tied a French bowline knot. Once he had the loop completed, he slipped the rope over her wrists, then tightened the knot. He stepped in behind her, trailed his hand over her ass, and gave it a slap before he made another knot. "Bring your right arm behind your back." She complied, and he put the rope over her other wrist. With only a small amount of rope remaining, he pulled Marley's wrists together. There he tied a square knot, stabilizing the hold.

He moved in front of her to find desire flashing in her eyes. Not a surprise. At the restaurant, she'd squirmed in her seat when he discussed the possibility of being bound, and her reaction told him she'd become aroused by the restraint. To be sure she felt safe, even if her eyes said as much, he voiced the question. "Being bound is a wonderful feeling, isn't it?"

"Yes, Sir, very much."

"I'm pleased to hear it, because you look stunning presented this way to me." He ran his fingers over the swells of her breasts. "It accentuates you here." He pulled back her shoulder, then grasped her hip. "You look even more beautiful when you arch your back a little. I want you to stay in this position at all times. Do not disappoint me by ruining my view."

"I won't, Sir."

Reed stepped back, content with what he saw. No flaws were present on her skin—only smooth white flesh beneath the dark leather, all inviting him to move forward with the scene.

He went over to the tray and grabbed his black leather cowhide flogger. This flogger was an appropriate choice for her—a light hit would cause some pain, but the velvety leather would provide only a minor sting.

Reed returned to stand in front of her. Marley's gaze focused on the flogger. "Ah, I see excitement raging through those beautiful eyes of yours." He positioned himself behind her, spun the flogger in his hands, and her breath hitched. Without another word, he smacked the flogger against her thigh to test her.

She gasped.

"On a scale of one to ten, tell me the pain level you experienced."

"Four, Sir."

"Only a four. I'll have to change that, won't I?" Her sweet ass clenched. With his empty hand, he smacked her on the ass with a flat palm. The loud hit echoed in the empty room, and she screeched. "Never anticipate what I will do to you. You'll never get what you expected, and I will punish you for such anticipation."

"Sorry, Sir."

"And so you should be." He waited for her to settle—for her muscles to loosen before he raised the flogger and hit her ass. "What's your pain level?"

"Three, Sir."

He smacked her again.

"Five, Sir."

He hit harder.

"Seven, Sir."

And harder.

"Ten, Sir," she shouted.

Reed studied her reactions to each hit. He witnessed the subtle way her muscles relaxed at the halfway mark. Her responses told him she liked a little pain, would find pleasure from the pain, but anything harder would be too much for her.

"You've held your position and answered my questions honestly." He moved in front of her and touched her pussy, swirled his finger in her juices before he inserted one finger, then pushed two through her damp lips. "Always stay honest, not only with me but yourself, and we'll do fine here." He slid his fingers deeper within her, settled them against her G-spot, and then he finger fucked her senseless.

Marley screamed. Her pussy clenched against his fingers, forcing him to grab on to her hip to keep up the rhythm he'd set. Her moans sent shivers down his spine and pooled heat into his thick erection.

She surprised him, though, by maintaining eye contact. So focused. So intent. He'd give her the first climax because of her natural submission to him and for how well she'd done.

He fucked her with his fingers more forcefully, and her screams morphed together in one long, desirable explosion. The sound of her climax stilled as wetness warmed his hand and her final cry of fulfillment rang through the air.

"Very good." Her pussy no longer contracted around his fingers, and the focus in her eyes returned. "You're responsive. I'm honored you came as hard as you did for me and so quickly." He withdrew his fingers, cupped her face, and crushed his lips against hers in a fevered pitch. Reed could find himself lost in her mouth, yet he pulled away to remain focused on his role. "By the time I'm done with you, I want to see your thighs glistening with your arousal. You won't fail me, will you?"

"No, Sir." She sounded breathless. "I won't."

Reed grinned. Not only was Marley undeniably beautiful, his type in every regard, but she had not fought him in the least. She'd been naturally everything he wanted in a sub. He'd forced her to come, not only to offer her a reward, but he'd wanted to see how sexually aware she was. Not all women were capable of having a G-spot release, but she'd done exactly that.

Damn, this woman aroused him, and he wanted her to experience the satisfaction of knowing she caused this reaction in him. He closed his body on hers to allow her to feel his heavy cock on her stomach, to give her that reward and show her she enthralled him. "The sight of you, the smell of you, your obedience—it all makes my cock fucking hard. You've made that happen and should be proud of yourself."

"Very proud, Sir."

It'd been some time since anyone had brought him to this level of arousal. Yes, they could cause a semierection, and eventually he'd grow hard and demand some attention, but not one had made him so hard, so fast—only Marley.

Reed approached the table again and grabbed the butterfly vibrator. He tucked the flogger under his arm and held the vibrator's straps up to show his intention. "I give my word the toy is new and has never been used on another."

"I understand, Sir."

"Raise your leg and place your foot on my knee." Reed lowered to one knee in front of her, and as she did as he asked, he got a full view of her pussy and the wetness that formed there. He raised her foot and ran the harness up to her knee. Once finished, he repeated the move on the other leg and pulled the straps up so the vibrator was positioned over her clitoris. Then he pulled the two clips together and attached them, so no matter where she moved, the vibrator would stay in place.

Reed went back to the table and snatched up the remote control. He purposely kept the device hidden in his hand to leave Marley unaware of his plan. "Hold your position like a good girl. Understood?"

Instead of waiting for her to respond, he hit the first button on the vibrator, and Marley gasped. After stepping behind her, he took the flogger from under his arm and held the remote in the other hand. He kept the vibe at a slow speed, raised the flogger, and smacked her ass lightly. He didn't want her to lose herself in the pleasure the vibrator offered.

He continued to flog her. The leather tails left pinkish color on her skin. Marley's moans deepened, and he saw her legs tremble, yet could also see her lean back, asking for more.

More he'd give her.

Reed set the vibrator to medium speed; Marley inhaled deeply, and her position faltered. He smacked her hard with the flogger, then switched off the vibrator. She cried out, either in frustration or pain, he assumed probably a bit of both. "Did I not tell you to hold your position?"

Marley righted herself, correcting her stance—legs spread, shoulders high, and back arched.

"Good. Let's remember to hold it next time, shall we?" He rewarded her by turning the vibrator back on to medium speed. Her muscles along her ass tightened, and she groaned but held her position. Pleased, Reed put the flogger to use again and whipped her ass in a steady rhythm, harder now.

He continued at this speed for a while to allow her to be comfortable with the force of the hits. Her ass cheeks grew redder with each hit, but not nearly enough to please him. He turned the switch on the vibrator to the next speed. Marley squealed.

Reed glanced to her hands, which now were clenched tight. However, he doubted it was from pain. He wanted to make sure she was holding up emotionally. "Pain level?"

"Three, Sir."

Her answer didn't surprise him. The rise of her pleasure forced the pain away; she wasn't feeling the hits as much as she had before. It told him to go harder. He used more force, increased his speed, and as the tails hit her ass, the beautiful sound of slapping filled his ears. Her head flailed from side to side.

Here he would teach her how pain could only intensify her climax—freeing her to unknown sensations. He clicked the vibrator to full speed. Marley screamed out against the brutal buzz tormenting her clit.

He left the speed set, stepped back, and positioned himself. At her limit of pain, he delivered fast slaps against her ass with the flogger, not letting her breathe and not letting her anticipate when the next hit would come. He had no doubt she'd soon orgasm. "You will tell me if you are going to come, and if I allow you the right to, you had better come hard."

"Sir, yes, Sir," she screeched.

Reed persisted with his movements for a few solid minutes before he saw the rise of her climax—the way her body tensed and vibrated told him she had reached her orgasm. Confirming his suspicions, Marley gasped, "Sir, I need to come, Sir."

Time for another lesson. He might have brought her to this state, but it didn't mean he'd grant her request. He pushed the switch off. "No, you're not allowed."

Marley cried out.

Desperation sounded all too sweet. He raised the flogger, came at her with a steady stream, and her yelps filled the space around him. She had the ability to pull her safe word and stop this, but he hoped she didn't. He wanted to show her how to push herself, fight against the pain, to understand that withholding her climax would make her release even stronger once she'd been granted it.

Through the hits, Marley cringed, roared out against his rough advances, yet never faltered in her stance. Pride filled him. She took each hit and breathed deep against it.

"I love this technique you're using." Reed admired how naturally submissive she had been. Most needed to learn the skill, and Marley did it without instruction.

Reed waited for her pain to be more evident as her ass grew redder and looked sore from his hits, before he pressed the vibrator back on to full speed. In one second, Marley gasped a cry and shook all over. "Sir, may I come, Sir?"

He grinned, not at all shocked by her response. She enjoyed being hit. It seemed to fuel her arousal, and it hadn't hindered the build of her climax. He suspected the intensity of the orgasm would be unlike anything she'd experienced before. "As long as you come like I have asked, then yes, you may."

Marley inhaled sharply. Reed used all his strength to deliver one slap exceeding her limits. As expected, she roared, lost her position, and stepped forward while she shuddered.

Reed turned the vibrator off in the same second. "You broke position again." He grabbed on to Marley's arm and forced her back into the right position. "I'm growing tired of having to remind you."

"Sorry, Sir." She panted, arching her back as he'd told her to before, but she shook with the lingering effects of her orgasm. "I'm sorry. I don't want to upset you, Sir."

He moved around to face her, found Marley's cheeks burning red with exertion, and her lovely green eyes were black with dilated pupils. He cupped her face and squeezed tightly. "Don't do it again and you won't."

Chapter Four

Marley had trouble gathering herself—not only had she received the most impressive orgasm of her life, but she'd had two. Reed had left her standing once he issued his demand to not fail him again as he approached the tray, and she wouldn't dare move.

No man had ever made her come like he had. She'd never felt such intensity, and she certainly never found herself wanting to beg for more. He turned back to her, staring with those captivating eyes of his that declared she didn't need to beg and he planned to give her more.

He stepped in behind her and rubbed lotion over her sore ass, repeating it on the other cheek. "I've enjoyed watching you, but I think I'll enjoy you more if you're spread wide."

The coolness of the cream eased the ache from the flogger, and his words melted over her in a similar manner to the cream, causing a burn to simmer between her legs. He removed the ropes binding her, and Reed snatched up her wrists, rubbing them a while, which eased the pressure from the restraints.

Marley sighed at his touch, not only soothing, but a thoughtful move she appreciated. As the throbbing lessened, he dropped his hands but stayed behind her. "Go and lie down on the box."

She approached the black box in the middle of the room and rubbed her wrists a little in hopes the circulation would return. She hadn't realized she'd strained against the bindings, but the dig marks along her skin proved that she did. At the box, she lay down so her shoulders rested on the edge and her head dangled over the side, while her back was supported and her feet were flat on the floor.

Reed held two longer pieces of ropes as he approached her. Marley's heartbeat kicked up a notch. "You have quite an interest in being bound, don't you?"

"Yes, Sir, very much." She had never known she'd be so hot to be tied up, but with Reed doing it, being held here as his captive, fire burned through her blood.

"I have a fondness for seeing you bound myself." He lowered onto one knee by her feet, took her leg, and placed her foot on his knee. With skilled precision, he wrapped her ankle with the rope, circling the twine while he looped it through a knot. Five wraps later, he pulled the rope tight against her skin.

He never hesitated or seemed unsure of himself. Every time he wound the rope, his hands trailed against her skin, and being already sensitive, it only teased her. She wanted him to look at her, needed that connection and approval, yet he never did. He seemed too focused on the ropes.

For the first time, Marley got a taste of what BDSM was really all about—the want to do right by her dom. Through all of this, past the orgasms and the pain, she felt a soul-deep need to please him. As much as she wanted him to offer her another climax, satisfy her, she hoped he got fulfillment from the experience as well.

Within no time, he had the other ankle bound, then glanced to her, and his gaze all but smoldered. She'd been on dates, had lovers before, but no one could make her flush with need by a simple look like he could, and she didn't even know him.

"Tell me, do you enjoy how the ropes feel on your ankles?"

"Yes, Sir, they feel wonderful."

He grinned. "I'm delighted to hear you say that, because you look exquisite."

"Thank you, Sir." Every time he offered praise, she marveled in it. She'd never thought she needed the approval of a man, but his appreciation made her soar and gave her a sense of serenity.

He took the end of the rope, pulled her leg up so her knee bent, and then he slid the end into the ring on the side of her corset. Now she understood his intention and what the loops where there for: it spread her wide and left her exposed. He bound the end of the rope to her ankle with a knot, leaving her knee bent but supported by the twine.

Once he repeated the move on the other ankle, he stood and smiled. "You're giving me a stunning view, one that arouses me. Can you see what you're doing to me?" He held his cock in his pants, pulled the fabric tight so she could see the outline of his erection.

"Sir, it looks quite hard."

"Painfully hard, sweetheart." Reed chuckled.

He stepped between her legs and touched her pussy, circling her clit a few times. The man had fingers of a god. He was so confident in the way he touched her, and his molten gaze left no doubt in her mind that he admired her.

As the pleasure began to take hold, he removed his touch, strode to the table, and grabbed something. He turned back to her, and she saw he now held a black crop. "You're going to be a good girl, use the technique you've displayed here so far, and handle the pain, understood?"

Oh God! Her imagination ran wild with thoughts of how the crop would feel against her skin. Would it be like the flogger? Or would there be more of a sting? All she knew was she wanted more and was eager for him to deliver it. "Yes, Sir."

He positioned himself between her spread legs and raised the crop to her foot. There he gave a steady smack against the arch. She gasped as the sting was, sharper than she had expected, and her eyes watered. His gaze held steady on hers; even a little smile crept up on his face. "Pain level?"

"Six, Sir."

"You've already proven you know how to handle pain, which is very good, but I'm going to teach you how to control it when it comes more intensely. Before I hit again, I want you to inhale and hold it. After the hit, exhale slowly and focus on my eyes. Do not look away from me."

"Yes, Sir."

Marley inhaled, and Reed hit the arch of her foot again, harder this time. The moment the smack echoed through the room, Marley's releasing breath followed. It surprised her that his instruction worked. Focused on his eyes, the desire and adoration she saw there made directing the pain easier, and her exhale allowed her to accept the ache.

"That's exactly right. Well done." He hit her thigh, light smacks as he traveled his way along her leg until he reached her center. He skipped her pussy and hit the other thigh repeatedly.

Within no time, the sting evaporated, replaced by a throb to her clit, a need for more, and a desire to lose herself in Reed's control. Clearly he recognized her wants, since he brought the crop back to her center and rubbed the flap over her clitoris, sending Marley to sigh as he teased her. "Have you been a naughty girl?"

"Sir, yes, Sir." She leaned her head back over the box, before she reminded herself he'd ordered her to keep eye contact with him.

"I should punish you for all the naughty things you've done." His smooth voice ran across her body like a warmed bath.

"Sir, I need to be punished."

He smacked her clitoris. Marley swallowed back her scream and bit her lip instead. She tensed against the ropes and fought the pain. The sting shocked her—such a sensitive area couldn't process an ache so intense.

"You did not breathe as I instructed." He stepped away from her, and she cried out, begging with her whines to continue. "You're being punished for disregarding my instructions."

"Sir, forgive me, Sir. I won't forget again."

His gaze narrowed, yet he stepped back in front of her. "I will forgive this once and only once, because you are new to the lifestyle. Don't do it again."

"No, Sir, I won't, Sir."

Reed circled the flat leather around her clit while he delivered light hits. Marley strained against the ropes. Her eyes stayed on his as his deep, intent gaze watched her in return.

After four hits, the technique allowed her to ignore the pain and focus more on the spike of pleasure given to her clitoris.

He ran the crop along her skin, slapping sometimes, other times just smoothing it across her flesh. "Your skin is turning an exquisite shade of red." He grinned. "It's lovely." He smacked her clit hard.

"I'm glad it pleases you, Sir," Marley shouted.

"Good answer from a good submissive." He all but purred.

Marley shuddered at the sexy sound.

"Do you believe I can make you come by using this crop?"

No, she certainly did not. So far he'd used his fingers, the vibrator, but her clit had never been that sensitive to actually orgasm from simple touch. Plus, being hit with the crop wasn't exactly what she'd consider orgasmic.

Reed tsk-tsked. "Oh, sweetheart, I see doubt in those eyes. Doubt I do not deserve." He lowered the crop. "Have I not warranted your trust and proved to pleasure you?"

Marley filled with anger at herself. The man had proven to be beyond capable, but he wasn't the problem. "Sir, it's not you. I'm not sure I can..."

His eyebrow arched as her words drifted off, and he shook his head in frustration. "You need to say what you want." He raised the crop and hit her pussy.

Marley gasped at the sharp pain and tried to remember his instructions.

"From now on, when I ask you a question, you will respond immediately. No more hesitation. Am I clear?"

"Yes, Sir." Marley groaned, still feeling the effects of the hit. Reed had made it clear before that she needed to use words instead of her normal blasé sound effects to answer him, but she'd had no idea how much it bothered him until now. That hit he'd given her did not arouse her—that one hurt—and anger wafted off him.

"Do not make me ask twice." He smacked her again.

Marley hissed.

"Answer the question."

Clearly this was another side of BDSM she hadn't experienced yet. The molding of how he wanted her to act, and she could see sense in it all, but she wasn't bold, and speaking so forthrightly was as a challenge. She gulped back her hesitation and blurted out, "I won't come that way, Sir."

A challenge flashed in Reed's gaze, one that made Marley's eyes go wide. "We shall see then, won't we?" He hit her clit, repeatedly.

Marley closed her eyes, and panic filled her. This didn't feel good; it hurt. Her safe word played on her mind—should she use it to get him to stop?

"Look at me," Reed commanded.

Marley forced her eyes to open.

"Breathe."

She wanted to listen to him, tried to focus on him alone, nothing else. Her muscles tensed in agony, but as she stared at him, she did what he'd asked her to do all along; she trusted him.

Each time he prepared to hit, she inhaled, and after, she released it. Her mind held the control here, and he gave her strength.

The pain lessened. His force still was hard, but she could manage it. "Yes, that's right; there you go," Reed said.

The sting turned into something else entirely now. Her clit throbbed, and every smack against her produced a wild sensation that had her arching her hips, asking for more. She needed to reach the climax she could feel building in her body. "Oh, Sir. Oh, Sir, I'm going to come."

Reed's eyes shone with pride. "Take it then—claim what you're after."

She did, not only her orgasm, but his claim over her.

My dom.

REED HAD CREATED this scene to be all about Marley, her needs, her wants, even if she didn't know them herself. But he couldn't draw his thoughts away from himself while he used the crop.

Not now.

The bindings on Marley's legs left her completely open to admire, and her pussy had been taunting him. He wanted to put his cock where his fingers had been. So tight and accepting—warm and inviting.

This woman held a power over him he couldn't make sense of. His throbbing dick overtook his logical mind. He dropped the crop and took off his shirt. "You've been a good submissive, a good girl, and you deserve to be rewarded."

"Yes, Sir. Reward me, Sir." Her voice was breathy, eyes sunk into desirable slits, and a blush formed on her cheeks.

He felt proud as he reached for the button on his pants, opened it, then slid the zipper down. For a woman never in the submissive role before, she fell into this lifestyle easily, and she enthralled him. She wasn't like any other woman he'd ever encountered.

Reed stepped out of his pants, approached the table again, and grabbed a condom—an item he kept around for safety purposes in case the need of one occurred. He hadn't fucked a sub since Samantha, and although he'd told Marley he wouldn't have sex with her, he couldn't deny his needs now.

He unwrapped the condom, slid it over his cock, and stroked himself, confirming he'd made the right choice—he needed to fuck her. Marley's eyes were wide and she panted, which indicated she enjoyed watching him jerk off, yet she raised her gaze to his as if he ordered it. "I'll never punish you for being turned on by my body. In fact, I'm pleased to see your eyes begging me to fuck you."

"Sir, I want you to fuck me."

Reed groaned and did nothing to hide his reaction to seeing such a luscious woman waiting for him. Marley exhaled deeply, a sound giving strength to his cock, a beautiful melody of arousal and apparent need.

He knelt before her, grabbed his heavy cock, then placed the tip at her entrance. Marley leaned up as much as she could in this position, grasped her thighs, and moaned. Reed slid in, and his eyes shut as he groaned. He heard Marley echo his sound. Nothing had ever felt so good.

"I'm delighted at how tight you are."

"I want my pussy to satisfy you, Sir."

He thrust into her. Marley's pussy tightened around his cock and nearly made him come. But he'd not waste the moment with her. No, he'd fuck her senseless so she'd never forget him, and he'd leave his imprint forever marked on her. "You will not hide your pleasure from me." He thrust again. "I want you to scream out in the way I deserve."

"Yes, Sir." The words barely sounded from her throat as her head fell back, showing off her long neck. The sight shifted Reed's arousal from blatant need to outright domination. *His.* He wanted to keep Marley. *My sub.* Tonight he'd leave a mark on her that no man could ever erase.

Her thoughts only of me.

Always of me.

He grabbed the ropes halfway between the clamps on the corset and the ones on her ankle and held the twine tight. Then he growled deep before he fucked her savagely.

Marley's screams ricocheted off the stone walls as loud smacks of skin against skin filled the air. She arched her back and gripped the box at her shoulders. Her breasts bouncing around on the top of her corset gave him a splendid view.

Heaven.

More.

Harder.

Deeper.

Reed couldn't get enough of her tight pussy, of the sight before him now. He thrust harder. Sweat gathered on his body, but he paid it no heed and continued with the powerful thrusts to satisfy his needs and hers.

His cock grew stiffer, his balls drew up, indicating impending release, yet he forced himself to wait—he needed her orgasm. He brought his palm to her clit and pushed hard. Marley roared and grabbed his biceps. She gripped his arms tight as her hands made a home in the valleys of his muscles.

He circled his palm against her clit, desperate to give her a release, while he continued to thrust in haste. Her eyes went wide, yet she hung there.

"You're going to come for me, and you're going to do it *now*." He pinched her clit.

Marley screamed. Her pussy clamped on Reed's cock as she lost herself in her orgasm, and he lost himself in his.

By the time Reed regained any sense, Marley must have latched on to his head and pulled him to her chest. Her small breasts made a pillow for his cheek, and the coolness of the leather gave an ease to the flushed heat on his face.

There he stayed—recovered.

When he felt her trembling beneath him, he remembered his responsibility to handle her aftercare. He raised his head, gripped the knot on her corset, and released it so she could lower her leg. As he expected, she moaned while the blood rushed back into her limbs.

Marley still hadn't looked up at him even after he released her other leg. Her head dangled over the back of the box; her chest rose and fell in rapid movements. He stood, tore the condom off his softened cock, and deposited the latex sheath in the trash. As he turned back to Marley, he grabbed the sheet used to cover the items and approached her.

Reed made quick work of removing the bonds on her ankles and rubbed them a little to gain the circulation back. The knot he'd provided on all her bonds tonight had been the kindest of knots but didn't provide too tight of a hold unless she fought against the restraints. The red marks covering her ankles showed she'd struggled.

He lifted her to him and wrapped the sheet around her. She needed time to recover, and he'd offer himself for however long she wanted it. He sat back on his legs and cradled her to his chest. But the longer he sat, the more his thoughts started to return, and he could hardly believe what had taken place. He had fucked her.

It'd been years since anyone had driven his arousal to a place where he couldn't control it, and the last time had been with Samantha. The part that surprised him most was that he'd enjoyed every minute of it and would do it all over again.

Even now, as he held Marley, rightness settled over him, an emotion that made him pause. He felt warm, not by heated flesh, but in his heart. A feeling he had not experienced in all too long. He wanted to stay here, with her in his arms, and he never wanted to let go. What had he done?

He created limits to avoid exactly this—never becoming attached. The realization that he had opened himself up to Marley slammed fear into his soul. "I must go now." Reed placed Marley gently onto the floor.

Her eyes fluttered open and went wide. "But—"

"I will send Raven to help you out of the corset." He turned on his heels, and her angry, confused eyes haunted him the entire way out.

CHAPTER FIVE

I t turned out Reed had arranged for Marley to have a room at the castle to stay overnight, which she appreciated—if she had driven, she would've crashed her car. Raven had assisted her in removing the corset, shown her to her room, and also run her a hot bath.

Marley should have been so exhausted from the experience that she slept, yet she never did. She was too pissed by Reed's reaction. She could have sworn something more existed between them. Of course, maybe every submissive experienced such an attachment to their dom, and even more so if it had been their first experience.

One thing Marley knew: her fantasy might have been a passing thought before, but now she'd indulge in the lifestyle again. She'd found something in herself during the time in that room—discovered happiness that fulfilled her in ways she couldn't have imagined and gave her the excitement in her life she longed for.

But why did her happiness seem to revolve around Reed? The thought of being with anyone else caused an ache to form in her stomach and made her cringe at the suggestion of belonging to another.

She'd finally found a man who made her feel, one she held an interest in, and one who could keep her happy, but the jerk-off had up and left her. Who knew if that was normal protocol in the BDSM lifestyle, but one thing was certain, if she ever did this again, she'd put that down as a limit. Her dom needed to stay and talk to her after, because him leaving her in the way he had was cold and cruel.

The drive back to Baltimore seemed quick. Marley assumed her mind was too busy to take notice of the time. She pulled into her driveway and sighed as she turned off the ignition. She glanced up at her house, aware the woman who'd left the home less than twenty-four hours ago wasn't the one who returned.

Before she could even open her car door, all three of her friends rushed from the house and wore equally impatient looks. Not a huge surprise—Marley had known they would be waiting for her and didn't doubt whether they'd stayed up all night.

She opened the car door and stepped out, and before she could say a word, Bella demanded, "Tell us everything and hold nothing back."

Marley laughed, closing the door behind her, and approached them. "Well, I'll tell ya this, the castle is incredible."

"Really, like in what way, incredible?" Sadie asked.

"Beautiful," Marley replied, "and busy."

"Who cares about the castle?" Bella waved the remark away with a flick of her hand. "Tell us about Reed."

"Can we go in at least? I don't think the neighbors need to hear about my X-rated evening."

Sadie grinned from ear to ear. "How X-rated?"

"Yes," Kyra exclaimed. "Like XXX-rated?"

Marley brushed past them, dropped her handbag by the front door, then plopped onto the plush couch. "Well..." Marley glanced from face to face. These women she loved, no better friends in the world, and maybe the feeling was even stronger now. If it hadn't been for their suggestion for the pact of seduction, none of this would have happened. "He was incredible." She sighed, sending her friends to giggle around her.

"How incredible?" Sadie asked.

How could Marley even put the experience into words? So much had happened for her, such changes in her soul that could never be erased, and all things she couldn't properly describe. "I've never met a man like him. He's so confident, sexy...and, girls, he rocked my socks off."

"Details, more details, you better tell us everything." Bella squealed.

No one here would judge her, but some things were her secrets, and ones she didn't want to share, so she stuck to the basics. "He had me dress in a leather corset, garters—really sexy lingerie. Used ropes to tie me up—stuff like that."

"Wow." Sadie's eyes hazed over.

"Wow's an understatement," Marley countered. She could tell them about it all, how he flogged her, used the crop along her clit in a way to render her blind, but she knew her friends only needed to hear one thing to satisfy them. "He gave me multiple orgasms."

Kyra's eyes went huge. "He did not!"

"He did," Marley retorted with a laugh, hardly able to believe it herself. "Trust me, I never would have thought it possible, but the man is gifted."

"Clearly." Kyra smiled.

"So did you sleep with him?" Bella asked.

The oddest sensation washed over Marley, which caused her to pause. It seemed too private, something special between Reed and her, and not something her friends needed to know. "No."

Kyra's eyes narrowed. "If you didn't get down and dirty with him, how did he get you off so many times?"

"With his hands and a vibrator." Marley told part truths. Sadie's mouth formed an O, and Marley laughed. "Insane, I know, but totally true."

"Will you do it again?" Bella asked. "You know, with Reed?"

"Yes, I'll do it again, but I doubt it'll happen with Reed."

Sadie frowned. "It sounds like you enjoyed yourself; didn't he? Why wouldn't he want to see you again? You're beautiful and a wonderful woman. What's wrong with him?"

Marley raised her hand to cut off Sadie's rambling. Whenever Sadie got confused, her motormouth came with it. "We never talked about getting together again because he kinda just up and left."

"Right after?" Bella demanded.

"What an asshole," Kyra said.

Of course her friends would be protective, they always were, and Marley understood their reaction. She was pissed too. But she didn't want them to put Reed in a bad light. No matter how he'd treated her after, the time they spent together had been incredible. "It's not what you all think. He never came in there with intentions of winning me over. We arranged this, remember? He actually seems sweet beneath his tough exterior. He even cuddled with me for a bit after; I didn't once feel like I'd been used or anything."

"Oh..." Kyra's furrowed brow softened. "Well, that's good, I guess."

Marley nodded. "I had the best time of my life with him. Really..." She looked to each of her friends. "I wouldn't change a second of it, and I'm so glad we made this pact."

"If you say so. I still think the man is an ignorant ass." The anger in Bella's eyes hadn't lessened, but she sighed and the tension eased along her face. "So that's it then. You've done your fantasy. Was it worth it?"

With Marley's fantasy done and over, Bella would be next, and clearly she needed the reassurance to dive in like Marley had. "Last night opened a new world for me, and I'm not about to give it up. I'm so experiencing that again."

"But not with Reed?" Bella asked.

Marley hated the thought of it being true, no matter how angry she was at him. "No, not with Reed." The sadness wafted off her tone. "Never again with Reed."

⌦⌧⌫

Reed hadn't slept, hadn't done anything but drive around for hours until he found himself back at home in the early morning. He powered up the computer, then pulled up Marley's profile in the forum and stared at her picture. Why couldn't he get her off his mind?

"Already on the prowl, are you?"

He'd been so focused on the screen he hadn't realized Kole had woken up and joined him in the living room. He spun the chair he sat in to face Kole. He wasn't about to tell Kole how foolish he was acting over a woman; his friend would goad him for it. Instead he stuck to the other thoughts in his mind. "How did the night go with Zoie?"

"Spectacular." Kole grinned. "Her tolerance levels are quite high. I suppose I should thank you for giving her over to me. She's going to provide me with some enjoyment, I'll tell you that much."

Reed inclined his head in response and wasn't at all surprised to hear Zoie shocked him by her pain levels; it had the same effect on Reed. Still, Zoie had been a special woman, and he needed to ensure Kole treated her right. "How hard did you push her?"

Kole plopped down on the couch beside the computer. "Not too far. Tested her limits is all. Tonight we've got another scene planned, and I'll push her a little more." He gestured toward the computer with a curious gaze. "Who is that?"

"A submissive I was with last night."

Kole leaned forward, examined Marley's picture, then whistled. "Just your type of woman—sweet and sexy. You think she's a keeper?"

Reed knew Kole would also understand the need to find one's own submissive. Even Kole, after all these years, hadn't found a submissive to claim as his. "We both know finding *forever* is highly unlikely."

Kole eyes went huge before he arched an eyebrow. "If I didn't know you better, I might think you were sulking."

Reed scowled. "I'm not sulking. More pissed at myself. I up and left her last night immediately after the scene."

"You didn't offer her aftercare?" Kole asked, a bite in each word.

The reprimand was justified—what he'd done was reprehensible. "I have no idea what fucking happened. We shared an amazing scene together; the woman is a born submissive, but then I panicked and ran like a damn coward."

Kole paused before he gave Reed a measured look. "Is she worth your pride?"

Marley had awakened a part of him that he'd thought long dead. She made him break the walls around his heart, and she left an impression on him he couldn't forget. "She is worth so much more." The entirety of the situation smacked into his thick head, past the pain of his damaged heart, because Marley *was* worth the risk. "I have to go to her and apologize."

Kole looked at him as if he were a complete idiot. "I would say that you do."

Reed deserved the harsh expression and, in fact, agreed with Kole. He had been a fool. After a short good-bye, he strode out of the house, got into his truck, and entered the GPS coordinates of the address he remembered from Marley's waiver. Baltimore streets flew by Reed's window while he drove at least twenty miles over the speed limit.

Half an hour had passed before he pulled up outside the red brick, two-story house. He cut the ignition and waited. His damned fears had caused him to run away, and he felt ashamed for how he'd treated Marley. He needed to apologize to her, and he wouldn't call to issue an apology over the telephone; he had to rectify what he'd done face-to-face. More than anything, he needed to explain himself to her.

Reed got out of his truck, closed the door behind him, and approached the house. It was around ten in the morning, and typical traffic filled the area—families out for walks with their dogs, people off to enjoy a sunny winter Sunday morning with their children.

Family.

The idea had never appealed to Reed—he'd not once thought himself capable of being a family man who would settle down enough to have such dreams. Now everything had changed—Marley had changed it all for him, and for the first time in so long, he had hope.

At the front door, he inhaled deep to prepare himself and hoped his thoughts came out clear and concise. He knocked, and footsteps barreled to the door before it opened to a pretty woman. Typical bleach-blonde bombshell, not his type and certainly not Marley. For a moment, Reed wondered if he had the wrong house. "Does Marley live here?"

The woman's eyes became suspicious as a protective note rose in their depths. "And you would be?"

"Reed." Those suspicious eyes flashed with total shock, and her lips parted to speak, yet nothing came out but a squeak. He stood for a few seconds, unsure of her reaction, but soon realized she needed a little help to move on. "Is she available?"

"Well...er..." The woman opened the door wider, and it gave Reed a view of the living room where Marley sat on the couch with two other women, all staring blank-faced at him.

Understanding hit him—these were Marley's best friends, the ones she'd spoken of when they first met. Clearly she had told them of the events last night, and his arrival floored them. He chuckled, unable to hold his amusement back. "May I come in?"

"O-o-h." The woman looked back to Marley. "Can he come in?"

In nearly the same move as her friend, Marley's mouth parted but nothing came out; her only response was a quick nod. Then she gave her head a shake and said in an even tone, "Yes, he can."

Reed kept his stare on hers and was pleased she had remembered his rules to use her voice. He stepped into the house, removed his shoes, then went over to the lone recliner resting next to Marley on the couch. He watched the women. No one blinked, yet no one said a word—amusement at its best. "Well, since you all seem to have lost the ability to speak, I'll go first. My name is Reed Matheson. I'm guessing you're Marley's best friends."

Each head nodded. Before Marley cleared her throat, the sweetest blush rose on her cheeks. "This is Bella, Kyra, and Sadie." She pointed to each woman at introduction.

"It's my pleasure to meet you," Reed replied. "If it wasn't for your pact of seduction, as you all called it, I'd never have met Marley."

Again silence filtered in around him, and their mouths dropped open. A good few minutes passed, and Reed had no clue what to say. In truth, he didn't want to share his feelings with a bunch of women; it'd be hard enough to tell Marley his deepest thoughts. So here he sat.

Blessedly after a few drawn-out moments, Kyra jumped to her feet. She yanked on Bella's arm and grabbed Sadie's hand. "Come on, girls, let's give Marley and Reed some alone time."

Bella struggled away, approached Reed, and glared. "You have some explaining to do." She poked his chest. "You don't get to leave her like you did last night, regardless of how good it was, then just show up here like some hero. Marley might be okay with what happened, but I'm not."

Reed glanced at her finger jabbing his chest before he looked back to her. He could count the number of times a woman had treated him as Bella did now on one finger. It took guts, and her tenacity amused him. "As much as I appreciate that you're loyal to Marley—and respect that you are looking out for her—I believe that is a conversation I need to have with her, not you."

Bella's eyes narrowed as she continued to poke his chest. "If I hear that you have done anything to not make her blissfully happy, I will hunt you down and make you regret the day you contacted her. Do *I* make myself clear?"

Her lips parted to issue another round of demands, but Reed interjected before she could. "I hear your warning." He removed her finger from his chest and then squeezed her wrist. "But I would recommend if you decide to follow Marley's actions and choose to fulfill a BDSM fantasy, lose the attitude before you go, or you'll have a mighty sore ass when you leave."

"I'm glad you heard me." The stern set of Bella's face vanished, her eyes went wide, and a blush rose to her cheeks. "Wait. What?"

"You're going." Marley gave her a shove toward the other women. "Right now."

Reed had never seen women move so fast; Sadie and Kyra practically ran from the room, and Bella stumbled as she followed. He focused on Marley, who had taken her seat again and still stared at him. Too many emotions ran across her face to pinpoint where her thoughts lay. He steadied himself to do something he'd never done before, dug down into his heart, and embraced his emotions. "I've come to apologize."

Marley blinked, the confusion clearing from her eyes, replaced by irritation. "Damn right you should."

Her curt tone stung, but he deserved her anger and would see to appease her. "I shouldn't have left you like I did, and I'm here to ask for your forgiveness."

"Ahh..." Her expression turned mystified. "Well..." She lifted her chin, clearly trying to hide the fact that his apology surprised her. "It's good you realize how much of a jerk you were."

"I do, and I'm more sorry than I can say. My duty as your dom is to handle your aftercare when a scene is over. It should've been me, not Raven, to make sure you were all right with what happened between us and to ensure you were settled. I left you at a vulnerable time and will forever regret my choice to fail you."

Marley laughed, showing her anger had lessened, which pleased him. "The word *fail* doesn't belong in what happened last night."

Either she wasn't as angry as she first put off, or she was too happy to see him to stay mad. Whatever it was, it pleased him, and the sound of her amusement sent a wave of warmth right to his heart. "You enjoyed the experience, then?"

"Immensely." She held his gaze in a way she never would have done when they first met. "Nothing happened I would change. I've never experienced anything so intense in my life. Well, except for the way you left."

He knelt in front of her and took her hands. "I didn't sleep last night contemplating what happened."

Reed joined her on the couch, rested his hand on her thigh, and squeezed, aware of her breath whooshing from her lungs. The reaction didn't shock him—his presence would unravel her. Now submissive, her mind would be drawn back to the events between them. Memories, he imagined, of what she had experienced. It pleased him to see her react so intensely, because he had the same feelings too. "There is something about you—something I want to lose myself in." He caressed her cheek with his thumb. "After we completed the scene and I held you, I didn't want to let go."

"You didn't?"

"No, I didn't." He'd never told anyone this. "You're the first woman I've had sex with since my relationship with my lifestyle submissive, the woman I loved, ended two years ago."

"You haven't been with anyone in that long?"

He chuckled at the surprise in her eyes—she had no idea what she did to him—and he inclined his head. "You, Marley, make me want to break my rules. I know enough to declare it now, or I'll forever regret it. I'm not a man who loves easily." He gave her a stern look. "My heart has been broken once, and since then I've never wanted to be attached, nor have I ever met a submissive I wanted to call my own—to control more out of a need for myself than a duty to the sub. Do you understand the difference?"

Happiness shone in her expression, and she smiled. "I do, but—"

He raised his hand to stop her next words of why and how. Of course, he expected her to doubt him. Hell, he'd doubted himself for the last eight hours, but in the end, she remained on his mind. "We don't have to rush into anything—all I'm asking for is a chance and some time to get to know each other outside of the lifestyle."

"You want to get to know me?"

"I do." Reed wanted to know all of her—every little piece that made up Marley. A spark had been lit, one he didn't understand and one he'd never experienced before—he refused to waste it.

The confusion showing in her gaze indicated her inability to accept what he said as true. "Are you saying you want to date me?"

"That's the idea." Date, love, dominate—he wanted it all.

"And what about *in* the lifestyle?" Excitement lit her beautiful eyes, and her cheeks flushed.

Reed squeezed his hand tighter around her face in a show of domination. "Last night you gave yourself to me and I accepted you. It would be my honor to show you more of what the submissive role could bring to your life."

"So you want to be my dom too?"

Reed shook his head. So much she needed to learn, but he was more than happy to teach her. "It's not a matter of want. I already am." He gathered her in his arms. "Where is your bedroom?"

CHAPTER SIX

Marley tried to get a grip on all this but failed. When Reed showed up on her doorstop, she'd tried to stay angry with him, but in truth she was blissfully happy he'd come. This all seemed like a big dream—one she waited to wake up from. Yet as he proceeded into her bedroom, kicked the door closed behind him, and set her down, she hoped if she was dreaming, it'd last forever.

The gentle man she'd seen minutes ago had vanished, replaced by the dominant one she'd witnessed last night. "Undress yourself."

Marley removed her clothing without hesitation, eager to please him, and waited for further instruction.

The silence drew on until finally Reed broke the awkward moment by arching his eyebrow. "I would hope I do not need to remind you of protocol."

Marley dropped to her knees, comprehending his statement. His gaze said it all; he now controlled the moment, and she understood what he meant about the difference between in a scene and out of one. A moment ago, he'd shown no signs of dominance, but here Reed was her dom. Not to be questioned, and by God, she relished his control.

She laced hands behind her back, stared at his knees, and remained that way even when he turned toward her dresser. He took something off the top, but she never saw what he had.

He strode back to her and stopped when his feet touched her knees. "Look at me." She glanced up to find he had wrapped her hemp belt around both hands.

Reed smiled. "I love how your eyes burn like they are now. It was my intention to arouse you by using this on that sweet ass of yours, yet you've pleased me by already getting there. Stand before me."

Marley did as he asked, instantly met by soft fabric against her breasts as he ran the belt over her taut nipples. Reed placed his hand around her nape to draw her close while he pressed his lips against hers. Marley sighed, parting her mouth to allow his tongue entry. His hand tightened to deepen the kiss to a point Marley had never experienced before. More than a statement to bring forth arousal—meant more to steal her thoughts and stop time.

He backed away, nibbled along her jaw, and treated her skin in the splendid embrace of his mouth. The swagger he possessed and the physical attraction she held for him set her aflame, but the confidence in which he kissed, as if he knew all her hidden places that made her tingle, was what sent her arousal to a level she could hardly control.

After a firm bite on her neck causing Marley to gasp, Reed reached down to her hand, placed the belt through the loop to create a handcuff of sorts, and pulled it tight.

"You have a fondness for being bound, and I plan to play on that desire." His voice dropped an octave. "But for now I'm limited since we're at your home." He pulled on the belt tied around her wrist and led her to the wrought-iron bed. "Though being limited doesn't mean I can't be creative."

"I want you to be creative—downright sinfully imaginative, Sir."

Reed shifted Marley into the center of the bed. He raised her arms above her head and looped the belt through the bars on the headboard. "I realize we're not alone in the house and I imagine you'll want to be modest, but if you won't scream your pleasure for me—I insist you had better find another way to show me your appreciation."

"Yes, Sir." The way Reed touched her so gently was such a contrast to the desire in his eyes. She squeezed her thighs together tight in response to ease the throb that reached her clit.

After tying the remaining belt around her other wrist, Reed stood. His gaze traveled like scorching heat along her body, and she squirmed under his scrutiny.

"It's a beautiful thing how much restraints appeal to you." Reed took a seat next to her, ran his hand up her leg until he nudged for her to part her thighs. He lightly touched her pussy, clearly pleased by her aroused state; his eyelids lowered and he groaned.

"You're going to earn your pleasure this morning. Last night was a taste of what I can offer you as your dom, but since I don't have toys here to make you earn your reward, you will appease me with your mouth."

Heat pooled in Marley's pussy—the pulse along her clit turned to a deep throb. "I want to suck your cock, Sir." She pulled against the restraints, more in excitement than a way to free herself, and suspected her expression begged him to come closer.

Reed rid himself of his clothing, and his naked form delighted her as it had last night. Spectacular muscles all rendered her speechless, his heavy cock awaited her, and she intended to give him some relief, but how?

He leaned forward to place his hand on the headboard, lifted one knee on the bed to bring his cock to her mouth. To taste a man such as Reed, to offer him the same sort of pleasures he'd given her—she could hardly wait to devour him.

"You may have five minutes to pleasure me as you see fit." His voice was a near growl as it dipped lower. "Then I'm going to fuck your mouth and take you as I need."

Marley parted her lips to invite him in. Reed angled his hips, closed the distance between them, and when the tip of his cock passed through Marley's lips to sit on her tongue, she sighed. He tasted sweet and smelled musky.

She closed her lips around the hardened flesh and gave a few steady sucks. Reed's hips thrust forward, pushing more of his thick, hard cock into her mouth. She didn't mind; she wanted to take all of him.

The position, though, began to frustrate her—she wanted to suck him, good and hard. She swirled her head, tickled his shaft with her tongue in hopes it satisfied him. His answering moan declared he enjoyed it, and the wicked glint in his eye, the tension in his jaw gave her the sense she did right by him.

After a deep suction, she lowered down slightly to keep only the tip of his cock in her mouth. She brought her cheeks in around him and bobbed her head. Reed moaned and leaned his head back.

He returned his gaze to hers, and the man before her now held a look she'd only fantasized about. More than possessive, even more than his need to come—this was primal.

"Enough," he ordered.

Marley gingerly moved away, rested her head on the pillow as Reed climbed onto the bed and straddled her. He grabbed on to the headboard, brought his knees up next to her armpits, and raised himself, bearing most of his weight on his hands.

"Tilt your head to open your throat." He placed his cock on her lips. "You will take me as deep into your throat as you can."

Marley's mouth stretched to accommodate his girth, but after a few slow thrusts, her lips relaxed, her tongue settled in a good position as her throat opened.

"Fuck, you're good at that," Reed said.

The position wasn't exactly comfortable, but she paid it no attention. His moans and the look of pleasure shining on his face sent shivers all through her. She also understood enough of BDSM to know that to give him the pleasure he sought meant she'd get it back tenfold. Besides, the position was so erotic it made her feel naughty in the best of ways.

His thrusts picked up the pace, and she noted that even though he told her to accept him in deep, he was being careful not touch the back of her throat. Trust. Yes, he'd push her to a point where it'd test her, open new doors for her, but he knew how much she could take and wouldn't go past it.

Each thrust was fast. He rocked his hips as he did exactly what he said he'd do—fuck her mouth, and splendidly so.

REED'S STOMACH TIGHTENED as his testicles drew up. Marley was talented with her mouth, and the way her lips felt as he slid in and out was enough to make him explode. Not something he wanted to do. He slowed his thrusts, then stepped back, and Marley made an unhappy noise.

He chuckled. "I have no qualm about fucking you this way until I come, but I want to feel your tight pussy clamp around my cock before I do." He could sense that her submissive nature didn't appreciate him stopping her. To not let her finish him would leave her feeling as though she hadn't fulfilled him.

Reed removed the belt from one of her wrists. "Turn over." Marley responded without hesitation. "Angle your hips up and show me that delicious ass."

She did as he asked and presented herself perfectly.

Not only did he get a marvelous view of her ass and thighs that he found sexy as hell, but she'd spread her legs wide enough to reveal her pussy.

He adjusted her hand on the headboard to make it more comfortable before he tied up the other again. As expected, Marley sighed, and her body relaxed—all telling him how much she enjoyed this. In time he'd increase the bonds on her, and suspected soon he'd be able to hog-tie her, leaving her completely restrained. The thought sent a thrill through him, but he needed to proceed slowly to reach that level of trust.

Once settled, he moved in behind her, positioned himself between her thighs, then buried his face in her ass. He licked his way along her damp flesh not only to taste her, but to awaken her desperation for him.

Reed traveled along her anus, down her folds until he found her nub. There he tickled the sensitive skin and teased it until she pushed back against him—squirmed as she attempted to find relief. When her moans became harsh pants, he applied a deep, firm lick back up until he reached her ass cheek, where he gave her a little bite. Marley cried out—not in pain, but in longing.

Reed straightened up, reached down to his pants, took out a condom, and applied it. He pushed on Marley's hips to lower her; then he straddled her thighs. He placed his cock at her entrance, waited only a moment before he pushed inside of her. His eyes rolled back into his head as the wet warmth of her surrounded him.

He gripped her hips and began thrusting, but pulled on her body at the same time to fuck him back. The sensation stiffened his cock further. Marley was a remarkable sight—her beautiful body made his restraint falter. Maybe now that he cared for her, he was overwhelmed with emotions, which continued to make his normal flawless control melt away into desirable needs.

He realized the urgency of his impending release, and not only did he increase his thrusts but deepened them. He placed his hand under her pelvis and lifted, angling her so his cock would rub against her G-spot. Marley's pussy went into convulsions around him. Her screams now were neither hidden nor controlled.

He suspected Marley could find another release in no time, but he knew enough of her now to know she'd not come as hard as he wanted her to. She loved the flogger, which told him she loved the sensation of pain intertwined with pleasure. It forced sensations to overload her, and that is exactly what he wanted. This he didn't need a toy for.

"You have the sexiest ass I've ever seen." He did not hide how he marveled over her in his tone. "Yet it needs color, I would say." He slapped her ass. Marley squeaked, which might at first have been a response but turned into a sound of shock thereafter.

Reed glanced down—his handprint marked her ass—and he grinned. Using both hands, he squeezed her cheeks firmly. Marley gasped but thrust back against him. She held nothing back, and she screamed out her pleasure for all to hear, only making him fuck her harder.

Every hit he delivered, he followed up by a hard thrust, not giving her a minute to breathe, overwhelming her with sensations. His efforts paid off. Her pussy tightened around his cock, which made him moan and nearly go cross-eyed with pleasure.

Still it wasn't enough for him—he wanted to witness Marley lose herself completely. He reached forward and pulled on her hair. Marley's back arched, and she didn't fight the move as the position gave him a better view of her face. As much as he would've loved to continue to deliver her with the hits that were making her ass a beautiful shade of red, his pleasure took hold, and he needed to finish them both off.

He kept her neck angled back, placed his palm between her shoulder blades to pin her and to give him leverage. Here was his prize. Marley softened beneath him; she didn't struggle in the least but found comfort in the inability to move.

A born submissive.

With her docile body beneath him, Reed gathered his strength and fucked her without mercy. Marley's shouts of pleasure urged him on and, with the added weight he applied on her back, made her breathing sound harsh, but it was bliss to his ears. Not only could he hear the sound of her climax building, but he could feel her pussy constricting his cock.

He groaned as the sensation made him cross-eyed. His balls drew up indicating he wouldn't last much longer. He'd not come now. He wanted to finish an entirely different way but needed her to return from her climax before he satisfied himself. As much as this was about her pleasing him—his thoughts remained of her as well.

He bit the side of his cheek to distract himself as Marley erupted into her orgasm.

Hold.

The moment her pussy released his straining cock, he pulled out, tore the condom off, then positioned himself near her face. "Open your mouth." Marley's eyes turned wicked as she shifted her head to the side to give him access and parted her lips. Reed placed his cock back into her mouth and pumped, hard and fast. He'd seen before that she wanted this, craved to be given the reward of his cum, and Reed wanted to offer it—a way to make his submissive feel proud.

As he continued to thrust into the wet space of her mouth, he grabbed on to her face, held her still while he fucked her mouth as hard as he had her pussy. In mere seconds, his balls tightened, body trembled, and with a deep groan, he gave Marley what she desperately sought.

She moaned as she drank his cum, so relaxed under his touch, regardless of how rough he'd been with her.

As the final shot of cum spilled from Reed's cock, he glanced into Marley's eyes and was surprised by what he saw. He pulled out as she swallowed, and he realized the gift had been bestowed upon him—if she experienced this level of gratefulness and honor, he could hardly wait to see where she'd be as a submissive six months from now. Luckily for him, she'd granted him the right to ride the journey with her.

Reed removed the belt from her wrists, flipped her over, then joined her on the bed while he massaged her wrists with his thumbs to help the circulation flow to where deep indentations were.

Marley appeared slightly dazed, studying him, while Reed recovered, feeling a bit hazy himself. After a long pause, she finally said, "You're too good to be true, you know. I've wanted a man like you for so long—fantasized over it. I wished for you, but these were my secret wishes; how can I believe this is real?"

Reed dropped her wrists, laced his hand in her long hair, forced her gaze to remain trained on his. "You're wrong. They're not only your dreams, because I wished for you too." And now that he had her, he'd never let go. He took her lips in a declaration that she belonged to him. She'd bow to him forever, and he'd carve her a path of seduction, holding her heart in his hand like she deserved.

BEG FOR IT

CHAPTER ONE

The warm scent of vanilla drifted through Bella's nostrils as the soft feminine body molded against hers. Raven's sparkling green eyes stared back at her, and even her silky, long brown hair invited Bella to take her pleasures.

Then why didn't she feel aroused?

Even the atmosphere called to her fantasies. Stone walls surrounded her, candles along the floor provided a romantic glow, and a large king-size bed fitted with black silk sheets rested in the center of the bare room.

Raven wore a mauve lace thong, matching bra, and sleek black heels. Her body was nothing less than a perfect ten. Her perky breasts along with her creamy-colored skin should entice Bella. But her dry panties declared her arousal was nonexistent.

Pushing her reservations aside, Bella, who'd dressed in crimson lingerie, pressed her lips against Raven's. Beneath her touch, the woman's skin was flawless as she ran her hands over a soft back.

A gentle mouth melted against hers, which was so different than a man's demanding kiss. Bella parted her lips and welcomed the light swipe of Raven's tongue; then Bella's muscles bunched as an unexpected bubble of emotion rose.

She broke the kiss and burst out laughing. "Shit. Sorry."

Raven dropped her hands that trailed Bella's arms, then frowned. "Is something about this amusing to you?"

"No. No. I *can* do this." She twined her fingers through Raven's silky hair and yanked the woman forward. "I want this." Pressing her lips against Raven's mouth, she swirled her tongue with Raven's and searched down deep to get her motor running.

Delicate hands slid along her back to rest on her ass and squeeze. Bella sucked in a harsh breath and fought against the reaction burning in her gut, but failed miserably. Her laughter tore from her throat.

"Oh God." She placed her hand over her mouth in an attempt to hide her smile. "I'm sorry."

Raven folded her arms. "This is getting old."

"I know. I thought I wanted this, but when I kiss you, it feels all wrong."

"Then let's end this. I won't be offended." Raven's tight features relaxed. "You tried something new, and I give you credit for that. But clearly, you're not turned on by women."

Bella's cheeks warmed. "Clearly not."

Raven strode over to her robe that rested on the floor by the bed. "You're a lovely woman, Bella." She grabbed it, dressed, then handed the other robe to Bella. "I hope you find what you're looking for. Preferably with someone whom you don't laugh at when kissing." With a sweet smile good-bye, she spun on her heels and left the room.

Bella sighed, stared at the now closed door, and wrapped the robe around herself. She was relieved to see Raven go to end this embarrassment, but she was pissed too. She'd made a mess of this, hadn't she?

The pact of seduction formed with her best friends hung over her. Tonight was her night to fulfill that promise. She thought a woman had been her ultimate fantasy. How wrong had she been?

Failure burned wicked in her body.

She entered the dressing area located at the back of the room, then dropped the robe and slid back into her tight black minidress. Leaving the robe on the bench, she strode out of the room and slammed the door with a loud bang.

Without a hitch to her step, she passed door after door to rooms that probably contained people treating themselves to their sexual fantasies, exactly what she should've been doing.

She hurried down the staircase, and the sound of her heels against the wood echoed in the open space.

After a nod at the bouncer who guarded the entrance of Castle Dolce Vita, she opened the thick wooden door and made it to her silver Honda Civic. Her seat belt was fastened, car was started, and she hightailed it out of the parking lot in a single breath.

Darkness surrounded her on the drive from Bowleys Quarters back to Baltimore, and that was fitting since it matched her mood. Each light she passed on the half-hour drive brought her closer to home, which only increased the pout on her face.

After she turned onto the tree-lined street of the two-story colonial-style house that she shared with her three friends, she pulled into the driveway. She parked behind Marley's SUV, cut the ignition, and heaved a sigh.

A warm glow spread out from the living-room window, indicating everyone was still awake. Not much of a surprise. They had all been on pins and needles when Marley went to fulfill her fantasy. They'd be waiting for her too.

What should I tell them?

Exhaustion weighed her down, leaving her needy and craving a hug. Not a state she enjoyed. She gulped back the emotions pinning her to the seat, exited the car, then approached the house. *Be strong, Bella.*

At the front door, she ground her teeth to keep from showing her disappointment and entered the home. All three of her best friends, who were watching a movie, looked toward her.

She forced a smile. "Hi."

"Why are you home?" Marley's green eyes narrowed on her. "And so soon?"

She shut the door behind her, shed her coat, then kicked off her shoes. Sadie and Kyra shifted along the cushions to make room, and she plopped down into the plush couch. "I couldn't do it."

Kyra made a face and flicked her black hair over her shoulder. "Couldn't do what?"

"My night with Raven."

Sadie leaned forward, which gave Bella an unwanted view of her newly purchased breasts. "What happened?"

She ran her hands over her face, then dropped them to glance between the women. "Well, we were kissing, and"—she groaned at the memory—"I laughed in her face."

A pause followed; then laughter erupted, and Bella couldn't help but chuckle too. The heavy weight in her chest released and her muscles relaxed.

Of course they'd understand.

"So you're not attracted to women," Marley said, her dark curls bouncing off her shoulders as she shook with silent laughter.

She grunted. "Not at all."

"What's the plan now, then?" Sadie glanced at Marley and Kyra before her warm chocolate-colored eyes focused back on Bella. "I mean, not that I don't understand, but we made this pact." Her look became knowing. "You'll have to come up with another fantasy."

She nibbled her bottom lip. "I don't have any other fantasies, though." She was aware that she hadn't looked at Marley. BDSM made her confused and curious all at the same time.

Kyra offered a kind smile. "You've got time to sort it out. Sit on it for the next week and see if you can think of anything." She waved her hand dramatically. "Lord knows the castle has everything and anything you could dream up."

Always the voice of reason, Kyra was. "True." She released her teeth that dug into her lip and pushed the frustration behind her, more than done with it all. "Is Reed's party tomorrow night still a go?"

Marley nodded. "Yes, and you're going." She gave a shit-eating grin. "If you're not getting all hot and bothered this weekend, you might as well get drunk."

At least there was that.

⋇

On Saturday night, Kole finished stocking the beer in the fridge and heard the crowd behind him grow louder. He grabbed a beer for himself and cracked it open.

After a big gulp of the brew, he moaned from the crisp aftertaste, then scanned his condo that he shared with Reed. Both were criminal lawyers with a top firm in Baltimore, but that wasn't their only shared connection; they were both sexual dominants.

The roommate relationship had worked out well, and with the shared mortgage, they could afford the luxurious condo.

Their living room was full of friends from the castle, some from the law firm, and others just personal friends. It always amused him to watch those who didn't live the D/s lifestyle mix with people who did.

For most, they'd never notice the way the submissives doted over their Masters, seated lower than the ones who commanded them. But Kole saw it clearly, and it created an ache in the pit of his stomach.

While he didn't want a submissive 24-7, he had wanted one when he demanded it. And he'd never found a submissive who intrigued him enough to start a long-term relationship with.

As he continued to survey the room, one woman caught his eye, and the tension in his muscles increased.

Bella sat on the couch, a gin and tonic in her hand, while her three best friends laughed around her. He'd never seen the woman look so depressed. She'd always been full of sass and the life of the party.

All the reasons he craved to have her under his command. As a man, he appreciated her saucy attitude and the strength she portrayed. As a Dom, he'd enjoy seeing her lose it when she gave him control.

More to the point, her beauty appealed to him; her long blonde hair flowed beautifully over her shoulders, and her tight body aroused him. But the submissive buried inside her tempted him repeatedly.

A low laugh dragged Kole out of his thoughts. He flicked his gaze away from Bella to find amused blue eyes staring back at him. Reed cocked his head. His dirty-blond hair fell over his eyebrow. "Hiding in here, are you?"

"Not hiding, watching."

"Ah, the Dom in you can't help but study." Reed grabbed a beer out of the fridge, opened it, then took a sip. "Who are we studying?"

Kole glanced over at Bella, and her gaze that normally sparkled with life only held dismay. "What's going on with Bella?"

"You just won't leave it alone, will you?"

He ignored the jab that Bella shouldn't intrigue him since she hadn't shown an interest in him for anything more than friendship or in BDSM. "I can't help but notice she seems out of sorts." He looked back at Reed. "And that's unlike her. She's always so put together."

Reed leaned his hip against the kitchen table and examined Bella. "From what Marley told me, she went to the castle for her night with Raven but couldn't go through with it."

Kole shifted on his feet, and his chest constricted at the thought of her being with anyone. "I could've saved her the embarrassment and told her that myself; she's not a lesbian."

Reed nodded firmly. "I'd imagine she realizes that now."

Kole gazed over Bella, pondering the complex puzzle that she was. He'd seen from day one that she had submissive tendencies. But it wasn't his place to inform her, nor was it his place to put her under his command, even if it'd please him.

With a grunt, he glanced at Reed. "What's with the long face, though?"

"Marley said she's frustrated because she failed." Reed's stare became pointed. "You know Bella. I'm sure her pride is playing a part here."

Kole took another gulp of his beer; then he shook his head in frustration. "It's bothering me much more than it ought to, knowing that I could guide her way."

Reed snickered. "Back to this, are we?"

It wasn't a secret that Kole had an interest in Bella. Hell, how could he hide it? Every time they all went out to a dance club or even met at a pub for *Sunday Night Football*, she teased him. But he wasn't the only one captured by a woman. "Marley spun you just as hard."

Reed inclined his head. "Got me there." Then, his expression firmed. "But this is different. Marley knew the lifestyle interested her. Bella doesn't. If you plan to stick to vanilla sex, then by all means"—he waved out toward Bella—"enjoy yourself. But it should stop there."

Vanilla sex didn't interest Kole. Even if Bella could use a good lay to brighten her mood, he didn't have it in him not to demand her submission, especially once he settled himself between her luscious thighs.

Reed continued, "If Bella finally realizes that her tastes extend to BDSM, then it's my responsibility as Marley's Dom—

and boyfriend—to place her with the right one." He lifted his chin, his voice deepening. "That's not you."

Kole snorted. "Thanks for the high opinion, jackass."

"You know what I'm saying, Kole." Reed's tone softened, and he placed a hand on Kole's shoulder. "You've never taken a newbie who's as innocent as Bella into a scene."

"I don't think she's as innocent as she puts off," Kole retorted. "There's a feisty woman in her, and that strength I'd imagine would make for a sub I'd enjoy."

"Strengthwise, yes," Reed countered. "But she's not submissive in nature. I doubt she has it in her to give you the control you want." He dropped his hand, folded his arms. "And then I'll be placed in a position to explain why she can't sit for a week since her ass will be marked for her disobedience."

Kole was well aware of who he was and that he enjoyed pushing his subs to extremes that Reed would never go in order to show their submission to him. Plus that he tolerated much less than Reed did from a submissive.

But something existed between him and Bella, and that told him that Reed's worries were irrelevant. He wouldn't be drawn to a submissive who couldn't give him what he needed as a Dom.

Reed stared hard into Kole's eyes and finally sighed. "Fuck, my talk is pointless, isn't it? You're going to go after her, aren't you?"

Nothing Reed had said would dissuade him. An opportunity had presented itself that he wouldn't let pass him by. Bella needed a fantasy. And he'd give her the one he knew she craved, even if she didn't realize it. "I'll introduce the idea and let her decide if she wants to pursue it."

"Introduce, huh?"

Kole grinned. "I'll awaken that dormant submissive in her, let her squirm awhile until she realizes I'm exactly what she needs."

Reed exhaled, long and deep. "Promise me you won't push her excessively if she doesn't submit to you as you'd like?"

"You know"—he glared at Reed—"for my roommate and friend, your opinion of me is discouraging."

Reed's expression was measured. "I'm well aware that you push subs when they're under your command." He gestured toward Bella. "Be careful with her, or Marley will rip into me, and I won't hear the end of it."

"I won't push past her limits, even if those limits are way too low." He cocked his head and sighed in exasperation. "Does that suffice?"

Reed nodded. "That'll do." He grabbed another beer out of the fridge, then left the kitchen to join Marley.

Kole leaned against the counter, pursed his lips, and regarded Bella. He had no doubt if he offered himself to her for a night of blistering hot sex, she'd jump on the chance, but getting her into a scene might prove difficult.

She clearly sensed his gaze on her, since she'd glanced at him. A pretty blush filled her cheeks, and she looked down at the glass in her hands. A reaction he enjoyed.

He suspected when Bella wanted a man, she didn't hold back and went after him. But when it came to him, she was a shy little thing who couldn't hold his gaze.

Submissive.

Tonight, he needed to open the doorway so she'd finally stop ignoring her interests in BDSM.

You've got your work cut out for you.

Good thing he loved a challenge.

CHAPTER TWO

O nly one thing would save Bella now—a stiff drink. Reed and Kole's parties were always fun, and it was nice to see new friends she'd made over the past month. But her mood was right in the toilet. It'd been that way all day and had only gotten worse since she joined the party. She shouldn't have come.

She cursed on a low breath. How in the hell was she going to get out of her current predicament? Originally, it'd been she who offered the idea of the pact of seduction, and she couldn't even commit. *Pathetic.*

Marley's giggle drew her attention, and Reed had pulled her onto his lap, nibbling at her neck. As horrible as it was, jealously surged. Maybe she had hoped that her fantasy would fill that empty void in her soul. Sure, it was meant as something sexually fun, but Bella craved something…

A part of her remained unfulfilled, even if she didn't understand exactly what was missing. All she knew, her life at this moment was boring with a side of totally sucks.

She glanced over at Kyra, who laughed with Sadie, and nudged her arm. "I'll be back. I need some air."

"Sure." Kyra's green eyes were a little glassy. The wine clearly had gotten to her. "Want some company?"

"Nah." She plastered on a fake smile. "I won't be long."

Kyra gave a nod, then turned her attention back at Sadie as the two chuckled about something Sadie had said. If only Bella had something to laugh about. She rose from the couch and made her way through the crowd.

As she passed, she noticed a man sitting on the ottoman and a woman knelt at his feet with her arms over his legs. The position appeared casual enough, but it also looked…different. As if the woman enjoyed being at his feet. Another spurt of jealously soared, and she gave her head a good hard shake. She was apparently envious of everyone who had a relationship. And since when had she been jealous of a BDSM relationship?

What's gotten into you?

She made her way through the living room and stepped out onto the balcony. The cool air brushed against her skin, and she shivered. Winter still hung on in Baltimore, but what a strange winter it'd been—snow one day, mild the next. Tonight was brisk, but that only seemed to help cool off the annoyance burning her blood.

With her glass in her hands, she leaned on the railing and glanced over the city. Reed and Kole's condo had an amazing view and the lights twinkled below.

She sipped at her drink and pondered her situation. How could she plan another fantasy when the only one she wanted she had yet to fully accept herself? And why was she acting like a bitter idiot?

After a long gulp that had her cringing from the aftertaste, a deep voice interrupted her useless thoughts. "I heard last night didn't go well."

She lowered the glass, licked the moisture on her lips, and looked next to her to find Kole. Like always in his presence, butterflies fluttered in her stomach, but she squashed them and kept her voice controlled. "That's putting it lightly."

His blond stylish hair framed a face worth a second look, and his dark blue eyes shone with a power that made her melt. He leaned against the railing beside her, cocked his head, and she felt the weight of his stare right down to her toes. "Tell me about it."

She sipped her drink, mortified to her bones that she had to admit this to Kole. "It wasn't Raven's fault. I"—she drew in a deep breath and said quickly—"I always thought my fantasy was to be with a woman, but clearly it's not."

"Ah, I see." He took a gulp of his beer before he lowered it. "You didn't get off, I'm assuming?"

She snorted. "If laughing in her face means that I didn't get off, then yes, I didn't get off."

He chuckled, the sound so seductive Bella quivered. In response to that odd reaction, she examined him and couldn't stop from admiring the view.

He was dressed in a pair of dark jeans that no doubt hugged his fine ass, and a black T-shirt that was snug around the muscles beneath. *Good God.* She licked her lips for reasons that had nothing to do with her drink.

"You didn't follow through with your part of the pact, then?"

Her gaze lifted to his face. The glint in his eyes declared he'd been quite aware of her admiring him. Hell, she'd lusted after him since the day they met. A strong sexual attraction existed between them that she hadn't experienced before with any man, especially a Dom.

She blinked and focused away from the warmth that formed between her thighs. "That's right. I bailed on the pact."

His gaze became penetrating as his tone dipped lower. "Why don't you arrange another night with someone else for your fantasy?"

"Because"—her muscles stiffened, and after a long sigh, she grimaced—"I have no idea what that fantasy is now."

"Such a problem for a woman to have," he mused.

She gulped at the way his voice seemed to carry into her soul; then she lowered her head to avoid eye contact with him. He raised his bottle to his mouth, and his arm brushed against hers. Tingles zinged through her, and she squeezed her thighs together to ease the throb of her clit.

How did he make her body do that? Every time he was near, she all but sizzled, and when he touched her, everything was amplified.

"I see that you need help, then, in finding what you're looking for."

It hadn't sounded like a question, which she was glad for since her tight throat made it impossible to answer. He slid his finger along her arm, slowly and with clear intent to unravel her.

She bit her bottom lip. "W-what does that mean?"

He tucked his finger under her chin and lifted her head. "I think we both know what I mean." Those eyes of his burned with the lust that he had obviously contained. "You enjoy my attention, and I'd enjoy you under my command."

Then he pressed a finger on the back of her hand and danced his touch up her arm. His gaze followed his caresses every step of the way. And damn him if she didn't close her eyes and shudder.

A scrape of his nail along her skin drew her eyes open, and he grinned with sin. "Look how beautifully you react to me." He finally reached her shoulder, and she trembled under the softness of his touch that seemed to contradict that power oozing from him. He tucked his fingers back under her chin, drew her head up, and stared intently into her eyes.

Searching for what, she had no idea.

His hold tensed, a shift in his gaze appeared that made her stomach flip-flop, and her panties were now soaked. He leaned in, pressed his lips against hers, and the world froze. His luscious and damn well perfect mouth molded with hers as his silky tongue swept her away. When had anyone ever kissed her like this?

Oh, right—*never.*

He kissed her thoroughly, leaving no part of her mouth untouched; then he backed away but kept hold of her chin. "It's time to stop ignoring what your body needs and accept that you want to be dominated."

Hell, how right was he? Maybe BDSM wasn't her fantasy when she made the pact of seduction with her friends, but after hearing about it from Marley, her interest had grown. She lifted a lazy shoulder to appear nonchalant. "I suppose if I set up a scene with you, that would be a solution to my problem."

"Not good enough." His gaze hardened. "Do you want me to take you into a scene, Bella?"

At his pause, she realized she needed to give a better answer, and she nodded. "I do."

He examined her for a long moment before he finally said, "Now what are your interests in BDSM?"

She melted at the way he stared at her now. So intense. So wicked. Was this a hint of what he'd look like in a scene? Her body flushed, yet she held her focus and lifted her chin. She had always prided herself on staying strong around powerful men.

Her job as a stockbroker in Baltimore's top lending investment firm meant she swam with the sharks. Most of her coworkers were authoritative men. If she'd showed weakness, she wouldn't be where she was today, and she'd worked hard for her position.

"I'm interested in"—her throat went dry. All these fantasies she hadn't admitted to anyone. Was she really going through with this? Her soaking panties declared it so—"ropes, sex toys, floggers, to be controlled, pleasure, and pain." She raised her glass to her mouth and tried to ignore the way her hands shook.

Before the rim could reach her lips, Kole snatched the glass from her hands and set it on the ground next to him. "If we're discussing this and you are serious, you *will* stop drinking."

A flare of irritation rose up that he'd be so bold to take her drink right out of her hands, yet Marley had said that Castle Dolce Vita Doms never allowed submissives to drink alcohol in a scene to ensure they were clearheaded. And since they were discussing what would happen between them, she let it go. "Okay."

He gave a short nod. "Now I want to make sure you're well aware of what will happen and what I expect of you." His gaze searched hers, seemingly looking right through her. "And I need to be sure that I'm the correct Dom for you."

"I don't want anyone else," she blurted out before she could stop herself.

His eyebrows rose. "I don't mind your answer, Bella." A small grin turned up the corners of his mouth. "But do tell—have you put more thought into this than you're letting on?"

Her cheeks had never burned so hot, but she wouldn't be *that* woman who'd stumble around a man. She stuffed her nervousness away, clasped her hands, and demanded her voice to be strong. "Maybe once or twice."

She'd been aware of the mutual attraction between them, so two could play his game. "Are you trying to deny you haven't thought about it too?"

He winked. "Maybe once or twice."

A flutter whipped around inside her, her palms grew clammy, and she squeezed her fingers. Why did he make her act so...knocked off her axis?

"One thing that needs to be discussed is my expectations." He glanced at her hands for a moment as if he took in her reaction before he looked back into her eyes. "From what I know of you as you are now, you'd struggle to meet them. And I want to make that clear so you know what you're getting yourself into."

"What's that supposed to mean?" she snapped. "Why would I *struggle* to meet *your* demands?"

He gave his head a slow shake. "I'm not saying it to insult you, but to give you a stern warning. I don't play lightly."

"Well, I..." Her entire face burned hot as if she had a high-grade fever. Marley had told her all about Kole. How he enjoyed pain play. How strict he was in how a submissive behaved. And all it'd done was increase the throb between her thighs. Solidified the fantasy. "I think I might like that."

He gave a delicious smile. "I have no doubt you would."

And then his lips were back on hers as he swept her away in another leg-wobbling kiss before those plush lips tore away from hers.

"You'll arrive at the castle next Friday at seven o'clock. I'll have a room reserved." He dropped his head, his eyes in the direct line of hers. "When you arrive, remove your clothes, kneel in the center of the room, and wait for me. Clear?"

Heat spread across her body at the images playing in her head. *Nude? Kneeling? Oh God!* She quivered in anticipation.

At his expectant expression, she nodded instead of offering him a breathy response.

"Good." He took her mouth again playfully, nibbled on the corners of her lips, and flicked her lips with his tongue. And when he had her body ramped up to a fever pitch, he backed away to trail his thumb over her lips. "Can you be honest and open with me?"

Drool, honest-to-God drool, formed in her mouth. Everyday Kole was sexy. Dom Kole was to die for. The sheer power that exuded from him, intensity in his features, it all captivated her. He'd asked her to be honest with him—how hard could that be? "I can do that."

He nodded in approval, skimmed her mouth again with his thumb, while his gaze stayed focused there. The smile he gave, the possessiveness held in the depths of his eyes, liquefied her insides.

Something sparked through his touch, only increasing with his kiss, and even more so by the way he looked at her now. One of those *duh* moments. Had what she wanted—desired—been standing right in front of her this entire time?

In less than a week, she'd have the answer.

CHAPTER THREE

The candlelight in the dungeon cast a lovely glow over Bella's naked body. Kole stood over her and loved the defiance in her eyes that appeared when he ordered her to look at the floor. Her frisky attitude aroused him as she presented a challenge.

Could he get her to yield?

Warmth pooled into his gut as she responded to his request, even though she fought against his command. He'd noticed submissive mannerisms in her before through their casual time together, but last week his touch awakened her. *Beautifully submissive.* His kiss had made her melt. *Responsive.*

To her tonight might be about indulging in BDSM to dive deeper into her desires. For him, a juicy piece of steak had been laid out in front of him, and like a lion, he planned to devour it. "Eyes to me, Bella."

Those lovely ocean-blue eyes twinkled in wonderment at him. Damn her, she'd mesmerized him, and his hard cock pressed against the zipper of his pants. He'd removed his shirt the moment he entered the room, leaving his black slacks on, and it was a good thing since the sight of her warmed him from head to toe. "Tonight, your safe word is 'thorn.' Use this if you need the scene to stop. Let me hear it."

"Thorn," she replied, and her nose scrunched up.

He grinned at how awkward that sounded from her. "Since you're new to the lifestyle, if I'm doing something that has you worried, but you don't necessarily want me to stop, you'll say 'rose.' Say it."

"Rose."

"Excellent. If you say your soft-limit word, I can take measure of you, see if I agree, and we can discuss how you're feeling." He leaned in and tilted his head. "I'll decide if I should keep going, or if we should move on to something else."

"I understand," she rasped.

He hadn't even touched her yet, and she was thoroughly aroused, her pupils dilated. The little spitfire held zero comprehension that she'd shine tonight. "I've asked you a direct question, so your response will be 'yes, Sir,' even 'okay, Sir,' or 'I understand, Sir.' If you want to make me very happy, you might say, 'yes, Master Kole.'"

A burn filled her gaze, and Kole understood. Bella had always kept everyone at a distance. He'd seen it time and time again. How she'd pushed everyone away with her brisk, snappy attitude, and he doubted she'd call him "Master." The "Sir" would suffice for now.

"Yes, Sir."

It'd been years since he had anyone new under his command. He usually enjoyed skilled submissives that he could push. Pain along with pleasure could leave women boneless. Yet he appreciated the innocence of Bella. Furthermore, he enjoyed Bella, the woman.

He inhaled and caught a waft of luscious woman mixed with cinnamon body spray. As he gazed over her naked flesh, his cock twitched. Her perky breasts with rosy nipples delighted him. The curves and hard lines detailing her athletic frame and shaved pussy invited him. His daydreaming over what she looked like beneath her clothes wasn't even close to how beautiful she really was.

Perfect.

Leaving her kneeling in the center of the room, he strode over toward the tray of items he gathered for the scene. Each item was chosen carefully from her list of limits she gave him when she signed the waiver required by the castle.

He grabbed the four leather cuffs with fur inside and also took the black ropes off the tray, then returned to her. "Stand."

She rose, awkwardly, which he'd not fault her for. Most times, he'd never tolerate such jerky movements from a submissive, but Bella wasn't his usual submissive. Something he reminded himself of as he wrapped the cuff around her left wrist, then repeated the move on the other. Her sharp inhale and the tremor that ran through her made him smile.

Very responsive.

Once her wrists were bound, he stepped in behind her and grasped her wrists at her back. Then, he laced one of the ropes through the loops on the cuffs.

Bella softened beneath his touch.

Lovely.

He pulled on the rope slightly until she backed up; then he attached the loose ends of the rope onto the wooden post in the center of the room. He added the cuff to her ankle and ran another piece of rope down to the loop on the floor to place her in an inverted Y position.

By the time he finished with the knot on her other leg, she panted in heavy breaths, and her muscles quivered. "Rose," she whispered.

"I'm pleased that you're aware when you should use your safe word. But I'm binding you because there's some trust between us since we've known each other for a while now." He brushed his fingers along her calf to soothe her. "If you go into a scene with another Dom, you're to refuse this until you trust him more." He tilted his head and studied her. "Now then, why are you worried?"

"I can't move, Sir."

"Breathe against your worry and grow comfortable within the restraints." He strode toward the wall to give her space, squatted down, watching for any sign that being bound was something she couldn't handle. The little woman trembled in fear, but those taut nipples couldn't lie. This aroused her.

Within a few minutes, the heavy rise and fall of her chest eased, and the redness in her cheeks faded. He approached, her wanton gaze and enticing scent drawing him to her. "You handled that well, Bella." A slow show of trust he appreciated. "You have your safe word. Remind yourself of that."

"I will."

He grabbed her chin, angled her head back to ensure he garnered her attention. "I explained my rules to you when we discussed your limits and have also given you a reminder a moment ago." Her eyes widen in slight, but he carried on. "If I have to remind you again of how to address me, you'll be punished"

"Yes, Sir."

She might have bitten out the word, but he expected nothing less. Right now, she was playing along to see where this would take her, not giving him the respect he deserved. He sought to change that. "Very good."

Drawing in a long deep breath, he considered her. From what she'd told him and shown him, she had a curiosity toward being bound and flogged, but she was skittish. *Proceed with caution, or she'll end this.* Not on his life.

This little hellion made him curious, and now having her here, a desire rose to show her what she'd been missing in her life. And that included him being in it.

Not pissing around any longer, he reached forward, palmed her sex, and silkiness warmed his fingers. "So wet already, Bella." Her lips parted, a soft moan escaping at his caress. "You might fear the restraints, but listen to your body. It likes it."

He pressed his palm against her clit, and her eyes rolled back into her head. Then he slid his finger into the warm wet space, and her inner walls squeezed against him as he worked her pleasure.

Her breath deepened; she sighed against every touch, and her body liquefied around him. Thrusting in deep, he rubbed the pads of his fingertips against her G-spot. With a loud gasp, her eyes went huge, and moisture flooded his fingers.

He chuckled and withdrew his fingers, and she made unhappy noises. *Greedy woman.* She wasn't used to a man stopping once he started. *Now this is fun!*

Leaving her bound to the pole, he approached a candle sitting along the stone ledge that ran across the middle of the room. He took the white pure paraffin wax candle and turned back to her.

Her eyes widened and her cheeks flushed. Stopping in front of her, he held the candle up to show her the wax pooled within. "Wax decorates a body so beautifully, and I enjoy seeing it on a woman's breasts."

That pretty gaze of hers stayed trained on the candle before she shut her eyes tight. "Rose."

Taking reflection of her, he lowered the candle, and once she opened her eyes, the worry of the unknown raged hard in their depths, changing the crystal blue to almost navy in color. "You're afraid." He said it more of a statement than a question, and she didn't reply.

He skimmed his fingers down the middle of her chest, circled one of her hardened nipples that awaited him, and sensed the tension in her muscles. But how this little lady burned with lust and trembled against his touch.

"The fear is caused from the lack of control in the situation." She released a lovely sigh as he continued to swirl the taut knot. "Remember, you have the power to stop this scene with your hard-limit safe word. Push past your need to bolt."

He gave her nipple a squeeze, and she gasped. "I'd like you try this once because I believe you'll enjoy it." He slid his knuckles over the swell of her breast. "This candle burns at a very low temperature. It'll be nice and warm. No pain." He playfully traced her creamy flesh. "If you don't enjoy the feel of the wax, we can move on. Yes?"

Her lips parted, but then she closed them, and took a deep breath through her nose. She finally said, "Yes, Sir."

"Excellent." He placed the candle on the floor, approached the tray, and grabbed the black blindfold. "I'm covering your eyes for no other reason than for your safety. Wax and eyes don't mix."

"Yes, Sir."

He placed the blindfold over her head and settled it into place, and then picked up the candle. Lifting the candle to her shoulder, he tilted it ever so slightly to allow a drop of the wax to land on her skin.

She inhaled a sharp breath, yet didn't pull her safe word, and the eager shakes of her body begged for more.

Moving the candle toward her breast, he then poured wax over her nipple. She groaned, a seductive sound of pleasure, and his groin tightened. He craved to hear it again.

He lowered his free hand to her pussy, slid his fingers into her slick heat, and pumped them. Then, he poured more wax onto the other nipple, and kept on pouring.

Nothing looked more beautiful than her shaking against the binds, her head thrown back, and the shouts that sang from her throat.

Leaving his fingers in her warm, wet space, he blew out the candle and tossed it to the floor. "Very good, Bella." He removed her blindfold. "You trusted me and pushed past your fear. That pleases me." He grabbed her waist and finger fucked her, hard and fast.

Her screams—mixed from her reaction to the wax and the force of his hard thrusts—drifted across him. Convulsions gave her pleasure away. But he had no intention of giving her what she sought. The moment her tremors increased, he withdrew his hand.

She jerked her head up and her eyes narrowed on him at his refusal of her climax. Yet, like a good girl she stayed quiet when he suspected she craved to order him to continue.

Progress.

Turning away from her, he grabbed the flogger off the tray. The cool leather was perfect in his hand. Once he approached her again, her cheeks were now flushed, but her features went blank as her gaze landed on the flogger.

He raised the flogger, her eyes went huge, and she sputtered, "R-rose."

Three times now she'd used her soft-limit safe word. He understood her nervousness thus far was all about her keeping control. Her issue wasn't her fear, but her inability to allow him to do whatever he wanted to her. Even if she didn't realize it, she was topping from the bottom, which was why he focused on reassuring her instead of reprimanding her for throwing out a safe word so quickly, but his tolerance now faded.

"While I don't mind that you're unsure about this, I *do* mind you overusing the power of words. If you say the safe word again, and if I don't believe you're honestly afraid, we'll be done."

She blinked. Her mouth dropped open before she whispered, "Forever, Sir?"

"You need to trust me." He tucked the flogger under his arm and stared at this beauty of a woman, making a statement of his own that he, not she, was in control. "Right now, you only trust your safe word."

He brushed his finger over her cheek, and he enjoyed when she leaned into his touch. "I won't hurt you, Bella, beyond what you can take. You've set out your limits in the questionnaire we did together. But you must trust me."

Her blink came again, and she stared at him with a vacant expression. "Okay, Sir."

He smiled. "The 'Sir' is coming easier for you now. That's very good, Bella." He raised the flogger and lightly tapped her thigh. No flinch. No squeak. No safe word. Not a surprise.

This woman had strength in spades, and if she allowed him the right, he'd prove it to her. Open her to new possibilities. How she could use the sensation of pain to give her extreme pleasures.

He tapped again, harder this time along the same thigh, and she groaned. Reaching forward, he pinched one of her wax-coated nipples; then he hit harder with the flogger. He lowered his hand and swirled her dampness along her clit before he pushed his finger through her heat.

She jerked against his touch and thrust her hips forward. Totally expected. He'd brought her to the very edge of her orgasm and had denied it. Now overwhelmed with foreign sensations to her with the wax and the flogger, her body responded.

"Holy fuuuccck!" she shouted.

Again, he dropped his hand. Instead of allowing her to climax, he raised the flogger and came at her with a steady stream of heavy thuds in a figure-eight pattern. Her loud shouts spoke to the uncomfortable nature of the hits since she wasn't used to the sensation. But she hadn't pulled her safe word, and pleasure shone in her gaze, making her eyelids hooded.

Lovely red coloration decorated her torso and thighs, and damn, she was a beautiful sight. Her eyes glazed over, not really seeing him. Not acceptable.

Continuing with flogging her, he reached up and pinched a wax-coated nipple hard. "Awareness, please."

Her gaze became alert, and after a couple blinks, her focus returned to him. "Ow," she snapped. "Ouch."

Oh, the sass. How he adored it. The flogger wasn't what she objected to, but the hard pinch he issued. "Stay in the present, and you won't get pinched."

He increased his speed with the flogger as the color of her skin along her thighs and hips deepened. A beautiful shade of red that impressed the Dom in him. Her head was lowered as she vocalized the intensity he pushed upon her.

Here was the limit she'd drawn. If she were any other submissive, he'd push her past this moment, increase the pain when she thought she couldn't take more, but he kept at the same intensity to avoid overstepping her boundaries.

He didn't intend to end this scene. Not now. Not with the woman who had enthralled him from a moment's glance was under his command. She'd yield to him by night's end. Or fuck, he'd die trying.

Dropping the flogger to the ground, he pushed his fingers into her slick heat, pumped them within her hot folds, and her body shook violently.

"Oh God!" she screamed.

"Not a bad way to address me, sweetheart." He gave a low chuckle, laced his fingers into her hair, and angled her head back. "Are you going to come, Bella?"

"Oh God, yes," she gasped. Her eyes were so deep and ravenous. "Oh God, Sir."

Holding her tight, unable to move from the binds around her extremities, and now her head captured in his hold, he lowered his voice. Here was her test. "Beg for it, Bella."

The pleasure widening her eyes faded. Her brow creased as if she fought herself. And that reaction didn't shock him. Asking that of her was pushing her to her very limits.

Bella had probably never begged for anything in her life. He suspected she'd think it a weakness. But here was his limit too. She either gave him total control, or he'd not touch her again, no matter that something existed between them. At her silence, he yanked his fingers from her pussy when her climax peaked. A whimper escaped her as she sagged against the binds. He dropped down, undid the rope on her feet, then tossed the rope aside.

Keeping a good hold of her, he unlatched her wrists from the pole. With her arms still bound at her back, he stepped in behind her, drawing her in close, and placed his arm across her middle. Damn, did her sexy body feel amazing against him. Little. Tight. Perfect.

He slid his hand over her curvy hip, reached her clit, and circled it with the pad of his finger. Quick movements that had her body quivering in need. He rolled, flicked, and pinched at the bundle of nerves.

Her deep sigh made his groin tighten further. He skimmed the hand around her middle, up to her chest where he tweaked a taut bud, and fondled her beautiful breast. Her answering moans implored him.

He pressed his lips against her shoulder, bit down on her soft skin, which earned him a loud gasp from her. She ground her pussy against his hand, and he smiled along her silky skin. Fuck, he enjoyed her.

Pushing hard against her clit, he rolled the bud beneath his fingertips until she panted. Keeping a hold on her, he leaned around her, slid his fingers through her soft, damp lips, and thrust inward.

Her wet pussy tightened around his fingers. Slowing his strokes, he used light touches to refuse her orgasm. Having no doubt that if he thrust in hard once, she'd erupt.

Her breath became ragged. Body visibly shook. Head remained bowed to the ground. "I can't keep doing this." No voice had ever sounded so exhausted. "I don't want to stop you, but..."

Too much?

He removed his fingers, stepped around to take measure of her, and kept a good hold on her arm since she swayed. Frustration rested heavy in her gaze but also held a hint of surrender. One wall was coming down.

Ah yes, she *was* unable to continue, exhausted from fighting against him, but she was also at the brink of handing him control. "You can. You will."

Her whimper didn't stop him from going right back to her splendid pussy.

Staying in front of her, he caressed her clit, moving it beneath his fingertip, and her eyes became hooded. She shuddered, and he thrust his fingers back into her center, groaning as she tightened around him. He wanted his cock right there, strangled by her orgasm.

Her eyes became dark before they shut. Although he would have demanded she look at him, he restrained the order. Baby steps would bring him to a final reward.

To deepen her pleasure, he moved his free hand up the middle of her chest, cupped her nape, and then pressed his mouth against hers.

Lips parted for his intrusion. Her tongue swirled and accepted his. Slowing his movements, he stroked her with a light touch. Tension radiated off her—an obvious fight not to give herself over to him.

Behavior he'd fix. A firm bite on her lip had her cringing, but a deep moan contradicted her body's reaction. He backed away and tangled his fingers in her hair, roughly shifting her head closer to him. "You like control, don't you?"

At her whimper, he added, "What does it feel like to not be treated like a princess that everyone tiptoes around?" Her pussy convulsed, and moisture flooded his hand. He jerked her head again. "To be handled as if you won't break?"

Her breath rushed from her lungs, her gaze wildly ravenous, and her cheeks were bright red. "I enjoy it, Sir."

He had no doubt she did, which was exactly why he upped the tension in the scene. To prove he wouldn't back down and, in fact, would only come harder at her if she refused. This power struggle she wouldn't win.

Tightening his grip on her hair, not allowing her to move, he stilled his hand. "Then enough fucking around, Bella." His voice was deep and threatening as he intended to push her. "Beg for it."

He thrust his fingers within her, fast and hard, as he called to her release. Demanded it. Made it impossible for her to refuse him.

Everyone bowed to Bella—he'd seen it with her best friends—because of her overpowering personality. Not him. A low sigh from her mouth echoed in the room before her pussy clamped down on his fingers. At the first sign of her approaching climax, he yanked out of her, and she cried out in frustration.

Before she had a chance to catch her breath, he thrust back in, demanding her orgasm to rise. Her pussy seized against his fingers, and his balls grew heavy.

"I'll count to ten." He stared intently at the struggling woman. "I'd learn to beg, or you'll be left here. Like this." Her eyes widened, mouth parted to no doubt argue with him, and he'd have none of it. "Ten."

"No—"

"Nine."

She shook her head frantic. "Wait—"

"Eight."

He thrust two fingers into her pussy.

"Seven."

He withdrew; then he pushed back through her heat.

"Six."

He flicked her G-spot.

"Five."

Her deep sigh sent a wave of heat straight to his cock.

"Four."

Her pussy vibrated against him.

"Three."

Her lips parted.

"Two."

She gasped a loud breath, and those eyes...oh, those sweet sexy eyes of hers cleared with determination. "Please. Sir."

He lifted an eyebrow. "Please, what?"

Blue beauties twinkled at him. And for the first time tonight, he witnessed her desire to give him control, her expression wide open for him. Fuck, he'd give her all he had; she only had to ask.

Her ravenous eyes begged him, but that wasn't enough. He needed to hear her submission. She finally sighed, everything about her went lax, shoulders sank, and her body softened against his. "All right," she whispered, sounding on the edge of fatigue. "Sir, I beg you to let me come."

Her submission empowered him in ways he didn't anticipate. He gazed at her, and within the depths of her eyes, he witnessed a Bella he hadn't met yet.

Soft and sweet. Willing and giving. He saw trust. In him.

"Now that sounded lovely." He tightened his jaw as he pumped his fingers, using the full force of his muscles to render the woman cross-eyed. But here was a powerful lesson for her too. "And that is exactly the type of behavior that gets rewarded."

Her slick heat tightened around his fingers, making him work harder, but no sound came from her mouth until she screamed, "Yeeessss."

As her final shout of release echoed in the empty room, he withdrew his fingers but rubbed her clit to intensify the lingering effects of her orgasm. Christ, she looked beautiful, all boneless and flushed.

He twined his tongue with hers, and she kissed him in return with no restraint. Elation soared through his soul. Her trust in him touched him. A warm sensation that made him smile.

Once he backed away from her, he discovered he wasn't the only one grinning.

"Wow." She exhaled with puffy lips. "I think I just came so hard that I, for all of a second, died." At his arched eyebrow, she added, "Thank you, Sir."

He chuckled. "That, my Bella, was to get you out of this"—he tapped her forehead—"and to get this"—he smacked her pussy with a hard hit, and she gasped—"warmed up."

CHAPTER FOUR

Tremors rocked Bella from the tips of her toes all the way up to her head as Kole removed the cuffs from her wrists. She was satisfied to her very bones. Never…not once…had she come like *that*. It was more than a wave of pleasure washing over her—nothing less than a soul-deep explosion of euphoria.

Every nerve ending awakened and seemed to detonate from within. She'd never felt more alive than under the command of Kole, experiencing sensations she'd never dreamed possible.

While she realized that she'd finally succumbed to him, and wasn't quite sure how she felt about that, she recognized it pleased him. And that in turn gave her unexpected pleasure.

Following him with her hazy vision, he strode over to the tray, then deposited the cuffs and rope. Her pulse kicked up a notch as she studied him. This man hadn't used his cock, and she about up and died.

What next?

More pleasure.

More pain.

More Kole.

Oh, such sweet delights.

Turning back to her, he held a long piece of black silk in his hand. He ran his hands over it, twining it between his fingers, and she couldn't look away. The heat that had settled between her thighs now flared back to life.

He slid the silk down her arm. *Good God!* The softness of the fabric was utterly sexy—thrilling.

He placed the loose fabric over her neck, and it rested against her shoulders. Then, he wrapped it under her armpits and around her back.

Using a crisscross motion, he fitted the silk around her until her breasts were supported and her torso was covered, with thin areas of her skin showing. The last of the silk enclosed over her hips, where he tied a knot at the back, fastening it tight.

He returned to her front, and his gaze zoned in on her breasts accentuated by the silk, and burned a trail of hot passion down her stomach. "You're lovely presented this way." He finally glanced back up at her eyes, his expression curious and probing, and the side of his mouth quirked. "Describe how this feels for you."

No one had ever looked at her as he did—pride, adoration, and wicked intent. She gulped to find her voice and considered how the smooth fabric held her. "Like I'm being hugged by soft hands."

He inclined his head, seemingly pleased that she understood his intent. "You presented like this makes me want to lay you out, spread you wide, and fuck you." He lifted an eyebrow. "Something you might want to remember for the future."

Future?

How to read that? Did he mean future as in tonight, or that he wanted more from her as in a relationship? Her heart pitter-pattered at the latter.

"Have you ever been spanked, Bella?"

His commanding tone dragged her from her thoughts, and he grinned at her. "I've made your thighs and hips a lovely color, but I'm fixing to make that ass rosy."

"No, Sir." And why did the thought of being spanked tip her arousal into full gear?

Stepping in beside her, he slapped her ass while he sank his fingers into her hair and pulled her head to the side. "Yes, that's a lovely shade on you." She exhaled, low and deep as her ass burned.

"Thank you, Sir." Instinctively, she shut her legs reacting to the sting that wouldn't go away.

"Legs out."

The barked order made her widen her stance, and he issued another blow to her bottom.

"I don't intend to treat you like a princess, Bella." *Smack.* "I intend for you to earn that sort of treatment by giving me your submission." Another hard hit stung her ass cheek, leaving her bottom to burn.

She gasped, desperately trying not to move, but each hit was fierce, and pain flooded her. But oh shit...so did pleasure, right into her pussy. "I like it, Sir."

"Of course you do." He chuckled. "I also know that you grow tired of everyone bowing to you." He latched on to a nipple, tweaked the bud and pinched it.

Gasping from the sharp pain, she attempted to move away, but his hold on her hair pinned her. "Ouch."

"Don't move, sweetheart. I like you right here." He gripped her breast and squeezed; then he released it to issue the same attention along the other nipple.

Gritting her teeth, she groaned against the sensation, all the while wanting to arch her back and beg for more.

"You have beautiful tits." He slapped each one, then smacked her ass and massaged her bottom. "And a spectacular ass."

"Thank you, Sir," she managed.

Keeping his grip on her hair, he stepped in behind her. "Your body tempts me." He rubbed the plump part of her ass before issuing another hit. "Makes me crave to add color to it." He slapped again, harder this time. "In fact, so much so, I'm enticed to put you on your knees, slam my cock into that slick, sweet pussy, and get a better view of your ass while I take my pleasures."

She squirmed and tried to avoid his hits, fighting all the while to stand still as he issued hit after hit. Each flat-handed smack on her ass caused more pain than the one before. But hot damn, she relished the sensation, and the way he spoke to her so roughly only increased her arousal.

"So rosy." His voice dipped low. "Fucking sexy."

Smack.

Burn.

Whack.

Her nerve endings awakened and became responsive to each hit, more aroused than ever. Kole didn't bring sensations forth; he demanded them with the hard blows, and her body rose to his claim. Overwhelming her. Making her crazed with need.

He rubbed her bottom with his palm in soft circles and pressed his hard cock against her thigh. "Be proud of how much I want you. Hard as steel, yes?"

"Yes, Sir, I'm proud." *Weak-kneed too.*

Two more blows hit her ass. God, she was becoming a desperate, entirely ravenous woman. Each hit only increased her need as his fingertips dug into her skin. One last hard hit rocked through her; then he stepped away. "Present yourself."

She stood still for a moment, wobbling slightly, and pondered. She didn't know much about presenting herself, only what Marley had told her in the few conversations they'd had. He liked her kneeling before. Would that please him?

In hopes that it would, she lowered to her knees and remembered what he said about the silk. She dropped her chest down to the ground, flicked her hair over her shoulder, and exposed her back so he'd get a splendid display of her skin wrapped in the fabric. She spread her legs wide and angled her hips to fully expose her pussy to him.

Oh my God, am I really doing this?

"Now that is a beautiful view." He slid his fingers over her aching folds. "A pussy made to fuck, nice and tight."

She bit her lip as he pushed in and flicked a sensitive area. "I'm glad it pleases you, Sir."

Withdrawing his fingers, he rubbed her bottom again, which was warm from his swats. His attention on her scorching flesh only seemed to cause more heat to rise within her. Then, he smacked her pussy...hard.

She flinched and was shocked again when another hit came upon her ass. It jolted her into a woman she never knew. Desperate.

Take me. Take me now.

She wiggled her bottom, imploring for more.

He slid his finger into her center and thrust in twice. "You've got a greedy pussy that's aching for my cock, Bella, don't you?"

"Yes, Sir." *Greedy.* It was downright painful with an ache that his fingers couldn't satisfy. She pushed against him, demanding more. Needing him to thrust hard and ease the building tension.

He issued another firm hit on her backside. "Not enough for you?"

She pressed farther back in a plea that he'd go deeper. Thrust harder. Do anything to free her from the insatiable need. "It's good, Sir."

"Now darlin', don't lie. Not enough for you?"

Even after he added another finger, it didn't appease her, and only made her desperation soar. Did he do this deliberately? Force her to near insanity until her arousal stole over her coherent thoughts?

No, she couldn't handle this torture. All she had to do was beg, and he'd give her what she wanted. "I want your cock, Sir."

"That sounds much better, and I see that you do." He issued another hard blow on her bottom, withdrew his fingers, then strode toward the tray.

There, he dropped his pants. His thick, long erection sprang free, and he slid a condom over his shaft.

Bella's mouth dried. Her gaze remained glued on his every step as he returned to her, his hand working up and down his erection in leisurely strokes. Nothing had ever looked *that* good.

"Ah, I see you approve of me." His voice held a husky edge. "Best I see to that ache of yours. We don't want a little submissive to whimper in need any more than she already is."

He grinned, and if Bella hadn't been on her knees, she would've ended up there. "I'm going to take my pleasure in you now, Bella."

That thick cock could drive her to places she'd never gone and she doubted she'd return from. "I think it's going to ease my ache...and then some, Sir."

A low chuckle followed as he stepped in behind her. His presence was now hidden. That was until he pressed the tip of his cock against her swollen, throbbing entrance.

With a gentleness that she hadn't expected from him, he inched his way in, slowly, letting her body adjust to his size. He stretched her so fully, and *this* was exactly what she craved.

Once seated to the hilt, he delivered another hard slap on her ass before he grabbed both of her cheeks, gripping firmly. He leaned down over her and all but growled, "I don't fuck gently."

He didn't give her a chance to respond. He straightened up and pounded his cock into her pussy. Skin slapped skin as his cock drove her to foreign sensations. Maybe it'd been too long since she last had sex, or maybe it'd been how hot he'd gotten her, but screams tore from her throat.

Where had her ability to breathe gone? And he wasn't giving her the chance to catch it.

One thrust after another rammed her from behind—over and over again—unforgivingly hard thrusts that she couldn't keep up with. The sound of his low groans filled her ears as her pussy tightened. Her eyes shut, and she drifted away with the pleasure.

A hard hit on her ass snapped her back into the present. "You won't come unless I allow it."

"Yes"—she gritted her teeth to fight off the hints of her climax—"Sir."

He spread her ass cheeks, and he drove deeper into her.

Oh fuck, I'm... "Going to come. So hard. Sir."

"No." His harsh demand echoed around her as he intensified his thrusts, pumping into her ruthlessly. "I plan to use you up, nice and good."

Her fists clenched, and she dug her fingernails into her palms, trying not to fail him. Kole was tough. But so was she. *I can't fail. I can take more. I'm his equal.*

He delivered another couple of smacks on her bottom, only awakening more sensations. Heat zinged from her ass cheek all the way to her swollen clit. "I'm inclined to do this for hours."

Hours?

Not possible.

She wanted to please him, to comply with his demand, but his cock continued to drive her to a place that left her mindless.

Biting her lip, she fought off her impending release and focused away from it. The wetness grew between her thighs, her inner walls convulsing, and her body gave her no escape.

A low chuckle sounded behind her. "You're right there, aren't you?"

As a last resort, she bit her palm, desperate to not climax.

Beg. Hell, that was the answer. "Please, Sir. I beg to come."

Had he sped up?

Another whack on her ass made her squeal as his voice echoed against the stone walls. "No."

Crying out in frustration, she panted against the way her muscles strained. The pleasure now turned to pain that burned awful. Her climax hung, forced by his brutal movement yet denied. It made her crazed.

He reached down, pinched her clit before he massaged the nub. "I love hearing you beg. Let's hear it again. Beg for me to let you blow."

She released her teeth from skin, and her voice sounded breathless. "I beg, Sir."

Smack. "No."

The sting arched her back, and she pressed herself against him.

Hard.

Intense.

Never-ending thrusts.

At the next hit he issued, her skin flushed too hot. Too out of control. Had she really given him this much power? To deny this? Had she lost her damn mind?

Slap.

His balls banged against her clit, and her breathing stopped. She couldn't fail. Not now. Not after *this*. But his cock, the pleasure, the hot burn on her ass—she was so wet, and her pussy contracted... *Need to stop!*

Before she could process what her mind was telling her and what her body wanted, she heard herself scream out, "Rose."

Kole was out of her in a second flat, leaving Bella nearly sobbing. He ran his hand over her sore bottom in a gentle, sweet embrace. "We're done, Bella."

She attempted to catch her breath and control her brain that appeared lost. "Wait! What?"

He continued to skim his hand along her back so delicately as if she'd break, and his voice was tender. "Stay there for a moment, darlin'." He strode toward the tray, deposited the empty condom, then returned to her.

"I warned you about using your soft-limit word again." Squatting down next to her, he offered a warm smile as he brushed his knuckles over her cheek. "But more than that, you've had enough for tonight."

No. This can't happen!

"I was a little overwhelmed and needed a break, which you said I'd get with the soft word." Oh Lord, she even sounded desperate. "Please, let's continue, Sir."

"You're right—I did say that about the safe word, but I also said that I'd take measure of you and determine if I agreed." His features remained tender, as did his tone. "In this case, I did, and you've had enough."

He lifted her and placed her on her bottom, the cool floor an utter relief to her tender skin. Then he removed the silk around her body.

Icy fingertips trailed up her spine as she cringed against the silk's departure. The sensation equaled to his hands leaving her body.

He grabbed a blanket off the tray, wrapped it around her, and gathered her in his arms, effortlessly.

Then he strode toward the back wall and took a seat on the bench and pulled her onto his lap, tucking her head against his shoulder.

"You've done well tonight." He stroked her hair. "Don't take shame that you couldn't handle the last bit there. It'll come in time."

But all she experienced was disappointment. Her body stripped of its release left her sickened, which only increased with the knowledge that she'd failed.

For the first time, she'd lowered her shields that protected her—that made her able to stand up to the arrogant men she worked with and hold her chin high—and she'd been proven not an equal.

"I warned you what would happen tonight and of my expectations." He tucked his finger under her chin, seemingly staring into the very depths of her. "You need to trust me, and this is how we gain that." He smiled gently. "I pushed you far tonight, as I told you I would. Be proud of what you've accomplished."

She dropped her head, not even able to meet his eye. Her body was used up, especially emotionally. Now with the sensations over, she realized she could have held off. Why had she panicked?

"Talk to me." His voice was soft and so unlike the demeanor he'd shown thus far. He forced her gaze back to his by lifting her chin. "How are you feeling?"

Her mind was so lost in the mess of confusion and anger. "I'm not sure what I'm feeling right now," she told him honestly. "But I know I enjoyed everything you did to me."

"Are you surprised by how compliant you were?"

Understatement!

It shocked the hell right out of her. "I didn't expect to enjoy it as much as I did."

He inclined his head as if he had already known her answer. "Nothing you didn't like?"

She shook her head, unable to say to him that she prided herself on being *strong*, and in the face of a test, she nosedived. Yeah, she fucking hated that.

"Lived up to your expectations, then?"

A lump formed in her throat, and she forced her voice to work. "It exceeded them."

Her stomach churned. Why had she done this? Her feelings for Kole were apparent before tonight. Now they were out front and center, and she couldn't keep up with him, wasn't enough for him.

He suddenly stiffened, and his hand tightened in her hair. A flash of emotion rushed along his face too quick to identify. "Tell me your thoughts."

Tell him or not?

She studied him for a moment to read him. To her horror, disappointment shone in his gaze. And that part of her that had doubts about giving him control rebounded. Her defenses rose, and she stood, holding the blanket over herself. "Nothing."

Darkness washed over his gaze. "Back to this, are we?"

"Back to what?" she snapped.

His eyes narrowed. "Bella, why do you get *tough* and shut everyone out?"

"I—"*Oh God, I have to get out of here.* "Thank you for this. For helping me fulfill the pact with the girls."

"Bella," he said sternly. "Answer me."

She stared into his eyes that demanded an answer, but now she only felt trapped. What had she done? How had she let this happen to *her?*

She'd given a man total control, weakened herself, and became *that* woman who offered herself like a doormat. "I should get home. The girls will be waiting. I'm fine."

He frowned. "Now that I don't believe."

She plastered a fake smile onto her face, something she was an expert at now. "Really, I'm great. Promise." The room closed in on her. *Exit. Where's the damn exit?* "I had an incredible time."

One sleek eyebrow arched as he stood with fluid grace. His hand closed on her shoulder. "Don't lie to me, Bella."

Reason, Bella. Give him a reason. "I-I just need some time to think all this over." *Never show weakness. Never get hurt.*

Kole had somehow stripped away the very fiber that made her what she was. He'd made her lose sight of the fight to always be strong. Why the fuck did she give him that control? For what? An orgasm.

"All right, Bella." He lowered his hand, and she exhaled, glad for the freedom. "I warn you that you better not be hiding anything from me." He gestured toward the door. "But if you wish, you may go off and think."

What had he meant by that? She wasn't lying. Not really. Just not telling him her innermost personal thoughts. That was different, right?

She couldn't care to figure it out.

Without a kiss good-bye, hug, or even a wave, she hightailed it for the door. She yanked it open and let it slam behind her.

Hugging herself, she hurried to the women's changing room. Confusion clouded her thoughts, leaving her unable to focus.

I need my girls.

CHAPTER FIVE

Outside of her house, Bella noticed the lights were still on the living room, indicating everyone was awake. No doubt the girls were excited to hear how the night had gone, considering how surprised they'd been when she told them of her arrangement with Kole. Marley's only response was "I sure as hell hope you know what you're getting yourself into."

Now she regretted this whole idea.

She hadn't ever thought of herself as a woman who needed a man to dote over her, but with Kole she desired it. Clearly, she cared for him far more than she'd thought she did, and seeing the disappointment in his eyes made her feel shunned.

With a long, deep exhale, she made her way to the front door; then she strode in. Kyra and Sadie were curled up on the couch watching a movie, but Bella was surprised to see Reed sitting on the recliner with Marley on his lap.

Kyra straightened up on the couch, nearly bouncing in her seat. "How'd it go?"

Bella's breath hitched. Dammit, she didn't want to break down with Reed here, but her hidden emotions were now exposed. Even the usual wall she threw up to stay strong crumbled.

In the comfort of her friends, she broke. "I..." She drew in a shuddering breath, then burst into tears.

All three friends were off the couch in a second and embraced her. Reed remained on the chair, but his stern gaze that normally would shut down all her emotions didn't have an impact.

Marley stared wide-eyed. "Jeez, Bella, what happened?"

Bella sniffed, tried to find her voice, but she was too afraid if she opened her mouth, it'd come out in a sob.

"Did it not go well, sweetie?" Sadie asked softly.

At Bella's continuing pause, Kyra looked around at the other girls with a wary glance, then focused back at Bella. "Seriously, why are you crying?"

She wiped her tears, gulping back the lump in her throat, and kept her gaze on Marley. "It was..." She tried to control her tears, but that only made her cry harder. "Kole, he...hurt..."

Marley's brow creased before she looked back at Reed. He stood with clenched fists, his voice all but a growl. "What did *he* do to you?"

Bella parted her mouth, but nothing came out. *I gave him control, and now I'm lost.* "He..." She'd always been the strong one of the group. Right now her soul was weak.

Reed approached Marley, his features tight, and he frowned. "I'll call you soon." He kissed her cheek, then strode toward the door.

"Where are you going?" Marley called.

Reed never responded, merely closed the door behind him with a slam.

Marley finally sighed, then pulled Bella over to the couch, taking a seat next to her on the cushion. "What happened?" Her gaze probed Bella's. "Did he do something bad to you?"

Bella wiped her tears and pulled herself together with a deep breath. "I just realized that I care..."

Marley gasped with fake surprise and held a hand over her heart. "Oh Lord, she's going to admit it."

Bella rolled her eyes. "Okay, so I've got a thing for him."

Kyra snorted. "When did you get your first clue?"

"Leave her alone," Sadie interjected. "I don't understand why you're so sad, though. You said he hurt you. Did he physically harm you?"

"Well, he hurt me...a little, but I liked it." The girls giggled, and she added, "He didn't do anything but give me a night I'll never forget."

Kyra's lip curled. "And this is a problem because..."

"Because he doesn't share the same feelings that I have for him."

"I don't believe that," Marley retorted. "Whenever you're around, his gaze follows you. Even if you haven't noticed, I have." Her look was knowing. "That man has been after your ass since day one. Reed even said as much."

Bella shook her head, her lip quivered, and failure sank deep into her gut. "Not anymore."

"What do you mean?" Sadie asked.

Lie?

Not an option. A vow of truth existed between the four of them and was the reason they'd been so close since childhood. "I used my safe word, and he stopped the scene."

Kyra's gaze darted to Marley and Sadie before returning to Bella. "I have no idea about this BDSM stuff, but from what Marley has said, isn't it a good thing that he listened to you?"

Marley nodded. "Exactly. I don't get why you're so upset about that."

Bella shrugged. "I think it's because I'm not enough for him. He didn't seem happy with me. You know how Kole is." Marley gave a nod of agreement, and Bella continued, "You've told me that he gets intense and likes to push his subs."

Rage burned in Marley's eyes. "So he did hurt you?"

The pain he offered wasn't the problem, and even that surprised Bella. How it made her so hot and brought her body to life in ways she'd never dreamed of, and offered new sensations that made vanilla sex boring in comparison. "It wasn't like that. He refused to let me orgasm, and I tried to hold off, but I couldn't."

"BDSM is weird." Sadie's nose wrinkled. "Why would anyone want to refuse an orgasm? Isn't that the point of having sex?"

"It makes it more intense." Marley dismissed Sadie's question with a flick of her hand. "Did he tell you he was disappointed?"

"No. But I saw it in his eyes."

"Hmm...well, I don't know why he'd be disappointed in you." Marley tapped her lip as she studied Bella. "But besides that, did you enjoy yourself? Are you feeling okay...you know, with it all?"

"I loved it." Bella bowed her head and tangled her fingers together, her heart breaking into pieces. "I enjoyed him."

A long pause followed as her friends just stared at her, offering comfort in their soft expressions. Then Sadie said, "Sooo...what did he do to you exactly?"

"'What didn't he do?' is more like it." She glanced between her friends. "Honest to God, I thought more than once I was going to die from pleasure."

Kyra laughed. "That sounds like a good thing, even if you'd never catch me being tied up and hit with anything. The man would have a black eye and a broken nose if he dared to boss me around."

"Oh yes, you'd just rather have two dicks," Marley countered. "You're up next. Let's just wait to see what *you* end up doing."

Kyra blushed right to her hairline and focused on Bella, diverting the conversation. "What went wrong, then?"

"I don't know." *God, how pathetic do I sound?* "He was being really sweet and stuff, cuddling me afterward; then when I looked at him, everything changed, and he was cold."

Marley patted her leg and gave a reassuring smile. "Kole is a tough Dom. Even, I, who've been in the lifestyle now for a little while, couldn't—and would never in my life be inclined to—be with him. He pushes in ways others wouldn't." She gave her a hard look. "I told you this about him when I first noticed this thing between you two."

"Yes, I remember, but I needed to fulfill a fantasy, and well...he was there, and I wanted..."

"His junk," Kyra finished for her.

Bella snorted. "To put it simply."

"But I'm still not getting what bothered him," Marley said. "Are you sure you're not misreading him? Did you not talk afterward? I mean, that's why you discuss things during aftercare, so you can figure it all out."

Bella gulped at the rise of emotions, which were ready to burst. "Yeah, we talked and everything. But it wasn't what he said that was the problem. It was the look he gave me. Like I failed him or something."

Yeah, that was what bothered her. A look she'd seen so many times from other men. Like she wasn't enough. Hadn't been strong enough to hold her own.

With Kole, she let him in more than she had anyone else, which included giving him total control, and he spat on it, or the disappointment in his gaze did.

Marley took her hand and squeezed. "It was your first scene, Bella. Cut yourself a break. Tonight, I'm sure you went through lots of emotional crap. I know I did the first time. It *can* be overwhelming, so let yourself just soak it all in." Her gaze firmed. "And let me tell you, if Kole is disappointed in you, he's a total dick, and you *should* stay away from him."

All this, though, wasn't about her night. It was about the ache in her heart and the hard truth that she craved Kole's approval. And she'd never needed anyone's approval of her.

For the first time in so long, she opened herself, gave Kole all of herself, and... *He let me down just like men always do.*

Not only the ones at work, but the list of men she dated and the relationships that had gone nowhere but down the toilet.

Marley smiled softly. "I'm really sorry that you came away from your scene so upset, but I'm sure Reed will get to the bottom of this."

No way. Reed was so *not* cleaning up her mess. She forced her emotions away, feeling foolish for crying over this. Good God, where was her strength?

She stood, pushed away the ache, and left the warmth of her friends and the comfort they always offered. "What's to find out? I couldn't keep up or give him what he needed. He wants a woman who can. Nuff said."

Marley's brow puckered. "Bella, but—"

"No," she interrupted. "I'm done talking about it. I'm feeling better now. I'm just tired, and I guess it overwhelmed me." She looked at each of her friends. "Sorry I got so emotional. Tomorrow I'll be a hundred percent. Tonight I'm just..."

"Sore?" Kyra offered.

She forced a grin, which made her friends giggle. "Exactly."

⌁⍀⍵⌁

Kole raised his beer to his mouth and chugged it back, as he sat at the kitchen table. He thought he'd gotten to Bella. It appeared that he'd made ground with her, and she opened up to him.

The woman he'd seen during their scene was the one he knew lived within her, past all those defenses she put up. Then, she clammed up and returned to the same old standoffish Bella.

He racked his mind trying to figure out what had changed. Was it something he said that put her on edge?

The change in her demeanor was obvious, and it disappointed him. He wanted the Bella he'd seen tonight. Who gave him control because she trusted him and even more so, was happy with him. That woman he adored.

Maybe he'd been foolish to think something more would come out of their night together. But there it was. He wanted her as *his* submissive. And he hadn't any idea what he'd done to fuck it up.

Damn it all to hell!

The front door of the condo slammed open and dragged Kole away from his thoughts. Reed entered the kitchen, fists clenched and veins protruding from his forehead. "What the fuck did you do?" Reed strode forward, and before Kole could catch up, Reed sucker punched him, sending Kole flying out of his chair to land on the floor.

Reed stood over him, his eyes burning with fury. "I told you to leave her alone, that it wasn't a good idea to take her into a scene." He pounced and attempted another punch, but Kole grabbed his arms, pulled him down to the ground, and tried to get the upper hand.

"It's not your business."

"It fucking *is* my business when Marley wrings my neck because of you. You promised you'd not be tough on her." Reed groaned as Kole kneed him in the gut. "What were you thinking?"

Reed pushed Kole's head to the side, squeezed his thighs around him, and Kole moaned as his cheek squished into the hard floor. "Get the hell off me!" He shifted his hips up, pushed Reed off, and reversed their positions.

"I warned you about this." Reed punched, but Kole dodged the hit by grabbing his arm and pinning it. "You played with someone you shouldn't have, and you broke her."

Kole jumped off, breathing heavily, but *that* statement surprised him. He held his hands up in surrender. "What do you mean I *broke* her?"

Reed pushed himself off the floor, and his fists remained clenched at his sides. "She returned to the house in tears."

Hot rage flowed through Kole's veins. So she had been hiding from him. But her reaction gave him hope too. Whatever had upset her, he didn't understand, but if something made her cry, it meant she cared more than she showed. "Is that so?"

"I will ask again only one more time before I beat your ass." Reed raised his fists. "What did you do to her?"

Not much of a surprise that Reed attacked first and asked questions later. Wasn't that what brothers did? And their relationship was that close.

"I didn't do anything to her." He drew in a deep breath, pondered this, and was unsure of where to go from here, only knowing Bella was in trouble—serious trouble.

"She's a lovely submissive, but she refuses it. I played with that and had her submitting after a while. Yes, there was some pain—not much, I might add—but she loved every minute of it." He'd not forget that simmering heat in her gaze anytime soon. "That's it. That's all, jackass."

Reed's stern features didn't waver. "I don't believe you."

"Believe it or not, I *could* care less." Kole shrugged. "What's it to you, anyway?"

"You, of all people, should understand the demands you make on a submissive. Whatever you did left her in tears, Kole." He huffed out a frustrated breath. "Why am I even having this fucking conversation? You're an experienced Dom. You *know* better."

"When she left me, she was the strong Bella, as always. Completely closed off and showing no emotion." He ground his teeth together. "She said she needed time to think, and I acknowledged that since she outright told me she was fine. Of course, she's a sneaky little woman and hides her emotions well."

Reed's expression became knowing. "You clearly got to her."

"I suppose. But she never said a word about it, even after I pressed her." He clenched his fists "And she certainly never asked for anything more."

A huge smile spread across Reed's face. "Say it ain't so." At Kole's arched eyebrow, Reed added, "You're in love with her."

Kole exhaled through his nose. Why deny it? They both knew it was true. He'd never believed in love at first sight. But he definitely believed in lust at first sight. He'd wanted Bella under his command from day one. Now that he'd had her, something else developed—his desire to keep her. "The woman has woven a damn spell over me."

"The challenge of her?" Reed offered.

Kole inclined his head. "I'll tell you this much—not once did I miss how far some submissives will go for me, and *that* surprised me."

"She keeps you content, then?"

"Bella could make me want no other." And knowing she was hurting created a heaviness like a rock in his gut, even if anger tinged it. "Fuck, she's in tears now?"

"Was when I left, but I'm sure the girls have calmed her down."

He grunted. "I could have helped her—talked her through it." He stared at his friend, and Reed returned the knowing look. "This hiding nonsense will stop."

Reed gave a firm, approving nod, seemingly agreeing with Kole's intent to make things right with Bella. "What's your plan?"

He stood and glanced down at Reed. "Her time to think things over has ended." Now he was fueled by motivation to fetch his sub and teach her a lesson. "I'm going to straighten her out."

"I'll call Marley and tell her you're on your way so that the girls don't kick your boys when you get there."

Kole said nothing more, wound up tight, and he exited the condo. He made quick time to his car in the parking lot and approached his black Dodge Charger.

The lights in the parking lot were dim, but the shine of the paint on his car glistened. Yeah, his car could make him smile, even though right now his unhappiness at Bella masked it.

Once at his car, he pressed the Key Lock button to open the doors, just as a voice sounded behind him. "Give me your money."

Kole slowly turned. "Pardon me?"

"Your money." The kid of no older than seventeen appeared hopped up on some hard drugs waved a gun at him. "Give it to me."

"Kid, go home."

Wide brown eyes stared at him so bloodshot and crazed. The teenager glanced around frantically before waving the gun at him again. "Now. Give it to me."

He heaved a sigh, wanting to get to Bella—to deal with her, not this shit in front of him. He reached into his back pocket, took out the four twenty-dollar bills in his wallet, then handed them to the kid.

"The credit cards too."

Kole narrowed his eyes. "No."

"No?"

"I've given you money. My generosity stops there." His fist tightened in preparation for the fight ahead, readying to knock this kid out. "Go home."

A long second passed before the teen lurched forward. Kole grabbed the hand closest to him and twisted to get him on the ground, but at the same time, the teen hit him above the eyebrow with the gun. Pain laced his forehead, and a warm gush of blood slid down his cheek.

He groaned, kicking the kid and sending him sprawling to the ground. The idiot, with gun in hand, scrambled away and ran.

Go beat the kid?

Another gush of blood along his face reminded him that he had a slice in his head. Cursing, he yanked his shirt off and held the cotton against the wound to stop the bleeding.

He opened the door to his car and sank into the seat. Then he glanced up into the rearview mirror and pulled his shirt away—the deep wound needed stitches.

Fuck.

He started the engine, tied the shirt around his head, and made a beeline out of the parking lot.

Stitches first, then Bella.

CHAPTER SIX

Heat burned through Bella as she replayed the night with Kole in her mind—the sensations he offered, ones she never knew possible. More than just getting off, more than just a simple orgasm, an explosion of sensations that held no beginning and no end.

The time that passed, which should have been her sleeping, was actually spent tossing and turning as she mulled over what happened between them. How her pride had made her leave him.

She had opened herself up to him, expected him to say...something. Ask her on a date, for another scene...just something. When all that stared back at her was disappointment, failure entered her soul, and her walls rebounded.

Never let anyone in. Be stronger than the men around you. Prove your worth.

She'd let Kole in more than anyone before. Let him overpower her, make her beg for him, and she had been exposed. His disapproval sickened her.

A creak of her bedroom door, followed by Marley's voice, interrupted her thoughts. "See, I told you he's not here. I waited a good hour, but when he didn't show up after you called, I knew something was wrong."

Bella rolled over just as Marley shut the door. Pushing off her blankets, she slid out of bed, dressed in yoga pants and T-shirt, then hurried out of the room to find Marley and Reed standing in the living room. "What's wrong?"

"Did Kole come to see you?" Reed asked. "I know Marley never saw him, but maybe he came and left."

She shook her head. "Why would he?"

Reed frowned before he focused back on Marley. "You're right. Something is wrong."

"What do you mean?" Her heart thumped. "What's going on?"

Reed never answered. Instead, he tucked his hand into his pocket and pulled out his phone. He dialed quickly, then raised it to his ear, and a moment later, he ended the call.

"He's still not answering. It's going straight to voice mail." He stared at Marley with concerned eyes. "This isn't like him. If he said he was coming here, he would have."

Bella couldn't catch up. "Kole was coming here?"

But before anyone could respond, Kyra's yawn sounded behind Bella. "Why are y'all being so loud?" Kyra said, peeking out from her bedroom door. "You woke me up."

"Kole's missing," Marley said.

Kyra strode quickly into the living room, wide awake now. "Missing?"

"We need to call around to the hospitals and see if he's there," Reed instructed. "His car wasn't at the condo."

"On it." Kyra shifted into serious mode, which fit her so well.

Reed continued, "I'll contact the castle and see if he went there."

Fury so intense and wicked soared through Bella's body, making her hands tremble. *He's at the castle with another woman—another submissive.*

Jealousy split her open like a knife in the gut. She should hope he was there, unharmed, but the thought of him being with anyone else crippled her.

Everyone was in a flurry of activity, unbeknownst to Sadie who remained asleep. Reed was on the phone with the castle. Kyra was in the kitchen calling the hospitals. Marley was pacing in front Reed. Bella just stood there, unable to move.

The past hours had been nothing but a whirlwind, leaving her mind a complete mess. *Kole's missing?*

Reed tucked his phone back into his pocket. "He's not at the castle."

Bella couldn't even process what that meant. Relief that he wasn't, but then where was he?

Right then, Kyra hurried into the room, breathless. "He's at Johns Hopkins."

"Why?" Bella squeaked, glancing from face to face, then finally settled back on Kyra. "Is he hurt?"

"The nurse wouldn't say." Kyra grabbed Bella's coat off the hook and shoved it at her, while Marley and Reed put their shoes on. "Confidentiality and all. But she told me enough that I got the impression he's not critical or anything."

Her muscles relaxed, heart slowed. Good news. She stuffed her feet into her clogs and fumbled with the buttons on her coat as her hands trembled. Why was she trembling? Drawing in a deep breath, she calmed herself. Reed smiled at her, then did up the buttons.

"Thank you," she whispered.

He gave a firm nod, opened the door, and ushered Bella and Marley out. "Let's go."

In quick time, they were in his truck and on the road. The late night was almost a blessing because the roads were dead. Reed paused at the red lights, but when the street was clear, he ran them.

Mere minutes passed before Reed squealed his tires, coming to a stop in the hospital parking lot. They were out in a flash and jogged to the front doors. The emergency room was full of patients all awaiting treatment. They hurried to the desk where a nurse sat talking on the telephone.

Reed tapped his hand on the desk, but the nurse raised a finger at him, not looking up.

Bella gritted her teeth as she listened to the nurse having a personal conversation, and even though only seconds passed, her patience fled.

She leaned over the counter, grabbed the phone from the woman, then slammed it on the receiver. The nurse jerked her head up and scowled. "Excuse me?"

"Where's Kole Walsh?" At the nurse's silence and continuing frown, Bella smacked her hand on the desk with a loud bang. "Where is he?"

Marley snickered. "Oh look, Bella's back."

The nurse pursed her lips, then glanced over a chart. Her sneer returned to Bella. "Room one hundred and twelve."

Without a thank-you, because the nurse didn't deserve one, Bella with Reed and Marley in tow dashed down the hall. Bella scanned the numbers on the doors until she reached Kole's. She took one step into the room, then froze.

Kole was lying on the bed, bare chested, one knee up and an ice pack on his forehead. Her breath whooshed from her lungs. The memory of their time together flooded her mind. Her body awakened, as if his presence ignited a spark in her that made her fully aware of him.

Brushing past her, Reed strode into the room, his voice deep and curt. "What happened?"

Kole turned his head to the side, and his gaze landed on Bella. He didn't look disappointed like he had earlier tonight. Fire burned in the depths of his eyes, but as he glanced at Reed, that rage faded.

Is he angry at me?

"Got mugged," he replied.

"Seriously?" Marley asked, stepping up next to the bed.

"Stupid junkie wanted money and pulled a gun on me."

Bella's heart skipped a beat. "Gun?"

Kole didn't even look at her. He completely disregarded her as if she hadn't said anything. As if she wasn't standing there worrying about him. Her own irritation flared to life.

What did I do to him?

Kole continued, "He knocked me in the head with his gun. Idiot was too high to realize shooting me would have done the trick."

Reed took a seat in the chair beside the bed. "Did you subdue him?"

"Thought about it." His fingers clenched and jaw tightened. "But I had other things to deal with."

"What happened after he hit you?" She asked, proud her voice sounded strong.

Once again, he didn't even acknowledge her, and her muscles tensed. She took a further step into the room and glared at him. "Stop ignoring me."

Reed glanced over his shoulder at her, frowning. Marley jerked her head to Bella and shook her head slowly, as if warning her. But she didn't deserve to be treated in this manner. She'd done nothing wrong and held her ground.

Kole rose up on his elbow, lowered the ice pack to display a good five stitches over his eyebrow, and pinned her with his stare. His voice flowed through the room, sounding smooth like velvet, but stern. "Bella. Take a seat. Stay quiet."

A wave of emotion washed over her, compelling her to listen. Normally if a man spoke to her in that manner, she'd curse at him and probably flip him off. But she found her legs moving her toward the chair and was shocked at herself when she sat down.

He finally removed his steely gaze from her and looked at Reed. "Came here thinking they'd stitch me up and send me on my way. Only to find out they had to report it to the cops, and I spent an hour answering questions. Then, the doc thought I should stay until the morning just to be sure I didn't have a concussion."

Bella clasped her hands in her lap, looking down, and a swell of emotion bubbled up. *Pissed* might have been an understatement. And his unhappiness with her now was worse than his disappointment.

"You should've called us, dipshit," Reed chastised.

Kole snorted. "It was late. I thought you'd all be asleep, and I wasn't in serious condition, so why bother?"

She peeked up at him under her lashes. His gaze was on Reed, and she'd never felt so ignored. She yearned for him to look at her, offer a glance of the appreciation that she'd seen tonight, and his refusal made her throat tight.

"All right." Reed stood. "Marley will drive your car home. Then I'll come back in the morning to get you."

Kole reached into his pocket, took out his keys, then handed them to Marley. "I parked in the far left corner of the parking lot. Wreck my baby and there'll be hell to pay."

"I'll drive carefully, and I'm glad to see you in one piece." Marley turned on her heels and started toward the door. She gave Bella a knowing look and whispered, "You, my friend, have pissed him off."

"Yeah, no shit."

Marley patted her shoulder and offered a kind smile. "Don't worry. His reaction tells me your concerns are for nothing."

"Which means?"

"He wouldn't punish you like that if he didn't care."

"Punish?"

Marley laughed under her breath and gave her a quick hug. "I'll wait for you in the hallway. Just don't go *Bella* on him and you'll do fine." Then, she left the room, leaving Bella to focus back on the men.

Reed squeezed Kole's shoulder, spoke in a soft voice. "Had me worried there, man."

"Got a bad headache, is all. Just added decoration to the black eye you already gave me." He closed his eyes and grunted. "Come as soon as you get up. I want out of this place ASAP."

"Sure." Reed turned away from the bed, then headed for the door. Once next to Bella, he stared at her intently, as if he understood why she was sitting in the seat not saying a word. Bella hadn't even understood the reasons.

He eventually freed her from his hard examination, and as he strode by, she stood and glanced over at Kole resting on the bed looking relaxed. Then, she turned to leave.

"Bella," Kole called, cool and collected. "Come here."

With a deep breath for bravery, she approached him as he said, "We have to talk, don't we?"

The curtness in his voice made her realize he really was angry with her. She had to wonder if it was because she disappointed him earlier, and now with the event he experienced, was he taking his frustrations out on her?

Instead of being enraged like she normally would be, she only experienced shame and sadness. Her heart bled. Now was the time to be honest. "I tried, you know."

"Tried, what?"

"To be what you needed." She heaved a sigh. "I know that you might find me boring compared to the others, but I can—"

He raised his hand, cutting her off. "Do you believe that I'm upset because of something that happened in the scene?"

"Aren't you?" Her lip trembled, and she hated that. She wanted to be stronger than this, to fight to prove that she could handle the likes of Kole. But her heart broke at his dismissal of her and left her feeling bare.

"Come sit on the bed with me." She settled in next to him, and he wrapped an arm around her as he continued, "You lied to me."

"I didn't lie."

"Oh no?" He arched an eyebrow. "You told me you were fine. Promised it, if I remember correctly. But then I find out from Reed that you arrived home quite upset." His eyes narrowed on her. "Explain that."

Heat burned in her cheeks. This was what it was all about—it had nothing to do with her pulling her safe word, and everything to do with why she kept him at arm's length. Would he make her admit she cared for him? "It's not what you think."

"Then what is it, Bella?"

Only the truth would save her now. "I like you."

He leaned back against the bed and stared at her, really looked at her as if she surprised him. "You *like* me?"

Glancing down at her lap, she twined her fingers and held on tight. "I..."

His finger came under her chin and lifted her head. His eyes were welcoming and warm, and his voice was equally soft. "Tell me."

"I know I disappointed you."

He frowned. "Don't read into me, especially considering you're reading me wrong." He tightened his fingers on her chin. "I'm disappointed with you for not sharing what was mine to hear. Those feelings you experienced revolved around my interaction with you. I deserved to hear your thoughts. Not your friends'."

"It's not so easy for me to admit this to you."

He swiped his finger so delicately over her jaw in a way that fully contradicted his last move. "We're finally getting somewhere." His mouth arched up ever so slightly. "I told you, Bella, I'm not going to treat you like a princess. I'm not a knight sweeping in to rescue you. You don't need it, and frankly, I'm not made for that."

"I don't want anyone to rescue me."

"Then speak your mind, woman. You're so very strong, but yet you hide away like a skittish cat. Why is that?"

"I don't know." At his arched eyebrow, she quickly corrected herself. "I don't enjoy looking weak. I've had to fight hard in my life to prove myself, and I guess...I wanted to prove myself stronger than you."

"Thank you for that honesty." He slid his fingers along her jawline. "And you thought that submitting to me weakened you?"

"I..." She shut her mouth, knowing she had been about to lie, drew in a deep breath, and tried again. "It scared me. I dropped all my guards with you. I wasn't expecting that. I didn't think I'd ever give that control to someone, and I'm not sure if I can give you what you need. So, yeah, that worries me."

"I believe that's for me to decide if you can give me what I need. Not you." His tight expression warned her not to assume on his behalf. "You don't have to be a perfect submissive, Bella. You need only to be *my* submissive."

The possessive claim sent sheer joy in a form of a quiver rippling through her. "But then why were you upset at me after?"

"You closed yourself off to me. You think I didn't see it in your face? Feel it in your body when you tensed?" He shook his head, slow and steady. "If you really listened to what I told you instead of hearing what you believed, then you would've understood what upset me.

"It's why the exchange of words is so important in a D/s relationship, because in that moment you'll be exposed, your emotions raw. You need to let me in, so we can work through it together."

His jaw clenched, and he continued, "But your issue with trust is something that cannot be overlooked." At her parted lips, he raised his hand. "I'm not talking about you using your safe word. That's there for good reason. I want you to use it if you're not comfortable."

Okay, that relieved her some.

"But you won't grow either as a submissive or in trust if you don't believe that I know what you need. You were overwhelmed and panicked. Totally understandable."

He understood; she hadn't expected that.

He gave her a measured look. "I had pushed you enough, which is why I ended the scene. You needed to see that I would listen to your safe word. That's how trust is earned, and I needed to earn that, Bella." He tapped the tip of her nose. "And you needed to learn that if you use those words, it comes at a consequence, which means you need to use them wisely."

"Oh."

He chuckled softly, leaned in, and kissed her forehead. "Now tell me, when I ignored you before, how did that feel?"

"Horrible."

He backed away, stared at her, and his gaze was tender. "And now you know exactly what I experienced when you did the same to me."

Awareness struck her. Marley had said he punished her, and that must have been what she meant. He'd done exactly what she did to him, so she'd fully understand what he experienced.

"Not pleasant to have someone ignore you like you're not there, is it?"

Odd way of doing a punishment, but it had the desired effect. "I was wrong."

"Indeed." He smiled in kind. "As to the other matter about how I felt, I was proud of you, in fact. You pushed yourself and submitted like a lovely sub should, which is exactly what I told you and seemingly that you chose to ignore. Thinking otherwise—that's all on you."

"I'm sorry."

Had she really concocted this all in her head? All he wanted was for her not to treat him like the men who'd hurt her before. And she realized in that moment that Kole was the first man who'd ever really seen her...for her. That he didn't want the Bella that she'd become from past experiences; he wanted the real her. More so, she finally understood that he deserved her heart because he'd never mistreat it.

He gave a low chuckle. "Now isn't this nice? And wouldn't this have been so much better if you discussed this after our scene instead of getting yourself worked up in a frenzy?"

At her nod, since she now realized how foolish she'd been, he studied her for a long moment, then said, "Tomorrow night we're going to fix this issue between us so we can move on."

Bella stared into that heated gaze, and her stomach swarmed with butterflies. How could he do that to her with a single look? But the only thing that truly mattered was what she wanted all along; he wanted more from her, and she could redeem herself.

"Yes, Sir."

CHAPTER SEVEN

The door to the dungeon room shut behind Kole. His cock went from soft to steel so quickly it stole his breath. Bella was nude except for a pair of shiny black heels. Her hair was pulled back into a tight ponytail that left the ends to sit at the middle of her back. Her legs were spread wide, and her arms were up above her head. Black silk had been wrapped around her wrists, binding her to the ring above, and covered all the way down her arms.

He had instructed Bella to prepare herself, and she had clearly gained the help from one of the assistants who worked at the castle. Her effort paid off. She had pleased him. Desire to take her engulfed him.

Once he approached her, he settled at her back, and the glow from the candlelit room made her creamy skin appear more delectable. Every line of her body was utter perfection.

Sliding his fingers down her torso, he caressed her side and down her hip. He inhaled, catching a waft of her cinnamon scent mixed with aroused woman. "You look lovely. Stunning, in fact."

"Thank you, Sir," she rasped.

Grasping her hip, he spun her around, and the metal ring holding her screeched as she turned. He scanned over her breasts, the taut nipples that awaited him, and the lines of her stomach that moved with her deep breaths.

When he looked back into her eyes and found them rich with desire. He grinned his approval, then slapped her thigh with a light hit. "Beautiful."

He turned away from her and strode to the tray of items he requested the assistant leave for him. He took the black crop, then returned to Bella. Her focus was on the crop for a mere second before her gaze returned to his. Oh, how the sub sizzled.

He slid the crop over each nipple, and she sighed and trembled, which made his cock jump. But as he stared into her pretty eyes, she appeared conflicted. She had clearly done some thinking since she left him at the hospital last night.

"I see questions on your mind, Bella." His voice was low as he intended. "Now is the time to ask them."

A pause followed, her expression thoughtful before she finally said, "How will this work? I mean with us...will we...do I...?"

He chuckled. "I don't want a slave, Bella. But you will learn when I demand submission. Good indicators would be when we're in the castle or in the bedroom. At all other times, then I'm Kole. Not Master Kole or Sir."

"Okay, well, that's good." She drew in a sharp breath, looked down, and avoided his gaze. "Do you have other submissives, Sir?"

He tapped the crop under her chin. "Eyes on me, Bella." She immediately lifted her head, but her features were tight. "There are more, yes."

Darkness seeped into her features before her focus went back to the floor. "I see, Sir."

"Is this something that displeases you?" He hit under her chin, harder this time, and she jerked her head up. "Speak freely, Bella."

She flinched from the hit; her voice held a slight tremble. "I don't want there to be anyone else, Sir."

He ran the crop over the swell of her stomach and enjoyed when she sucked in a deep breath. "You prefer me to give them up?"

Her gaze zoned in on him, focused and intent, and the Bella that he'd grown fond of appeared, the strong woman who knew what she wanted and dived headfirst to snatch it up. "I would, Sir."

That's my girl. This Bella in front of him was who he adored. Not the frightened one who ran from him.

"You're interested to see where this goes, then?" He tapped lightly along her thigh, and her muscles tensed. "You want to be exclusive?"

"Yes, Sir."

"What you ask of me is not to be taken lightly." He ran the crop up her thigh, along her pelvis, tapping her clit with the flat part of the crop, and she moaned. "Tell me, why I would place my subs with another Dom for only you?" He intended to, but she needed to understand what it meant for him to do that.

Another hit had her drawing in a breath through her teeth. "Because there's something between us—something special—and I think we need to explore this."

He marveled at her strength. "You're much more beautiful when you're honest. And I agree with you, but Bella, you've already proved to be disobedient when you weren't truthful in our last scene together."

"I was unaware, Sir."

He moved the crop lower down to rest at her entrance. With his free hand, he palmed her clit to show her that her answer was exactly right. "Explain why?"

"Because..." She hummed as he rolled the bud beneath his touch. Her eyes fluttered closed for a mere second before she snapped them open. "Because I never talked to you. If I had said how I felt and asked if you were disappointed instead of assuming it, then this wouldn't have happened."

He lowered the crop, then slid his fingers through her damp folds and worked her center with prodding fingers. "And because of your behavior, what happened?"

"You withdrew from me and punished me by not acknowledging me to show me how you felt when I did that to you." She dropped her head on her arm and thrust her pussy against his hand. "Which I deserved, because I clearly shouldn't assume what others are thinking."

He pulled his hand away. The chain above Bella protested as it carried some of her weight with a loud clang. "Are you aware now of what will happen if you behave in this manner again?"

"We'll be over."

He snapped his fingers in front of her face. "Just like that." He tucked the crop under his arm. "If a Dom and sub don't have openness and trust between them, the relationship will fail." He cupped her face and leaned in, his lips nearly on hers. "No lies. Total honesty. Yes?"

"From here on out, Sir."

He smiled. "Nice to hear." He slid his hand along her jaw, took her chin, and held her firm. Her sincerity pleased him. And she'd understood his actions at the hospital. Sometimes experiencing something firsthand was much easier than explaining it. And she learned from it, but here was her test to see if she was truly honest with him. "Now that you've had time to *think* things over like you requested..." Her eyes widened, unease filled her features, and he expected such a reaction from her. "Answer my question. Why do you get *tough* and shut everyone out?"

"What—"

He narrowed his eyes. "Now, now, don't going ruining how well you've done and make me punish you in ways that are unpleasant."

Restraining his grin proved difficult, seeing the full-body shudder she gave at the idea of his punishment. "I was very kind last night to simply ignore you. My generosity will not happen again."

She nibbled her lip for only a second before her shoulders relaxed. "I've been hurt before." Tears welled in her eyes, and his heart clenched seeing her pain. "I suppose because of that, I closed myself off so you couldn't do the same."

All things he expected to hear, but it was refreshing that she finally spoke the truth. "Does it feel good to always be forcing others away?"

She shook her head, and more tears fell. "No, Sir."

He couldn't stand not touching her any longer. He cupped her cheeks, and brushed away the wetness. "If you feel that you need to protect yourself, then yes, I believe shutting out anyone who would mistreat you is wise." He swirled his fingers along her cheeks. "But am I a man who will disrespect you?"

"No, Sir."

His heart warmed at the softness of her. Sweet woman. And he wanted to lash out at the men who had mishandled her emotions "We're in agreement, then, that those walls you put up to protect yourself don't belong when you're with me?"

"Yes, Sir."

"That sounds much better, darlin'." He reached up for the hook above her and unlatched it.

As she lowered her arms, she sighed, and he caught the sound with his mouth. He swiped his tongue in a perfect rhythm with hers as he cupped her nape. A perfect, wet mouth he could get lost in.

She melted under his touch, squirmed against him, and damn, she tested his control.

Backing away from her, he rested his forehead on hers and kept his hand tight on her neck. "It's not a question of will I give up my other submissives for you." He stared into her eyes that had entranced him at first glance and hoped she read his emotion. "It's that I always needed more than one to satisfy me. With you, I need no one else. Bella, I'm in love with you, sweetheart."

"I love you too."

He grinned. "Not just *like?*"

She laughed, the sweetest sound he'd ever heard. "No, Sir, love."

He took her mouth and kissed her as if tomorrow was his last. Her tongue followed his as he guided her. He enjoyed the soft, wet mouth of hers that he could hardly wait to have around his cock.

Once he'd thoroughly kissed her to leave her panting and shivering in excitement, he backed away. "Further questions?"

"None, Sir."

He ran his hand over her stomach, and a tremor rippled beneath his touch. "We'll use the same safe words. 'Rose' as your soft limit. 'Thorn' as your hard. Yes?"

"Yes, Sir."

Leaving her there, trembling in her arousal, he strode to the other side of the room, then pulled two thin benches with cushioned tops to the center of the room.

After positioning them with a gap between them that would be comfortable for her, he crooked his finger at her. "Come to me."

Once she was before him, he removed the silk from her arms, then helped her on top of the benches. On all fours, with her left side supported by one bench and her right side supported by the other, she was spread wide. He took four ropes off the tray, then, he strapped her arms and her calves to the benches.

"Tonight I'm going to push your limits, Bella. I'm going to show you that your fears about not being able to keep up with me are without merit. You enjoy a little pain with sex as much as I enjoy offering it, yes?"

"I-I think so, Sir."

He held her gaze as he removed his pants and tossed them into the corner of the room, along with his socks and shoes. He returned to her and grabbed the crop off the floor.

"Now then, you have your safe word in case things become too much for you. I *want* you to use it if you need to." At her nod, he continued, "But trust that I'm giving you what you need, not what you might want. Your body has told me enough that you will enjoy this."

"I trust you, Sir."

Had anything ever sounded as beautiful as that?

Stepping into the open space between the benches, he positioned his erection in front of her face, and she stared at it. His cock jumped at how she licked her lips, at the way she practically fucked him with her gaze.

His voice took on a husky tone even to his ears. "Your plush lips are made to suck cock. Soft. Warm. They invite me."

She looked from his cock to his face. Her eyelids were lowered, cheeks a perfect pink, and her mouth was parted. "Yes, Sir."

"Off you go, Bella."

With a soft moan, she leaned forward, yet the rope along her limbs stopped her. She frowned at him. "I can't reach you, Sir."

"Looks like you're going to have to work harder then." He smacked her ass with the crop, and she flinched. "And take this as a warning I do not approve of being frowned at."

"Yes, Sir." Her tongue flicked out, reaching for the tip of his cock, and it barely made contact. "I want to taste you, Sir."

"I as well, darlin'. Best you find a way." He raised the crop and hit her bottom in endless slaps. "The longer you take to suck me off, the more hits you'll receive. I want to take pleasure in your mouth, and I'm growing impatient."

Groaning from the force of his hits, she reached for him. He glanced at the binds on her arms and calves, and they dug into her skin. Her tongue connected with the tip of his cock, and she moaned as she drew his precum into her mouth.

Then she licked the slit of his cock, and he threw his head back, relishing in her slick tongue. Wet. Skilled. Impressive. Fuck, she was good at that.

He lowered his head, stopped the force of the crop, and looked at the binds along her arms.

Discoloration informed him that she strained. It must've hurt, which proved to him that, as he thought all along, she could handle more pain than she gave herself credit for. Her trembling, her face flushing hot—oh yeah, she enjoyed some pain with her sex.

"That's very good, Bella. Now take more of me into that hot mouth of yours." He raised the crop and smacked her ass, and she gasped. But she returned immediately and deliciously caressed the head of his cock.

Another hard hit caused her bottom to flame. Damn, he liked seeing her ass rosy.

Good thing Bella had an attitude that would no doubt warrant punishment often, especially once she grew more comfortable with him, because he'd take enjoyment in seeing that ass red often.

Her tongue snaked out again, as she desperately tried to please him. He appreciated her effort. "Yes, sub, you do that well and make me want to fuck your mouth."

Taking a step forward, he closed in on her. Her gaze remained on his, and he glanced over her blonde hair trailing along her creamy skin. Her smooth back and red ass all enticed him enough that he reached down to tweak a nipple.

She rubbed her face over his erection. His muscles tensed, and fuck, the woman could make him come by doing just that. Instead, she parted her lips, and he pushed the tip of his cock into her mouth.

The feel of her lips—the feel of his Bella—on his cock compared to no other sensation. She bobbed on the tip of his cock to suck him dry, and she was well on her way to doing just that.

When she slid forward, taking him all the way into her throat, he grasped her head and held her there.

Her ravenous eyes remained on his, and she massaged him with her tongue. "Bella, you are enjoying this far too much."

Whack.

Smack.

He grunted as he slid out from her, only to return to the very spot that he had now decided was paradise. Her lips created a suction that made him feel strangled and ready to blow.

She slowly released him, and she'd never looked so beautiful. Nothing had ever appealed to him so much as this little spitfire bound, ready for him. *Damn this. That pussy is mine.*

In haste, he rid her of the ropes and grasped her arms, lifted her off the benches, then placed her on her feet. He took her in a forceful kiss that tangled his tongue with hers. She gave him an answering moan, and in greed, he ate those moans, ready to intensify them. She squirmed against him, her stomach stroking his cock, and she whimpered.

With a nibble on her bottom lip, he backed away from her sweet mouth, staring into the eyes of the one woman who made him want no other. To give up every submissive so he only controlled one. The one woman whom he thought he'd never have and now had no intention of ever letting go.

"Know this, Bella." He pointed to her and then to him. "This thing between us I've wanted for some time. Nothing pleases me more than to have you here, under my command, and have your body open to my pleasures, as well as your heart."

She smiled, a bit playful yet full of emotion. "I'm yours, Master Kole."

The floor had dropped right out from underneath him. It wasn't what she said that thrilled him. It was her voice, her soft expression, the willingness, the acceptance, and the way she fully trusted him.

He pressed his body against hers to overpower her as her submission spilled over him. What started out as friendship, curiosity between them for maybe more, had now entered into a full D/s relationship. "That show of respect is one I welcome."

Then he spun her around, brought her back against his chest, shoved his erection into the seam of her ass, and walked forward to grab a condom off the tray on his way.

At the wall, he pushed her against the stone, trapping her with his hand between her shoulder blades as he ripped the condom wrapper open with his teeth. He sheathed his cock and kicked open her legs, then angled her hips.

After he placed his cock at her entrance, he pushed through her tight center. A sound of pleasure and relief sounded from her throat as he thrust upward.

He ran his hand up her shoulders and held the base of her neck, pinning her to the wall. And she melted under his touch. Her pussy contracted against him as her wetness spread over his balls. The earlier scene had no doubt aroused her beyond measure, and fuck, if it hadn't done the same to him too.

"Don't move." His voice sounded on a throaty growl as he spoke in her ear. "Now I will take my pleasure in this sweet little cunt, my Bella."

CHAPTER EIGHT

Sweet Jesus!

Kole's weight pressed against Bella's neck, and she'd never been so comfortable. Safe. Here under his hold, her world aligned. And her body was set aflame.

She'd never been so wet—so wanton—and the lingering pain from the ropes on her arms and calves only amplified her need for him, awakening every nerve ending in her body.

His cock was pushing inside her, stretching her in ways that no man had ever done before, touching her as she'd never been touched.

Her heart burst wide open, and for the first time, she was doing exactly what she knew was missing in her life. It wasn't anything she needed to find; it was something she needed to give in to—to put all of her trust in Kole and allow him the right to take care of her.

Being here. Just like this. Restrained under him and open for his pleasures. His submissive. And that part of her that refused his claim on her settled because she wanted to give him all of herself.

He deserved nothing less.

Skin slapped skin as sweat coated her body, and the dampness of Kole's flesh brushed against her own. His low groans remained right by her ear as he thrust exactly as he had before, ruthlessly.

The grip he held her by was firm. Her face pressed against the cold stone wall, his grip holding her so tight she doubted her cheek would get scratched, because he wasn't allowing her to move enough to warrant it.

Kole grunted, and she mirrored the sound as his moves became easier, faster, and smoother. Everything tightened. Her muscles clenched with her impending release. Light danced behind her closed eyes. Flutters tickled up her legs and spread warmth into her belly. Legs trembling, she attempted to fight it off, but the sensation rose and took hold, overpowering her.

"Sir. Need. To. Come."

He smacked her ass with a firm hit, then squeezed her cheek as he continued to thrust into her savagely. "No."

She gritted her teeth. Her breath sucked back into her body as that hit awakened her nerve endings to soar into a soul battle that shook her bones. All her muscles surged with awareness. She parted her mouth, and a scream of frustration spread throughout the room.

Through her fight she suddenly realized the lack of sensation. She hadn't known Kole had pulled out and hugged her from behind. Too lost in the battle against her orgasm, she knew nothing but the high he denied her.

Backing away from her, he squeezed her neck. "Stay in this position." His skin left hers and she mourned the loss. How her legs trembled and insides quivered.

He approached the tray again, and she closed her eyes, listening, needing to understand what he was up to. She heard him remove his condom, which didn't please her, but heard the rip of another wrapper. Then a click, almost as if he opened a bottle.

The moment he returned to her and slid his hand over her bottom, his intent became clear. She tensed. "Rose."

His hands stilled, his body leaned against hers, and he came close to her cheek. "Shh...only touching, for now."

Continuing his descent, he slipped his fingers between the seam of her ass and pressed his finger against the tight bud, smoothing a warm liquid over her skin. "Your ass has never been touched."

It didn't sound like a question, and she didn't respond. Fear crept up. Her pulse hammered. No, her ass had never been fondled or fucked. Not that she wasn't interested or curious, but no man had ever asked before.

She debated pulling out her hard-limit safe word, but the ache in her pussy disagreed. Kole wanted his pleasure. And his pleasure he would take.

She might not know what this sensation would be like, but she trusted that it'd bring her some type of pleasure, as Kole had proven to do effortlessly.

His voice was so low it vibrated right through her and raised the little hairs on the back of her neck. "Relax." At her exhale, he pressed against the bud, his finger demanding entry. "Objections?"

"No, Sir," she squeaked.

Gently but quickly he slipped the tip of his finger through the rim. Bella whined, in slight hesitation and also in wonderment over the odd feeling. No pain, but pressure. Pleasure, slowly building.

"Feels good?" he whispered

"Different, Sir, but not unpleasant."

He withdrew from her, spun her around, and pressed on her chest so her back met the wall. He squatted, angled her hip back, then placed her leg over his shoulder. He inserted his finger again—and his tongue discovered her clit. And Lord, he discovered it well.

Her eyes fluttered closed as he licked her clit from side to side, pressed against the little bud, and flicked it. She swirled her hips, asking for more from both his finger and his mouth. An odd sensation, but more… Yes, she needed more.

His chuckle sent a warm breath of air over her scorching pussy. "Frustrated?"

"Not enough, Sir," she groaned.

He removed his finger and then stood, but kept her leg hooked on his arm. His dark gaze sent flickers of sheer need between her thighs. She tried to listen to his instructions to relax as he placed the tip of his cock against her straining ass. "Objections?"

Pressure. Her body clenched, and muscles tightened to refuse him. *Too full.* "Rose, Sir. Rose."

He stilled, leaned away from her, and stared at her for a moment before he said, "Are you wanting to use your hard-limit word, but are worried to?"

"No, Sir." She sucked in a deep breath, realizing she was about to be less than truthful, and corrected herself. "I'm afraid enough right now that I think I might use it." Even to her own ears, her voice sounded shaky. "I've just never done this before, and I'm scared—like seriously very, very nervous."

"When we discussed your limits and I brought up anal sex, you squirmed in your seat. Your mind might be stopping you because of fear, but your body wants this. You are so very wet, Bella."

She nodded in agreement. Why lie? They both knew it was true. Clearly, her body was far braver than her mind. "I've always been curious. I like how erotic it is. I'm just trying to figure out how to relax enough to let it happen."

"All right, Bella." He lowered her leg, then strode over to the tray.

He returned a moment later and squatted down at her feet. "Lift your leg and step into this, darlin'. If fear is so present in your mind, then we'll just have to remove it."

"Yes, Sir."

Glancing down, she put her leg through the strap, and her heart skipped a beat. He was placing a vibrator against her. *Oh hell…*

He slid the harness up her thighs, then fastened it around her hips and positioned the vibe over her clit.

"All set." He smiled a grin that could have been from the devil himself, then offered his hand. "Kneel, sweetheart."

With his assistance, she lowered down, and he nudged her knee with his foot. "I want a good view of your pussy, Bella."

After she complied, he gave her a once-over, then nodded, seemingly approving of her look. "I'm not expecting anything from you here." He turned and headed toward the far wall. There, he crouched, and his focus remained on her. "You don't need to hold any position. Just enjoy."

Before she had a chance to ask what he planned, he raised the remote control in his hand and turned the vibrator on. Her eyes widened. "Oh…good…God."

"Ah, she likes the vibe." Not only the device—hell, she'd used them herself—but with Kole watching her, enjoying her, pleasure rocketed into every molecule of her body. "Now then, let's see how much you like it."

The buzz increased as he clicked the vibe to a higher speed. She clenched her fists at her sides, the sensation all but making her cross-eyed.

Lowering her head, she breathed through the first zings of pleasure spreading through her.

Another click.

Her head snapped back up and Kole grinned at her. Dark, seductive eyes stared back at her. Her vision grew hazy, and she blinked to keep her focus on him while the vibe tormented her clit.

Wetness spread between her legs. So much, in fact, that it became uncomfortable. She squirmed, but that brutal buzz followed her. And when Kole clicked the speed again, she jolted up fully on her knees, unable to sit back on her legs.

"Oh." A shudder rocked through her. "Oh. My. God."

Kole stood then, approached the tray, and grabbed some long ropes, then returned to her. "Look at you, darlin', practically purring like a kitten."

With her legs spread wide, he slid his hand below the vibe, dragging his fingers through her damp folds until he reached her anus. There, he inserted his finger, then another while he worked her pleasure to unspeakable limits.

She gripped his forearm, and his muscles bunched under her touch. She trembled as an orgasm different than the one before, not so deep but equally as wonderful, built.

Her body quivered as her climax reached its peak; then Kole surprised her by removing his finger in haste and lifting her off the ground.

She could barely focus on the world around her as he took the ropes and wrapped her body in them. The sound of the rope sliding across metal, and the tug against the binds on her skin, informed her he was tying the rope to the rings on the wall.

With a skill that would have impressed her if she wasn't focused on the vibe, he strung her up. Her body was completely suspended off the ground, spread wide open for him, and her bottom was now at the level with his cock. Her weight against the rope burned yet only added more sensations building her pleasure.

Leaving her hanging there, ready and in near desperation for him to take her, he returned to the tray and grabbed the flogger. He spun the flogger in his hands, and Bella struggled for breath as he stood in front of her.

"That was to get you excited." Those powerful eyes of his stayed trained on her. "This is to make you forget everything around you entirely."

Without a chance to catch her breath, he hit her with the flogger, along her thighs, breasts, and stomach. At first, slow taps that brought no pain and only increased her arousal. Then, he increased the speed, now doing just what he said. Pushing her past a place that she thought she could handle or enjoy.

Thud. Thud. Thud.

Each hit of the flogger made heat soar through her—the leather feeling like nothing less than a hundred fingertips caressing her body in the most beautiful of ways, the hits bringing forth a stinging sensation that zinged straight to her pussy.

And he didn't stop.

Not once.

Never slowed.

He continued to rouse her body and force her mind to be aware of only the sensations he gave her. That he wanted her body rosy and warm for the flogger. Relaxed and accepting of what he wanted to take from her.

And she wanted to give it all to him.

He increased his speed and she arched her back even in the binds, offering herself. The burn that touched her skin only fueled the pleasure inside her—a slow buildup to a fast, hard urgency, imploring for more.

She had lost sight of him now. Her eyes must have closed as her body tingled from head to toe. Heat scorched her skin and made her feel more alive than ever. The pain of the hits had morphed into awareness all through her. As if time slowed, her breathing became more shallow, and her heartbeat a mesmerizing rhythm in her ears.

A sharp pain awakened her, and she gasped, snapping her eyes open. She blinked once, then saw Kole grinning at her as he tweaked a nipple hard.

"Well on your way to subspace, weren't you?" His eyes, though raging with lust, appeared wide with surprise. "Sweetheart, you're not quite ready to go there, but I'm pleased by how easily you could have gone under."

Her head moved from side to side, everything in her body loose and needy. Subspace? She couldn't even comprehend what that term was. It sounded familiar, but thoughts were unreachable now.

Kole lowered down, held on to the ropes holding her open for him, and pressed his cock against her anus. "Focus on the vibe."

How could she not? He had clicked the last speed of the vibrator before dropping the remote to the ground, and nothing mattered except easing the pressure building inside her. Pressure that rapidly increased as his cock pushed through the rim.

She was no longer tense against him, and it took only a moment for the tip of his cock to dip through the tight rim. Little flickers of pleasure mixed with the pain in her bottom. It all seemed to conflict against each other rising euphoria that she couldn't control. She groaned as her anus stretched to accommodate him. The width of him made her ache, but she relished in it.

More.

All this blissful pleasure, the tingle of her skin from the flogger—it all brought her to a place that she'd never gone, a ride she never wanted to come down from.

"You're there."

Kole's strangled tone forced her eyes open, and she noticed his pelvis pressed against her bottom, now fully seated inside of her. He started to move, slowly easing himself in and out.

With her arms semibound, she placed her hands on his chest, caressed the squared pecs, and ran her hands down, exploring the valley of his muscles. Until now, she hadn't been allowed to touch him. And how she'd been missing out. Kole was all man—hard, delicious, and drenched in sweat.

His deep moans filled the air, causing goose bumps to form along her skin. The enjoyment and rich pleasure he received rested hard in his features. Pride from within intensified the heat building inside her. And when Kole grabbed a nipple and twisted, pain shot through her, yet the force threatened to bring forth a climax powerful enough to make her eyes go huge.

"You won't come until I allow it, Bella." His voice dropped an octave. The speed of his thrusts increased.

Her breath was lost—only he remained.

He grasped her ass cheeks, squeezed so tight it stole her silence, and a scream raged from her throat. He delivered a round of gentle but quick thrusts, jolting her into full awareness of her body. Removing her from the sensation of hanging on the very edge. He smacked her ass, and it forced her back into the present. Right; she couldn't come yet. And as before, the same overwhelming sensation rose within her as her body fought to release. But she didn't want to disappoint him. She wanted to be the submissive he needed, and he enjoyed pushing his subs. She could do this.

She panted in heavy breaths, struggling for the very last ounce of control. His gaze stayed focused on hers, and his eyes shone in silent approval of her submission. And she was aware he appreciated that she fought against the very tremors that rocked her to the core.

Now she understood what he wanted from her. He was never going to go easy on her. It didn't matter that the last time she pulled the safe word was during straight intercourse. He wasn't going to repeat the same scene to get her past it. He set up a scene that tested her further and pushed her to the very limits she set.

This wasn't about the orgasm. This wasn about her fully submitting to him. He had upped her pleasure to unspeakable limits and now expected that she'd give him all the control.

The pressure in her bottom and the buzz on her clit made tears rush down her cheeks. Her body was on the edge of an explosion, but here, locked in his gaze, she'd not fail him.

He asked this of her—no, demanded it—and she gritted her teeth, focused away from the tightness engulfing her, and gave him utter control over her body.

He grinned, a delicious smile that held so much pride. "And there it is. Beautiful submission." He increased his speed, pumping into her, and only his gaze on her allowed her not to erupt around him.

Reaching forward, he grasped her nipples and twisted, holding on so tight. "Beg for it, sweetheart."

The pain tightened her jaw but sent a zing straight to her pussy. "Master Kole, please, may I come?"

The smile that swept along his face was one of sheer adoration for her. However, a note of pure sin appeared in his gaze before he twisted her nipples further, and agony drifted across her in a marvelous embrace.

"Hold your breath, darlin'. This is going to be intense."

After she inhaled, he released his fingers on her nipples. Blood rushed into them so quick that the pain jolted her body into the highest level of pleasure. As her scream filled the air, he squeezed both breasts and thrust his cock into her. "Come. Now."

The sensations slammed into her like an order she couldn't dare refuse. Her back arched, body tightened, and eyes leaked with tears of satisfaction.

She jerked against the ropes, convulsed against his body, and screamed as if that would free her from the intense release bombarding her. Heat exploded. Light danced before her eyes. A rush of pleasure soared through her, releasing all her tension. And with a loud roar, Kole buried himself in her ass and soared into his own climax.

When her muscles loosened, the aftereffects of her release left her a quivering mess. A tremble so deep in her soul that if she opened her mouth, she had no doubt her teeth would have chattered.

Kole panted in heavy breaths as he rested his forehead against hers. "Good girl, Bella."

After a long pause, he kissed her cheek. "I'll be only a minute, darlin'." He shifted his hips, pulling out of her, then strode toward the tray. After he removed the condom and cleaned himself with a wipe, he returned to her; then he cleaned her.

Once he deposited the wipe in the garbage, he proceeded to remove the ropes from her body. She hissed when he placed her feet on the ground, as all the blood rushed back into her body from where the ropes had restrained her.

He dropped to the ground, sitting against the wall, and pulled her onto his lap. She inhaled his scent of sandalwood mixed with sex and sweat. Her chest rose and fell as she fought to catch her breath.

He pressed his lips against hers, softly, not rough like before. Tongues tangled in a dance as his plush lips made her heart warm. Safe. Adored.

"You succeeded," he whispered with an amused tone, drawing her out of her haze.

"Succeeded, Sir?"

"You didn't come when I pushed you." He chuckled, low and throaty. "You could have come very hard many times during our scene, yes?"

"So hard, Sir, and a lot."

"Be proud of yourself, Bella. You overcame something that you couldn't do in that last scene. That's very good." Skimming his lips from her neck to her cheek, he licked his way to her mouth, where he pressed his lips against hers. His kisses weren't a simple embrace; they held meaning and told her she pleased him.

After a nibble on her bottom lip, he backed away and stared at her. "Any worries now that you can't keep up?"

She shook her head, dazed, but now understood why he'd done this scene tonight. He was shedding her worries that she wasn't enough for him. He hadn't held back, and he issued a lot of pain and refusal of orgasms, which she managed. Pride in herself, yes, she was touched by that.

"None at all. And if *that* was any indicator of what I've been missing out on trying new things, then gimme more."

He grinned. "How about I take you to dinner first?"

"Better idea"—she licked his bottom lip—"skip dinner, and how about you tie me up for dessert?"

He gripped her chin, darkness seeped into his eyes, and power radiated from him. "Watch that mouth, Miss. I don't take to kindly to demands made of me and have more than a few ways to make sure you remember that fact."

"I'll be sure not to forget." *Although. Maybe...* "What would be my punishment if I forgot, Sir?"

"Something entirely wicked and kinky." He gave a dark, seductive smile. "And you'd enjoy that, wouldn't you?"

"Yes, Sir."

BET ON ECSTASY

CHAPTER ONE

"Prick." Smith slammed the pool cue down on the table, cursing the game that had cost him a thousand dollars. The muscles in his neck ached, as did the throb in his head from concentrating on winning for the last twenty minutes.

His business partner, Brock, laughed. The black ball spun in the corner pocket, and the white ball swept up the table to hit one of Smith's two remaining striped balls. "Pay up," Brock stated.

Smith scowled at the glow in Brock's blue-gray eyes. He mentally flipped Brock off for his satisfied smirk. With a snort, Smith grabbed his wallet from his back pocket, then tossed the money onto the pool table. "You got lucky."

"Lucky!" Brock gave a booming laugh. "It's all skill, buddy."

He cursed again under his breath, dropping down into the leather seat in the corner of his office. Perhaps he shouldn't have purchased the new pool table. Then he wouldn't have had his ass handed to him.

His secretary had thought he'd lost his mind when he asked her to place the order. Smith figured it made total sense. A game in between the long hours he worked kept him sane, which made a thought rise. "Did you go through the last stack of résumés?"

Brock nodded. "Sure did, but no one stood out."

Smith pointed. "You're too damn picky." He'd seen at least four résumés that fit exactly what they were looking for to hire new employees to ease up their workload.

Brock grinned. "Perhaps." He hesitated, then gave a halfhearted shrug. "Why change something that works."

Even if the month-long search grated on Smith's last nerve, he also couldn't deny the truth behind Brock's statement.

MDR Software had been built upon years of hard work and sweat, not only from Smith, but from Brock too. When the company had celebrated its five-year anniversary, it had grown into a million-dollar venture in Chicago. After the takeover a year later of fellow software company HighDot, located in the heart of Baltimore, MDR's worth tripled.

Brock leaned against the pool table, his gaze glowing. "New bet?"

"You emptied my wallet, who says I want another bet?"

While Smith did have money in the bank, he didn't have any other cash on him. It had taken a good year to stop the memories of living paycheck to paycheck and pinching every penny. Though he'd grown more comfortable with money, he'd never forget when they first opened the company, he ate hotdogs for an entire month.

"Not interested in winning your cash back?" Brock asked, stretching his arms.

The sardonic look Brock delivered usually raised the stakes in their bets. A competitive streak had remained healthy between them, and not only in business. For the most part, Smith enjoyed betting on *things*, except when he lost. "Possibly."

Smith laced his fingers behind his head, catching a glimpse of the Baltimore skyline out the large panoramic window. The dark night was typical. There wasn't a day he, or Brock, didn't put in a ten-hour shift.

Hard work made for a solid company. Yet the long hours had also been the reason why Smith had been pushing for new employees. He wanted a life, not more time in his damned office.

The telephone next to Smith rang once, and Brock's grin became sinful. Smith's irritation at the loss of the game morphed into a new type of heat, pooling low in his groin. He reached for the phone on the side table, then held it to his ear. "Smith."

"Kyra Garner is here to see you," the security man, Antonio, said. "I realize it's late, but she said you were expecting her."

"Send her up." Smith placed the phone back on the base, spotting Brock's expression shift in intensity. Smith also sensed the growing impulse to control and conquer. It'd been a long day waiting for Kyra to arrive, and now Brock's question held a stronger appeal. "I take it she's the bet?" At Brock's nod, he added, "What's the wager?"

Brock smirked. "Ecstasy."

Smith had always understood why women flocked to Brock; his charisma, handsome features, matched with a lighthearted personality impressed the ladies. Smith witnessed the toughest businesswomen crack under the assault of that smile. "Bet on ecstasy, hmm?" He rubbed his jaw, considering the proposition. "I'm intrigued, but why that one?"

Brock lifted a lazy shoulder. "Any other bet would make us assholes."

Smith nearly offered a bet on who Kyra would take an interest in, perhaps who she might want to date when the night concluded. It had happened before. Smith had attempted to date two of the women he'd met through ménage adventures with Brock. The last woman had become near obsessive, causing Smith to shut her down when she showed up at his office. The only thing that resulted from any relationship lately was money-hungry women who wanted a certain lifestyle he wouldn't give them.

Even the women he dated who weren't into ménage relationships ended up more interested in where he took them for dinner. The social circuit in Baltimore had been disappointing and hadn't given him anything other than a one-night stands.

After consideration, he dismissed the thought of his idea for the bet. Anything too emotional crossed a line neither him, nor Brock, would cross. He preferred no-strings-attached sex, but he wasn't a coldhearted bastard. "Interesting bet. Indeed."

Brock ran a hand through his sandy-colored messily styled hair, which amused Smith. No matter if they were surrounded by millionaires, at work, or watching Sunday-night football, his hair always remained disheveled. "Christ, she'll reap the rewards anyway."

From what Smith heard out in the hallway, Kyra was nearly at his office, her high heels clicking along the marble floor. "No one loses," Smith agreed. "Well, except one of us, which will be you."

"Dream on." Brock jumped off the pool table as the sound of her heels against the floor drew closer. "You in?"

Smith nodded. "Double it up."

The clicks of Kyra's heels sounded right outside the door. One second passed of silence—far longer than he expected. He wondered if she searched for bravery. When she finally entered through the opened door, the sight of her stunned him, and his entire body came to life.

His cock hardened to steel, causing him to groan as raw primal need tensed his muscles. He experienced a pull to her that shocked the wind right out of his lungs—it was more than lust; it was raw chemistry. Kyra was beautiful.

Standing at the doorway, she offered a sweet smile that held a mysterious edge. Her green eyes were a stunning light color he'd never seen before. Her long black hair would drape beautifully over his thighs when her puffy lips pleasured him.

"Hello, Kyra," he murmured.

She strode into the office with a confidence he favored in women, chin high, gaze fixated directly on him. Once in the center of the office, she licked those lovely glossy pink lips. "Smith." Her gaze cut to the right. "Brock."

"Pleasure to meet you." Brock winked, a playful smile teasing the corners of his mouth. "I mean to say, in person, and not through e-mails and texts."

Her laughter was as lovely as the women who owned it. "Yes, exactly."

Smith stood from the chair in the corner, gesturing to the leather couch. "Please take a seat."

Kyra approached the couch, and her scent carried to him. Smith inhaled the mix of flowers and spice that suited her. Sweet with a slice of fire. He reveled in that combination. "Would you like a glass of wine?"

Her smile was polite. "Yes, thank you."

Smith chuckled under his breath, unable to stop himself. An outsider would think she arrived tonight for business. Kyra looked all too proper in her rose-colored blouse and black pencil skirt, but her killer legs were anything but appropriate.

The meeting tonight had nothing to do with discussing software.

Brock closed the office door and locked it before he dropped down into the couch across from her, while Smith retrieved her wine from the small bar in the corner.

"Do tell us, Kyra, about this pact of seduction you made with your friends," Brock said. "I must admit, I found your ad at the Castle Dolce Vita...appealing."

A personal ad Smith and Brock had stumbled upon late one night on the Web site's forum. Castle Dolce Vita was located out of Bowleys Quarters, a half-hour drive from Baltimore. The castle catered to everything from ménage encounters to BDSM to just about anything the mind could conjure.

Smith poured her wine and corked the bottle. He turned to hear her reply in a strong voice, "It's a silly pact between friends to live out our ultimate fantasies. Call it boredom, or maybe insanity, but that's the gist of it. Two of my friends have already completed the pact, and so, here I am."

Smith enjoyed the strength Kyra portrayed. Most women wouldn't voice such thoughts so freely without a stumble in speech or mere hesitation. Impressed by her, he approached, eyeing her silky calf crossed over her knee, envisioning exactly where and how he planned to touch her.

Smith reached her, raised his attention to her face, and she bewitched him with her elegance. He offered her the wineglass. "You all joined the Castle Dolce Vita to fulfill this pact?"

She accepted the glass and as she did, he brushed his fingers over hers. Kyra's eyes widened, breath hitched. "Yes, we all joined. It seemed like the best place to find others looking for similar ventures."

The perfect place, Smith thought.

Though that interested him, he couldn't take his eyes off her, more than pleased he wasn't the only one affected by the clear heat between them. Tonight would be enjoyable for all, if her reactions were anything like she'd shown from the simple touch.

He and Brock had both been members of Castle Dolce Vita since they relocated to Baltimore. Of course, they also had visited many sex clubs around the country who catered to sexual exploration. He'd reveled in the freedom. No emotions. No needy women. He could have fun, then walk away.

While both of them had numerous relationships throughout the years, some lasting longer than others, all failed miserably. Their tastes included an active sexual appetite. Smith had never met a woman who fulfilled him enough, and none of their ménage relationships had ever worked out. The women they'd been with had thought they could handle two men, but it always turned out two was just a little too much.

"Why are you members?" Kyra asked.

Simple question. Simple answer.

Together, they weren't only solid partners in business and excelled at their work, but with a woman between them, they shone. They'd shared their fortune, success, and enjoyed sharing their women.

Smith watched as Kyra took a sip of her wine and her eyes fluttered closed, indicating she enjoyed the taste of the wine. At six hundred dollars a bottle, Smith wasn't surprised. He sat down in the leather chair to her left, gazing over the long lines of her shapely, silky legs.

Images of them wrapped around his waist while he drove into her could be his undoing. He forced his gaze onto her face again, which was currently turning a lovely rose color under his examination.

Smith liked the effect he had on her.

He fought to remember her question and cleared his throat. "Our business is our top priority. This tends to mean our time is limited. The castle has provided a means for us to enjoy sex without involving relationships. Also, it has the highest form of privacy." Even he heard the cold distance in his voice and saw her eyebrows rise.

Every person who joined the castle signed a waiver swearing to keep things private and not share identities to nonmembers, and everyone went through STD and AIDS testing. Smith preferred knowing his sexual partners were clean rather than having casual sex with strangers from a nightclub, and the privacy of the castle offered a sense of freedom.

Kyra took another mouthful of her wine, then with a twinkle in her eyes, tipped the glass at him. "Understandable. Privacy is something I can appreciate too."

Woman, you are to be appreciated, and then some.

Brock chuckled at Smith, clearly reading his thoughts. He turned to Kyra. "Tell us a little something of yourself. More than the basic details in the profile we saw when we discovered you, kitten."

The side of her mouth arched at the nickname indicating she didn't mind, and why would she? Smith had no doubt Brock lowered his voice to inflict a straight attack on her hormones.

"I'd prefer if we kept the small talk to minimum," she said.

Smith leaned back in his seat. He'd never met a woman who didn't want some type of intimate connection before they had sex. Not in any of the encounters that had been arranged through the castle, or relationships out of the castle for that matter.

He lifted his chin. "All business, then?"

She drank a larger sip of her wine before she lowered the glass. "We're not here to get to know one another, are we? We're here to fulfill my ménage fantasy." Her eyebrows rose higher. "That is what we agreed to, yes?"

"All action. No talking." Brock's grin widened as he rubbed his jawline. "Damn, kitten, you're my type of woman."

While Brock seemed eager and accepting of her response, Smith wasn't so easily swayed. Women, even if they came in different colors and shapes, were still women rich with emotions. Right now, Kyra acted more like a man, void of any emotional connection. "Are you comfortable with that arrangement, Kyra?"

Her deep swallow displayed her nerves, but she sipped her wine in haste controlling the reaction. "I prefer it."

Smith grinned at her while she shifted uneasily in her seat. He enjoyed that he unnerved her, since her presence gave him a hefty erection. Plus, she made him far more interested than he'd ever been in any woman.

While he believed she had, in fact, lied to him with her answer, he wouldn't speculate as to why. He also wouldn't argue it out with her either. Her emotions belonged to her. "Fair enough."

He paused while she drank her wine again. Once he had her fixated on him, he leaned forward, resting his arms on his elbows. "It's important you're aware of what's ahead of you tonight. Before you arrived, Brock and I decided to make a bet on you, if you're agreeable."

Suspicion darkened her eyes as she lowered her glass onto her lap. "What sort of bet?"

"Your orgasms," Brock declared.

A blush crept over her face, yet her expression didn't hold any wrath at such a bet, which Smith would've expected. She blinked. "E-excuse me?"

Brock added, "The wager is simple: orgasms for points. Whoever gains the most points from your pleasure by the end of the night wins the money."

Her pupils dilated, and her lips arched up into a sexy smile. "Might I ask what the value of this bet is?"

"Two thousand dollars," Smith stated.

All the heated reaction vanished in a millisecond replaced by wide eyes, and her mouth fell open. She glanced around the office as she must've realized their wealth. Maybe only now she realized they didn't just work at MDR Software, but they owned the company.

Smith had seen the reaction many times—fancy things impressed women, sparkly things even more. What he hadn't ever seen before, once the surprise faded from her eyes, she didn't seem at all interested in that. "Seriously, a two-thousand-dollar bet on my orgasms?"

"Yes, kitten, we're quite serious." Brock grinned. "Are you willing?"

Christ, Smith could only grip the armrests to stop himself from going to her, tossing her legs over his shoulders, and having himself a snack. No woman had ever made him this damn hard.

In a slow, seductive slide of her finger she traced the rim of her glass as she regarded them. "I'm agreeable to join the bet." Her cheeks flushed a color that wreaked havoc on Smith's cock, making it ache in need. "But I'm afraid there's a problem."

Smith forced his attention away from her slender finger that he hoped would make a similar move on his dick. He also ignored her pinkish cheeks that he prayed burned deeper while she writhed beneath him. "Which is?"

She hesitated, then said on a quick breath, "I don't orgasm easily."

Smith smiled. As if that would be a problem. But it was glaringly obvious she *pretended* to be a sex kitten who was, in fact, more or less, in way over her beautiful head.

He could see himself respecting a woman like Kyra.

He exchanged a look with Brock, who gave him a firm nod, indicating their thoughts ran on the same line. Smith turned to Kyra again, and he noticed how she squirmed in her seat.

Exactly how he wanted her.

Smith appreciated a confident woman who fought to be brave, and he respected the trait, yet without a certain vulnerability to her, the appeal would fade. He loved pink cheeks and a stunned speechless woman under his touch. More to the point, enjoyed when a woman unraveled in his presence. To hold such heady power fed a greedy part in his soul.

In the minutes Kyra had been in his office, she'd given him all these things.

He tilted his head, regarding the treat awaiting him on the couch. "Quite the dilemma, isn't it?" He stood from his seat and approached her. It delighted him how she sucked in a deep breath, and how ragged it sounded from her parted lips.

Once in front of her, he took the wineglass from her hands. The stunning clarity in her eyes mesmerized him. "Sit on the desk. Do not cross your legs."

Her eyes blazed with reservations, even as she licked her lips. "Why?"

Smith scanned over her long, beautiful neck, her silky skin stretching over her hammering pulse. "We take our bets seriously and need to know what we're up against. It's a lot of money to wager if it's bound to fail." He leaned down into her face, his cock pressed against the zipper in his slacks. "Get on the desk, Kyra."

CHAPTER TWO

In two-point-two seconds, Kyra leaped to her feet. Her blood burned, even if Smith intimidated her, since she stood eye level with his chest. His tall stature was the first thing she noticed in his profile at the castle. Well, also his photo, where he looked like some Wall Street hunk.

The photo hadn't done him justice. Good glorious Jesus, the man was hot as hell.

Not to say his appearance had been his only appeal. She was used to dealing with handsome and powerful men. Her employment with the PR firm Silverholt had *those* types. What had sealed the deal for their night was something she'd seen in his eyes, something that made her want to know him.

Now something else concerned her.

After what she'd heard and seen from these men, she wondered if she'd made a mistake by accepting their invitation. She lifted her chin, staring into Smith's warm chocolate-brown eyes. "Are you doms?"

Smith shared a puzzled look with Brock. His gaze held a certain depth that Kyra decided was a healthy amount of confidence. He frowned when he said, "I suppose some might perceive us as dominant men."

"No, not dominant men," she corrected, saying the words slowly and carefully. She didn't want any misunderstanding. "Doms. BDSM. As in, bossing women around, refusing orgasms, and demanding submission."

Brock barked a laugh. His eyebrows arched over his piercing eyes, which to her annoyance, held an equal amount of haughtiness. "Do we look like men who would enjoy what you've suggested?"

Kyra scanned over Brock, noting the hard angles of his jawline. He reminded her of a fitness model she'd seen grace a cover once. Hell, he fit the model type with his sandy-colored hair, masculine but beautiful features, and his athletic frame.

Even he had caught her interest from the get-go. More than the little tickle between her thighs at the idea of being with Brock and Smith, she couldn't quite pinpoint why she'd been so dead set on meeting them.

There was just *something* about them that drew her in like a bug to a light.

Smith had a thicker frame, like a man who'd spent hours in the gym. His jaw was softer than Brock's, yet his lips were more defined. She didn't doubt for a moment both men had six-packs and a plentiful display of muscles beneath their tailored suits.

What concerned her was the self-assurance they portrayed. Arrogance she'd seen all too often in the form of her best friends', Marley and Bella's, boyfriends. After another quick look at their stern expressions, she nodded with conviction. "Yes, you both act like doms."

Smith appeared to fight his smile, but his voice was rich with amusement. "Would you like us to dominate you? I've never refused an orgasm, or expected submission, but if you wish—"

"No, I do *not* wish." Kyra's fingernails dug into her palms. "I'm not looking for a dom." She hesitated. "Or I should say, two of them."

Brock gave her a long look. "Beyond being the most peculiar conversation I've ever had with a woman, why would you assume we live that lifestyle?"

"Well..." At Brock's question and Smith's amusement, her cheeks warmed. Now, she was horrified to her bones, realizing her assumption was wrong. "My best friends from the pact live the BDSM lifestyle, and you both seem"—she hesitated, then shrugged—"bossy."

Smith chuckled.

Brock's grin remained. "You're safe with us, kitten. We want to give you orgasms, not refuse them." His smile faded. "Besides, if I, or Smith, physically hurt you in any way you didn't want, I'd hope you'd have us arrested."

She relaxed her fists. "You realize, then, if you give me orders and if I respond, it's not because I'm submissive."

"A kitten who hisses." Brock winked with a dark, seductive look. "I like it."

Smith's mouth twitched. "It appears your friends are big players in the BDSM lifestyle, since you're so adamant in pointing that out. But yes, Kyra, we understand you're not submissive to us."

Brock added, "You're more than welcome to boss around right back. In fact, we expect it and would enjoy some interplay from you." His eyes positively glowed. "We prefer a spunky kitten than a timid one." His head tilted. "Can we move past this BDSM issue?"

She nibbled her lip, glancing from one man to the other. "Yes, of course." With her point made, embarrassment crept up. "You were bossy, and I assumed—"

"We wanted a sex slave." Brock smirked.

"Right, silly," she muttered.

Months ago, she wouldn't have accused anyone of such a thing, since she'd never heard much of the lifestyle. But after hearing endless stories of D/s relationships, it seemed her mind just went there, even if she'd rather not. "Perhaps I need to stop listening to my friends' stories."

"Perhaps," Smith agreed.

Brock still grinned. "Now then, since we've moved past that interesting conversation, I suspect I won't forget any time soon, it's time to get your sweet ass on the desk, kitten."

While their intention for putting her on that desk was clear-cut, she had signed up for this, hadn't she? Small talk had been out of the question. She didn't want to know these men after tonight. She wanted...wham, bam, thank you, two hunks! The less she knew, the better. For whatever reason, she felt emotionally rattled by the men. That if they got too close, she wouldn't be able to run.

Never get emotionally involved, especially when you're dealing with fancy men. A lesson she'd learned from working at the PR firm. Tonight she was down to all business. She'd fulfill the pact, live out her fantasy, and never look back. Besides, these two men were hot, and she planned to let the wild part of herself come out and play.

With that mission in mind, she approached the desk. When she reached the large cherrywood desk, she turned to the sexy beasts behind her. Two men, who no doubt planned to devour her. Desire flickered through her.

The contrast between them startled her. Who were the men behind the photos she couldn't stop looking at? Smith seemed reserved and strong, while Brock appeared playful and arrogant. The mix of the two provided stimulation without any foreplay. As if one man lacked a quality on his own, but together, they were perfection.

A dangerous situation, reminding her to shut her heart down.

She settled her bottom on the edge of the desk, the tips of her high heels supporting her weight. Her skirt rode up slightly on her thighs and she didn't have to look down to see her garters showed.

Brock's gaze went straight to her thighs, and his eyes flared with heat. "Stop right there, kitten." He stood from the couch, slow like a predator ready to pounce. "I do believe some of your clothing needs to go. Don't you, Smith?"

Two could play at this game of seduction. "Skirt off, then?"

"No, Kyra," Smith murmured. "Entire outer layer." His eyebrow arched in a silent challenge. "Unless you're too shy to undress while we stay clothed."

Both men approached her with the same controlled power and settled in front of the desk. Shyness had left her the second she signed up for this insane pact and joined the Castle Dolce Vita. One promise she'd made to herself tonight: no holding back.

The fantasy she'd always dreamed of would only happen once in her life. She'd never be so ballsy to do anything like this again. Here, she held her chance to be sexually free with two drop-dead gorgeous strangers she'd never see after tonight. That meant she'd push herself to limits she never would dream to go.

Leaning away from the desk, she steadied herself on her heels, then reached for the first button of her blouse. Smith's gaze held hers, as Brock's examination did a full sweep of her body, stopping on her fingers.

With leisurely slowness, she undid each button, her body heating as they watched her.

Once the garment draped open, she pulled the hem of her silk top out from her skirt. She slid herself out of the fabric, placing it behind her on the desk. Under their stares, she realized it wasn't the act of her undressing turning her on, it was the power in the depths of their eyes.

Smith smiled. One of those *I'm about to eat you, dear* types of smiles. "You look lovely, Kyra."

Marley had picked out Kyra's lingerie for her tonight. The black lace balconette bra made Kyra feel sexier than she ever had in one of her push-ups.

With the aroused masculine gazes on her, Kyra drowned in confidence, and she reached back to unzip her skirt. When the garment pooled at her feet, Brock gave her a full once-over again—more than a study of her, an outright appreciation of the micro black G-string only held together by the two bows laced low on her hips, and her garter belt and stockings.

Kyra paused, glancing at them. When neither of the men said a word, she peeked at their crotches, noticing big bulges. She smiled, loving the moment of control she owned, and the sexual kitten inside purred with pleasure. "Back on the desk, then?"

Smith's eyes darkened. The brown wasn't so warm now, but fierce and attentive. "Yes, Kyra, get on the desk."

Once she obliged him, pressing her bottom against the cool wood, Brock took the final step, closing the distance between them. A charming smile grazed his lips that no doubt won his way into many beds. "Widen your legs."

She did as asked, and if it weren't for the appreciation flaring in their eyes, she never would've been so bold. Their arousal fueled her bravery. Brock reached toward one bow that held her panties in place at her hip, while Smith took the other. In almost the exact moment, they pulled on the ends, and the light fabric lowered to the desk, exposing her heated flesh.

Kyra couldn't breathe; being touched by them moistened her lower lips.

Brock removed her G-string, dropping it to join her skirt on the floor. He stared at the junction between her thighs, as did Smith. While Bella had talked Kyra into going to the spa a few days ago, the entire Brazilian wax wasn't an option. Kyra had settled on a triangle shape of trimmed pubic hair, leaving her to feel like a woman, not a girl.

The men didn't seem to mind her not bare, since their nostrils flared as they gazed over her mound. Then as both men glanced up the length of her body with hungry looks, something in how they watched her, in a way so ravenous, made her hot. At the same time, emotion she attempted to force away struck her hard in the chest, hitching her breath.

What is it about you two?

Kyra had never been the clingy type. She had never chased after a man. Since seeing their pictures she couldn't get them out of her head. She'd wondered if their appeal would fade when she actually met them, but that was not the case. They consumed her.

"Let's see to this problem of yours," Smith murmured, raising his finger to her mouth. "Suck."

A slow delicious heat slid low in her belly as she wrapped her lips around his thick finger. She drew his digit deep into her mouth and sucked with a hard pull. The side of his mouth curved when he withdrew his finger from between her lips, her saliva coating his skin.

Brock offered his finger next. She repeated the move, adding a little swirl of her tongue, which made him groan. Hell, she liked playing with the big boys, and these men were two very *big* boys.

Smith's touch came first. He slid his hand up her knee and continued his journey to her inner thigh, all the while watching her. As he travelled higher she held her breath, unable to move. His gaze turned hotter, intense. "Kyra, you make me want to fuck you in every way I can."

She found herself equally affected. Both men were made of dreams. In appearance, they were her type, athletic and handsome, but not too pretty.

Each man had a feature that melted her bones—Smith with his warm eyes, and Brock with his charming smile, which he used in full force as he placed a hand on her opposite thigh. She shivered, as for the first time after fantasizing for so long, she had two men touching her. Brock's body temperature ran higher than Smith's, the warmth of his skin burning straight through her.

Smith's hand never stopped, still slow and measured, making her tremble in anticipation. Brock nudged her thigh when he reached the top of it. "Nice and wide, kitten."

She widened her legs, craving their hands all over her. She wanted them inside her, touching her, and pleasuring her. The scents lingering in the air around her were confusing, at best. Brock smelled like citrus. Smith held a sandalwood scent. The combination of the two intoxicated her. She couldn't decide which one to focus on, so she drowned in both.

Smith's touch neared her lower lips, but Brock didn't hesitate. He placed his thumb directly on her clit. Her eyes fluttered closed as he swirled the swollen bud.

The mix of Smith's patient touches and Brock's determined advances spun her with an incredible force. No doubt these men could turn her world upside down, and tonight, she'd happily allow it.

Brock grunted, a low primal sound, as she circled her hips in time with the movements he made on her clit. She opened her eyes, and the hot-as-hell grin he offered took a turn straight to devilish. "Fuck, you're sexy, kitten."

The tip of Smith's finger teased her slick heat, and her breath whooshed from her lungs. Each swipe of his finger against her slit sent sparks of desire across her hot flesh, filling her with desperation.

She didn't know much of anything except for the two men focused on her. The intensity in their stares became potent stimulation, driving her wild.

"Ah, now that's a look we love." Smith's smirk was pure sin. "Wicked and greedy." He slipped one finger inside, removed it to moisten another finger, then pushed both inside with slow precision.

A scorching hot shiver raced through her from head to toe. The pressure on her clit increased as Brock caressed her nub harder. She read in his superior stance he planned to win this bet. Not as if she cared. If they wanted to use her body to win some testosterone fueled contest, she'd play along.

Quivers and tingles erupted within her. Moans she couldn't control poured from her mouth. Smith pressed his free hand against her pubic bone when his fingers shifted in and out of her with a gentleness that didn't match such an intense man. There, in the depths of his eyes, he held a look so sure she'd orgasm, she believed him.

Perhaps she'd never been with men who cared enough, because only one ex-boyfriend had ever brought her to orgasm. Her climaxes always came from her vibrator. However, she didn't doubt for a second if they continued to give her those heated looks, her orgasm wasn't that far off. Brock increased the circles on her clit to include pinches and quick flicks.

These men were intent on their mission, as well as damn good at it.

"Sweetheart..." Brock leaned forward, slid his nose against her neck. She shivered under their attack of pleasure as he whispered in her ear, "You're much more responsive than you think."

Smith applied pressure on her pelvis, angling her bottom. He wiggled his fingers, then grinned. "We'll call this one a tie since you're enjoying Brock playing with your clit." The authority in his gaze made her heart skip a beat as his voice became as soft as velvet. "The next one is all mine."

He increased the speed of his fingers, moved in hard and deep, and her breath caught in her throat. Her fingernails bit into the desk beneath her, and she held on to the wood in a death grip, overloaded with sensations. The fast swirls on her clit from Brock, and the hard pressure building inside her pelvis from Smith, all rocked pleasure deep inside her.

Their fingers were notably different in strength and force, and she couldn't process the contrast. The sensations brought her to a state of incoherence. Her screams became nonexistent, stuck in the haze of her confusion. Now, only pleasure in its richest and highest form assaulted her.

Low in her belly, heaviness formed, and a new need rose, one she'd never experienced. She reveled in the sensation captivating her, well aware of what awaited her.

The men drove her higher, and on the very brink of shouting *stop*, she burst wide open. Pleasure flooded her in waves she shouldn't be able to survive. Her eyes screwed shut, and now her unleashed screams became the only sound echoing around her as two hands belonging to different men pinned her to the desk.

About the time she noticed her scratchy throat, she realized she had dropped from her climax. She discovered Smith had removed his fingers, but Brock squeezed her sex tight. The pressure against her hot flesh eased the deep contractions still vibrating through her.

"Looks like our bet won't be an issue," Smith stated.

He looked down at his fingers as he trailed her moisture along her inner thigh, which had never come from her body in such delicious amounts. When he removed his touch, he brought his finger to his mouth and sucked on it.

All she could do was watch him as her satiated body shockingly awakened yet again under the promise of pleasure. More so, under the touch of these men. Brock squatted in front of her and used the flat of his tongue to lick up any evidence of her climax.

By the time he reached her clit, she had become a shivering mess. She craved more of them, of their talents, and of this dirty game. "My turn," she said, shocked by the huskiness to her voice. "Gentlemen, all your clothes need to go."

Their answering smirks made her wonder if she'd unleashed demons, but her soul wasn't up for grabs; they wanted to own her orgasms. With an impressive speed, shoes and socks were toed off, jackets were gone, buttons were flicked open, pants, boxers, and shirts were off, exposing beautiful masculine bodies. Smith had the body of a man who spent hours in the gym. His shoulders were wide, biceps thick, and his squared pecs demanded attention from her hands.

On a deep swallow, she turned to Brock, who had the body of a runner. Thin, trim, and all muscle mass. But the slenderness of his frame made his muscles more defined, sharper, and damn well delectable.

As her attention drifted lower, she noticed their cocks. Brock was long. Smith was thick. And both cocks were aimed toward the ceiling, hard and ready to be buried deep inside her. Lord knows, she had confidence walking through the office doors, undressing in front of them, but now... She had doubts she'd survive her first ménage experience. Maybe even had doubts she'd come out of this not emotionally wanting more. Though the promises of the greatest sex of her life, the intensity in their features, and their robust bodies that exuded strength...

A quiver danced through her. "Bring it on, boys."

CHAPTER THREE

Brock might've been stunned speechless over the woman if he wasn't hard as a rock and ready to pump into Kyra until she writhed in pleasure. While he found her beautiful and so stunning in her lingerie, the playfulness in her personality, as well as her confidence, did more for his hard cock than her appearance.

When it came to Smith and him, women could be intimidated and usually were. He hadn't had a past girlfriend who at first wasn't a little vulnerable around him. Exactly why his relationships never lasted. He liked a woman who could be soft, yet held a confident twinkle her eyes. Even his lovers hadn't had that spark, which is why they'd remained only lovers.

Kyra showed no hint of nervousness. Brock preferred a woman with a bit of a hard edge, kind, but not too soft. He liked her to be feminine, yet in a room full of men, she held her chin high. Kyra had proved in a matter of minutes she had all those traits. He found her strength and poise more alluring than her spread wide.

However, at her small smile as she pushed off the desk and slid onto her knees, he wondered if she had possibly bewitched him. His muscles tensed as he stared down at her on her knees. She crooked a finger. "Come closer."

Brock took a step forward, as did Smith next to him. When she wrapped her hand around his shaft, Brock couldn't restrain his groan. He tossed his head back and a deep rumble rose from his chest.

He forced himself to look at her. Kyra glanced from his cock to Smith's. Her strokes were slow and light, playful. Brock could only assume she'd fantasized for a long time about having two cocks in her hands. And he liked how she looked when she touched him, determined to pleasure him, but enjoying the ride as much as he was.

She licked her lips before her head lifted, and her eyes had darkened. Christ, this woman *loved* having more than one cock to enjoy. Not all women did. Brock had seen some women play as if it had interested them. Some felt naughty being stuffed full by two men. But other women *needed* two men and found contentment and happiness under two hard bodies instead of one.

Kyra was the latter.

His groin tightened as he watched Kyra take Smith's cock deep into her throat, and Smith moaned. Brock grunted himself as her hold tightened around his shaft and he closed his eyes, relishing in her soft strokes.

When he heard her mouth pop off and release Smith, he snapped his eyes open and equaled Smith's near growl as she drew his dick past those luscious lips. He watched himself disappear into her mouth, and he enjoyed how her lips, painted with pink lipstick, looked around his cock.

Brushing his hand over her hair, the silky strands danced through his fingers, and he inhaled sharply when she sucked him hard. The scent of her arousal engulfed him, creating a wicked aroma from three hot bodies, all driving his desires higher.

The beautiful view of Kyra only fed fuel to the fire. He couldn't tell what about her he found so enthralling, only that right now, he stared at perfection. In fact, he couldn't take his eyes off her. Something he definitely hadn't felt in some time. Not since his high school sweetheart. The same woman who dumped him on his ass when he told her he wanted to have a threesome.

After a long, slow pull on his cock, Kyra released him and grinned. Her gaze flicked from him to Smith as she jerked them off with fluid strokes of her hands. "Two are definitely more fun than one." With a wicked glint in her eye, she once again devoured Smith, and his loud grunts followed.

Brock might have missed that mouth, if her hand wasn't equally as talented. Kitten was a multitasker. She had no issues keeping up the sensual strokes on his cock as her head bobbed on Smith.

Hearing the sounds of Smith's pleasure next to him, Brock couldn't stop himself from running a finger over her shoulder, needing to touch her. Craving beyond anything he would even dare to control, he yearned to feel the silkiness of her flawless flesh calling to him.

When he trailed his finger against her silky skin, feeling perfection under his touch, she mistook it for an order and moved away from Smith. He shook his head. "Keep on Smith, Kitten." He hadn't meant to distract her, but he'd been compelled to put his hand on her body.

Brock couldn't remember the last time he'd been so motivated to feel a woman more than to merely take pleasure in her. It'd been years since he had anything he'd call a relationship, and he was perfectly content with that decision.

He hadn't met a woman he could not only trust wasn't with him for his money, but also accepted his sexual preferences. Yet, he experienced a draw to Kyra, a pull he couldn't understand, and one forceful enough he wouldn't run from it.

The sounds of Smith's harsh inhale snapped him out of his thoughts, and he blinked into focus, watching Kyra release Smith's cock. She turned her head and devoured Brock's dick. Her tongue wrapped underneath, her lips slid over his shaft, and he threw his head back with a long groan.

When she moved her tongue around his cockhead, he looked to her, noticing Smith stepping away from her. They had shared enough women that Brock understood Smith's desire to take things a step further. And well, he also experienced Smith's urgency; this woman was the most fuckable thing he'd ever seen.

While he moved away from Kyra's mouth, she remained on her knees, giving him a cute quizzical look. Brock winked before he approached the leather chair near the coffee table as Smith grabbed his pants off the floor and took out his wallet.

Brock smiled, dropping down into the chair, the cool leather easing his overheated skin. With his gaze zeroed in on Kyra, he crooked a finger. "Come to me, kitten."

A sexy smile curved her mouth as she crawled toward him. For a woman who adamantly rejected BDSM, she didn't seem to mind some of the light play that went along with the lifestyle. Brock suspected if he pointed out she had crawled to him, she'd bash him down with a lecture, but he knew well enough her mindset was more on sexual exploration.

Kyra had crawled because she knew it'd be sexy.

She was right—it made him burn.

Settling in between Brock's spread legs, she ran her hands up his thighs with a wicked twinkle in her eyes, when Smith called, "Not kneeling, Kyra, on your feet."

She glanced over her shoulder, and Brock heard the hitch in her breath. He followed her gaze and noticed Smith putting on a condom, explaining why her hands were trembling against his legs, in what Brock assumed was anticipation mixed with excitement.

Smith applied the condom, and when he approached them, he tossed a foil package, which Brock caught. Kyra turned to Brock and once again swallowed him whole. Continuing to suck him off, she rose to her feet. Brock didn't wait; he reached up and pulled her bra cups underneath her breasts, letting her spectacular tits hang out.

He loved a naked woman, yet Kyra had gone to the trouble to dress up for them, and he appreciated her lingerie. He had no doubt if she stood, her breasts would look incredible with the lace underneath. Besides, he hoped to draw out their bet tonight.

In fact, he was already thinking of setting up another night.

When Smith settled in behind her, Kyra's mouth became more urgent on Brock's cock. Smith placed a hand on her back and angled her hips, placing Brock's raging hard-on farther into her throat. A groan, deep and low, hummed from his throat.

Every swipe of her lips, feel of her tongue along his shaft, and pressure she set with her hand tightened his muscles. With clenched fists, all he could do was admire the beauty going wild on his cock, her long black hair curtaining his thighs. Her lips tightened, so Brock glanced up to a smirking Smith.

"I like you wet, Kyra," Smith said.

She inhaled a sharp breath through her nose as Smith fingered her, bringing her into no doubt another mind-blowing orgasm. Though Smith's smart-ass grin declared his intention was more than to make Kyra wet, he had gotten in the first point.

Dipshit.

Loud moans drifted around Brock as Kyra's mouth popped off the head of his cock and she rested above him. Her eyes were closed and her lips parted as she trembled against him, clearly suffering the aftershocks of her climax.

Brock looked to Smith and mouthed, *Fucker.*

Smith inclined his head, his eyes shining in victory.

Brock had to up his game.

Kyra's long exhale drew him to her. Her eyes were fixed on him, her dark pupils captivating him. Some women looked pretty after they climaxed, but Kyra...a beautiful sunset had nothing on her.

He froze a moment, lost in the depths of her eyes—innocence, compassion, and strength. He read all those qualities within her, and he found himself compelled to be closer to her. Time slowed around him as he brushed his thumb over her cheek.

She leaned into his touch, and then her pretty eyes widened. Brock didn't have to look at Smith to know he'd pushed his cock inside her. Kyra's flushed cheeks told him enough, and that look on her topped anything he'd seen so far, making all bets off. Right now, he didn't give a shit if Smith won; he simply wanted her mouth on his cock.

He slid his hand along her cheek and then tangled his fingers into her hair, guiding her down toward him. Once again, she drew his greedy dick past her lips and sucked, bringing him pure pleasure. He reached down between them and cupped her breasts. He pinched and teased her nipples, and she moved even quicker now. Her lovely moans washing over him.

Brock raised his gaze to the reason for her noise, and Smith fucked her ruthlessly from behind. The hard slaps against her fine ass echoed in the office and hardened Brock's cock between those amazing lips. His teeth clenched, and his need to be deep inside her erased any patience he possessed.

He brushed his finger over the side of her face, drawing her attention to him, then as he stood, her mouth popped off the tip of his cock. Moving to the side, he put the foil package in his teeth, and as he opened the condom, Smith pulled out of her. He positioned himself in the chair, with his hips resting off the seat, and Kyra straddled him.

Brock glared.

Smith winked before he thrust his hips and pummeled her from underneath. In defeat, Brock took the foil from between his teeth and closed his fist around it. He moved in next to the chair, positioning himself by Kyra. If he wasn't going to bury himself inside her, he'd definitely take anything he could get.

Oddly enough, the distance bothered him. He liked being close to her. Almost as if the air was just a little bit warmer with her near.

He settled in next to her, and Kyra grabbed his cock. She stroked him in the same rhythm that Smith set, rapid, urgent strokes. The scent of her arousal sped through his nostrils, and he clenched his jaw, watching Smith fuck the woman boneless. Neither Smith nor him were gentle lovers. They had no time for it. Anything they did, they put 100 percent in to, and that extended to a woman's body.

While Kyra continued to stroke him, Brock nudged on her shoulder to straighten her. In an instant, her tits jutted out, and the image he thought he'd see of her breasts resting atop her bra didn't compare to the real thing. She had great tits with hard rosy nipples, and a tight body he wanted beneath him.

Smith gripped her hips while he continued to bang her savagely. Brock slid his fingers down the center of her chest, and he loved the feel of her soft skin. He continued to the middle of her bra, slid his hand lower along her toned abdomen until he found her swollen clit. The noises she made entranced him—soft moans, yet sounding rich with desire.

Beneath her, Smith pumped hard, each thrust building in intensity. Brock saw the effect it had on her and that she enjoyed this position. Her screams drew out thicker, raspier, before her eyes screwed shut.

She gripped Brock's cock tighter as if to carry him along with her, but he wouldn't come this way. No way in hell. He'd be buried deep inside her when he blew. He pulled her hand off him and placed it on Smith's chest, while Smith continued to slam into her.

Her scream elongated, and Brock rubbed harder against her clit, swirling faster, until she shouted, "Stop."

Brock jerked his hand away from her clit, and Smith had her off his cock, standing over him almost in the same instant. A long silence followed, as Smith exchanged a look with Brock. Kyra, with her hands on Smith's chest, panted.

Smith tangled his fingers in her hair, drawing her head up. He asked in a soft voice, "What's wrong?"

Kyra gasped, breathless. "You've already had me, so now let Brock have a turn. I want you to finish"—she slid her fingers over her mouth—"right here."

Smith's eyes searched hers, and Brock stayed silent, knowing Smith hated what she proposed. He didn't enjoy coming in a woman's mouth, nor did Brock. Buried deep inside was where they both preferred to finish.

Though Kyra had cornered Smith, hadn't she?

Brock restrained his chuckle, seeing the fight Smith suffered. Typically, Smith would flip the woman over and fuck her until they both lost themselves in orgasm, but Kyra made it a point to say that she wanted some of the control. He wondered what Smith's move next would be.

It came only a second later when Smith assisted Kyra off him. He removed the condom, put it in a tissue, then deposited both in the trashcan beside the couch. "All right, we can do this your way."

Smith settled into the seat again, legs spread wide, and Kyra bent over as she reached for Smith. Her long hair draped over Smith's thighs as she took his cock into her hands.

When Smith raised his hand to grab her head, she said with a sly grin, "No touching me. Put your hands on the armrests. Don't move."

Smith exchanged a bemused glance with Brock, who chuckled at the bossy woman. Kyra, without any doubt in his mind, held her own against them, and Brock found that endearingly sexy.

Apparently, so did Smith, since he gave her a sly grin. "By all means, darlin'..." He rested his forearms on the armrests. "Please, indulge yourself."

Brock didn't wait for an invitation. He wanted to feel Kyra squeezing him to climax. Without hesitation, he opened the condom wrapper and sheathed himself. He settled in behind that sexy round ass, decorated in the garter belt. He rubbed his hand over her fine bottom before he gave her cheek a slap, loving the pinkish color it left.

Each rub against her bottom had Kyra wiggling her hips; every firm grab of her cheek had her arching up into his grip, and every slap against her flesh had her moaning. Unable to wait any longer, Brock placed the head of his cock at her slit, and slammed home.

She threw her head back as he no doubt startled her, but he didn't give her a chance to recover. He gripped her hips and pumped into her with the intention of spilling himself inside her.

Skin slapped against skin, and their moans all morphed together as she also worked Smith's cock. Brock held a determination to get one more climax out of her. With that mission playing on his mind, he pressed against her lower back, angled her, and shifted his hips to rub against her G-spot. He cursed Smith, because he looked into Kyra's eyes while he took her this way, this hard, this raw.

In fact, he wouldn't stand for it.

He grabbed her hair, then angled her head to the side. "Who's fucking you now, kitten?"

"You are," she gasped. "Oh God!"

Locked in her stare, he spotted the heat she experienced from his cock, only his touch. He liked knowing it was him bringing her to this level of arousal. He loved being the reason why her eyes were so rich with desire, so much so he didn't want it to end.

I want more of you...

Though when Brock looked at Smith, he stared at Brock with the dark look he'd gotten used to seeing when Smith was on the brink of his climax. Kyra might think she controlled Smith now, but she'd be wrong. Smith had allowed her that control, even if she didn't know it. Smith could've easily persuaded her, yet he allowed her to think she owned his choices.

Both Smith and Brock needed control in their lives and craved to control their women. That didn't mean they couldn't allow a woman some freedom to think she owned the show...for a little while. They weren't successful in life by luck. They knew how to get what they wanted.

Now, Brock saw in Smith's gaze, he fought off his orgasm. Brock wasn't nearly done with Kyra tonight. He wanted more time with her. Having sex once wasn't enough to get his fill of her. Though he suspected Smith wanted the same, by how he looked at Kyra with such fierceness.

Releasing his fingers from her hair, Brock murmured, "Finish Smith, kitten."

She wrapped both hands around Smith's cock and lowered her head, but the intensity with which Smith looked at Kyra shifted. The control he'd given her a moment ago, he clearly wanted back. To ensure she forgot what she had asked Smith to do, Brock slammed forward to steal her train of thought. In the same instant, Smith wrapped his hands around her head, then thrust up from underneath.

With Smith taking her mouth, Brock continued to pound against her sexy ass. Each thrust forward gave him quite the view as her bottom jiggled. Each withdrawal showed his cock glistening in her arousal. Her inner muscles tightened around him almost immediately after he started thrusting, which didn't surprise him.

This was her fantasy.

While Kyra loved to be a bit bossy to show her strength, she clearly also loved being sexually dominated by two men, even if she didn't want to admit it.

Smith tightened his fingers in her hair, and she moaned which sent her inner muscles clamping against Brock's cock. He gripped her waist and thrust forward, ruthlessly. His balls drew up tight against his body, causing a hot wave to rush over his spine, making him thrust faster. The squeeze of her inner walls against him made him pump into her harder. The moans she made around Smith's cock encouraged Brock to render her cross-eyed from her climax.

His muscles burned as he pumped into her mercilessly. Kyra stiffened under Brock's hands and around his cock. Her body quivered and shook as Smith bucked and jerked against her mouth.

The moment her lips popped off Smith's cock, she screamed, exploding into a thunderous orgasm that, without warning, brought Brock's climax. Flickers of flames rushed up his spine, making him roar as he blasted into orgasm.

Beneath his hand on Kyra's back, he sensed the aftereffects of her release. The little jerks of her sweaty sexy body milked his spent cock. Unable to support his weight, he pulled out from inside her and dropped to his knees.

Smith panted, as deeply as Brock. Kyra now lowered to her knees, her head against Smith's leg, as if she couldn't possibly move. Brock concluded he couldn't either and rested his forehead against her damp back.

Long minutes passed as all their panting turned into quieter breathing, before Kyra shifted away from Brock. She stood, looking down at them with a dozy grin. "Jesus, that...was amazing!" She approached her clothes, which gave Brock a great view of her ass wrapped in that sexy garter. "By the way, boys, who won the bet?"

"The bet isn't over," Smith muttered.

"Oh?" She reached for her skirt, glancing over her shoulder, her eyes twinkling. "Why would that be?"

Brock looked at Smith in curiosity, wondering the same damn thing, since his brain hadn't fully recovered. Smith's eyes narrowed. "You know as well as I do, you sassy thing, that it's a tie."

Kyra laughed as she dressed in her skirt. She put her shoes on in no time, then finished up with her blouse. "Is that what you think?" She gave a smart-ass smirk, which included a wink. "Interesting."

Brock counted and now realized her orders hadn't been without purpose. She had stopped Smith earlier because she knew she was going to come, and that would've tipped the scales in Smith's favor.

She hadn't asked Brock to take her because she wanted it— or maybe that had been part of it too—but more so, it evened the score. She'd ordered Smith not to touch her at all, meaning Brock had made her come, not Smith. Brock believed any way this played out, she would've ensured the result was exactly what had happened.

Saucy little woman had outsmarted them.

"Thanks for the fun night. I'll never forget it." She blew them a kiss, spun on her heels, and her laughter followed her out of the room.

"Brat." Smith grunted.

Brock stared at the empty doorway in stunned silence. She was a smart kitten, not only in regards of the bet, but... "Did she just walk out on us?"

"She did."

Warmth slid through Brock. "A challenge?"

Smith gave a crisp nod. "She's...different, hmm?"

Brock considered Kyra, and she *was* different. By all appearances, she wanted nothing more to do with them. Never, in all the years that Smith and Brock enjoyed women together, either dating or merely as lovers, had one left them after sex. In fact, it'd always been the other way around, and women tended to be clingy.

He and Smith were two of the wealthiest bachelors in Baltimore, which usually brought women who were after status and money, more than anything else. That reason had been exactly why they'd joined the castle. It kept their sexual preferences private, and they never intended to find a woman worth a deeper look, or had plans to settle down.

He wanted a longer night with Kyra, and she'd just walked away without giving him the chance to ask. Though did he want anything more with her? Did her confidence and independence somehow bring forth a hunger to see her again?

The answer was glaringly obvious. "I'm not done. You?"

"Not nearly finished." Smith got up from the chair and gathered his clothes off the floor. After he grabbed his slacks, he threw Brock his pants. "There's something about her that's—"

"Unique." Brock dressed, leaving his shirt off, as did Smith. Oddly enough, Brock felt used by her...and Christ, he liked it. More so, she had no idea how intriguing she was, to have the both of them pawing after her. A very interesting development, indeed. Little did Kyra know neither he nor Smith took no for an answer. "Besides, she didn't let us finish the bet."

"Quite unfair of her." Smith gave a firm nod, arching an eyebrow. "We need to settle the score."

Brock grinned. "And kitten just upped the ante."

CHAPTER FOUR

The next night, Kyra sat atop her bed with her laptop, reading an article on Smith and Brock. RAGS TO RICHES: THE STORY BEHIND THE TWO ORPHANS WHO BUILT AN EMPIRE. She scanned the article, now understanding their closeness—even if it didn't explain why they enjoyed ménage encounters. They'd been adopted by the same woman and had grown up together, and they'd taken their self-made software company and made themselves multimillionaires.

Impressive.

Kyra clicked on another article: SAD NEWS FOR BALTIMORE'S WOMEN. MDR SOFTWARE'S TWO TOP BACHELORS ARE GAY! She burst out laughing and read some ridiculous tabloid that claimed Smith and Brock were homosexual. While she could understand how someone would come to that conclusion, since she doubted they'd had many relationships considering their *tastes*, the tabloid had it so wrong.

Shaking her head, she continued to search. After a minute of clicking through some boring business articles, she landed on another tabloid: GAY? DREAM ON. LADIES, THE TWO MOST ELIGIBLE BACHELORS ARE BACK ON THE MARKET!

Kyra wondered over the tagline. Was that what they were...*back on the market?* Were they even eligible? Could they have a proper relationship? How could they share a woman so easily?

She heaved a sigh, knowing exactly why these questions remained so heavy on her mind. For the hundredth time, she picked up her cell phone off the mattress next to her and read the text message that Brock had sent just after nine o'clock.

We'd like to see you again, kitten.

The choice is yours.

She pursed her lips at the message from Brock before she placed her phone on the nightstand. Using her mouse, she opened the original e-mail from them offering the night that had brought them together.

Once the e-mail popped open, she scrolled down to their photos. Brock's piercing blue eyes pooled heat low into her body, which only increased as Smith's deep, warm chocolate-brown eyes stared back at her. Her night with the men flashed into her mind, making her temperature rise. Their hands on her, their voices seemingly still whispering in her ears, and the sheer pleasure they'd given her all made her mindless.

Her fulfilled fantasy ended up being so much more than she had expected. Maybe she thought it was naughty having two men at the same time, but more happened that night. Rightness settled deep into her soul, giving her clarity that she needed two men instead of one.

How confusing was that?

She shouldn't want two men in her bed.

Only problem?

She did.

"Still staring, huh?"

Kyra gasped. "Oh. My. God. Bella." She gripped her chest, attempting to control her hammering heart. "You scared the frickin' crap out of me. Don't do that!"

Bella chuckled, leaning against her door frame dressed in her pink nightie. "I knocked twice." Her blue eyes held more happiness and contentment than Kyra had ever seen in her friend.

"Oh." Kyra's cheeks warmed. Had she seriously been *that* lost in their eyes, and her thoughts? "Sorry." She took one final look at hunk one and hunk two, then closed her laptop. "What did you need?"

"I went to the bathroom and saw you were still up." She plopped down on the bed in typical Bella behavior, as if this was her bed, not Kyra's. Her long blonde hair looked a mess, and Kyra didn't even want to consider the cause of that messy hair. "I had a realization tonight."

Great. One of Bella's insights usually meant another crazy plan, like the pact of seduction. It'd been Bella's idea, even if Kyra and her other two roommates agreed to it. "Which was?"

"You weren't supposed to have your fantasy next." Bella's eyes narrowed with suspicion. "But then, I remembered tonight Sadie was supposed to go, wasn't she?"

Kyra thought back to the conversation when Bella had returned from her fantasy night with Kole, and she remembered when Bella suggested Kyra was up next. "Originally, when we drew straws, Sadie was supposed to go after you."

Bella glanced to the floor for a moment before she looked to Kyra with a furrowed brow. "Why didn't you correct me?"

"When you said it, Sadie didn't object, and the way she looked at me..." Kyra hesitated. "Almost like Sadie begged me to go next. Clearly, she needs more time to be okay with this all. I figured I had to go anyway. So, why wait?"

"Ah, I see," Bella drawled.

"Don't make a big deal out of it either." Kyra pointed an index finger. "I don't want you saying anything to Sadie."

"I won't. Promise. I feel bad for Sadie, maybe she doesn't want to go through with it." Bella blew out a long breath before she glanced at Kyra's phone on the nightstand. "Anyways, something to figure out later. So have you responded to the text?"

"Not yet." Kyra lifted her chin, not to look like the wimp who couldn't send a dang text message. "But I will."

A low chuckle sounded from the doorway. "Scared shitless, aren't you?"

Kyra gritted her teeth, not even wanting to look over at Bella's boyfriend, Kole. She knew exactly the expression she'd meet. Though when his chuckle stopped, she figured it safe enough and turned to him. She pinched her lips together as she greeted his smart-ass wink.

Kole was dressed in only his black boxers, and his muscular physique glistened with sweat. For a man who'd only been dating her best friend a short time, he'd clearly grown comfortable in her, and her best friend's, house. She liked Kole, but she could do without his opinion. "I'm not scared."

His eyebrows rose over his intense blue eyes. "Then why haven't you responded?"

"I'm..." She glanced at her clock, seeing that it was midnight, which meant she'd been reading articles about them a lot longer than she realized. "I have no idea what to say."

"Hey, I'm up to fucking you two beasts again," Bella stated. "When can we meet?"

"Bella!" Kyra snapped, covering her warm face with her hands. "Honest to God."

"That's my girl." Kole laughed.

When Kyra finally lowered her hands, Kole's grin faded. His look became more controlled, stern, which was typical Kole. He was a dom after all. Kyra figured that look just went with the territory.

"There's no reason to be nervous," he said, in what she assumed was meant to be a soothing voice. Coming from him, it sounded more like an order that she calm down. "They've invited you for another night. It's a given."

"I'm not worried about being rejected," Kyra countered. "It's just...this is confusing. I thought it'd be one night. That's it. And they're so..."

Bella wiggled her eyebrows. "Sexy?"

"Yes," Kyra admitted. "And well, *normal*."

Kole's head tilted, his eyes searching hers. "Do I look the type of person to hold the interests I do?"

Said interests were painful things that Kyra didn't even want to consider, which included floggers, wax, and ropes, among other things that horrified her. She'd heard enough of Bella's experiences with BDSM to sing a song in her head every time Marley or Sadie made her talk about her *adventures*. "Um..." She rolled her eyes. "No."

He gave a firm nod, but before he could clearly push his point further, Bella interjected, "You can always say no, you know."

That was certainly an option, one at the top of Kyra's list.

"But you don't want to, do you?" Kole asked in that maddening observant voice that both he and Marley's boyfriend, Reed, possessed. Kyra looked down at her white duvet and played with a loose string. She'd be a fool not to accept another night with Brock and Smith, but that wasn't the deal. The plan had been to live out the one fantasy that was always a naughty secret; the one that she'd spend the rest of her life remembering in the comfort of her bed with her favorite dildo.

"I don't know what I want," she whispered.

"Sure you do," Kole stated. "It's time to stop stalling."

Kyra lifted her head, and while his tone held a sharp edge, warmth rested in his features. She'd grown to like that about Kole. Part of him scared her with all his intensity, but there was depth to him that if she hadn't seen him with Bella, she doubted she'd ever noticed. She also expected most people never saw the softer side to Kole.

There, in his fierce gaze, was a strength telling her to make a decision. She thought back to why she made the pact in the first place. With no prospects of love and a few boring one-night stands, what did she have to lose?

Not a damn thing.

What could she gain?

Another sexual experience that equaled no other.

In the arms of one man, she found no fulfillment. In the arms of two men, she tasted satisfaction. The thought of Smith and Brock focused entirely on her made her shiver, sending heat rushing from head-to-toe.

Kole's mouth twitched. "And there it is." His voice took on a sharp edge as if stating for a fact he recognized her desire for the men.

She exhaled a long, slow breath, still trapped in his stare. "But how can this work between us?"

"They're not asking for your hand in marriage." Bella patted Kyra's leg. "Just more hot and sweaty sex."

There was the *other* problem. She couldn't stop thinking about them all day. Was it just sex to her? Unemotional play that kept her safe? She rubbed her eyebrow, knowing the answer was staring her dead in the face. "But what if I start"—she swallowed—"liking them?" This was the serious problem— something about the men made her feel so safe, so comfortable. Becoming attached didn't seem difficult, and that scared her.

Kole leaned his shoulder against the door frame and folded his arms. "So, what if you do?"

She looked to Bella, waiting for her to agree that a ménage relationship could never work, but Bella remained silent. Kyra finally looked to Kole. "How can a woman want to date two men? It's wrong...weird."

"Get *normal* out of your head," he replied with little heat to his voice. "Is my liking to restrain Bella and flog her *normal?*"

Her immediate response was *no*, but that'd just be rude to her best friend since for Bella it was normal.

At her silence, Kole inclined his head. "In the context of our lives, it's right because it's what we want. Just as, in your life right now, you want these two men."

"Besides," Bella cut in. "From what you've said they're stinkin' rich, which means fancy dinners and presents." She slapped Kyra's thigh. "Enjoy it. You deserve to have some fun."

Kyra glanced down to the string on her bed that she fiddled with, and she contemplated. Why was she rejecting the idea of spending more time with men who could satisfy her to her bones? Sure, she entered dangerous territory since it'd been a long time since she had this kind of chemistry with a man...or two men, for that matter.

Would she have regrets if she ignored Brock and Smith's offer? Could she keep herself distant enough to not let feelings get involved? Part of her doubted it. She felt butterflies thinking about the two men she didn't even know. The other part of her—the stronger part—declared she could keep this strictly sexual.

"All right." She raised her head to Bella, then said to Kole, "I'll message them."

"Glad to hear it." Kole gave her a direct, probing stare. "Nothing wrong with going after what you need, Kyra."

"Right, what I need," she muttered, which were two gorgeous men, two hard cocks, four hands, and...

Dammit, she needed to stop shivering. Kole's smile widened, and he clearly fought against his laughter.

Bella bounced on the bed. "I bet once you get sandwiched between those two hotties again, you'll wonder why you sat here staring at them on the computer for so long, contemplating this instead of fucking them."

Kyra grunted. "Bella, you're such a pervert."

"I know." Her grin was sure-as-shit satisfied before she jumped off the bed and leaped at Kole, who caught her in his arms. She wrapped her legs around his waist while he tucked her nightie over her butt to fortunately hide a view Kyra didn't want.

Kyra shook her head, laughing. Her heart warmed at their happiness. Maybe she was slightly envious of their relationship; she wanted that—to find true love. Nonetheless, she was thrilled that Bella had found Kole. "Night, guys. Thanks."

"Send that text," was all Kole said before he took a giggling Bella back down the hallway.

Once she heard Bella's bedroom door shut, Kyra placed her laptop on the floor and tucked herself into bed. She grabbed her phone off the nightstand and drew in a deep breath. Before she could chicken out, she got right to it.

I'm in.

She hit the Send button and went to place the phone back on the nightstand when a loud beep echoed in her room right before Brock's text popped up.

Hello, kitten. Are you always a night owl?

Butterflies rushed through her as she could almost hear his voice. It would appear that way since she was up late, but she was so far from that.

No, I'm not usually up late. Are you?

Yes, always.

She blinked at the screen having no idea what to say next. She frantically thought up something, since the pause was awkward and she knew he was sitting on the other end, probably smiling, waiting for her to respond.

Why?

She hit Send and groaned. This wasn't about talking and getting to know him better. This was about raunchy sex...again. She needed to stick to the plan. Hadn't she already told herself the smart part of her was stronger than this?

I'm best on six hours of sleep. About our date, when are you available?

She exhaled, so relieved that he'd shifted back to the *important*. Even if she wasn't quite sure she liked the idea that he called it a *date*. That wasn't what they were planning, or she hoped. Another meeting at their office would do just fine.

Tomorrow is good.

Terrific. We'll see you at Blackfoot at 5:00.

Her heart hammered. This sounded like a date. Was it a date?

Before she got the courage to somehow ask that and set him straight that wouldn't be happening, another beep came from her phone.

Oh, and Kyra…

She paused, holding her breath.

Wear something sexy for us, kitten.

CHAPTER FIVE

Blackfoot, one of Baltimore's restaurants, was fine dining at its best with its modern design and five-star cuisine. Brock had many business dinners sitting at the corner table he now shared with Kyra and Smith. Though none of those dinners included him thinking lewd thoughts.

He couldn't quite keep his hands off Kyra. Maybe that's why he sat in next to her to ensure he didn't have to deny himself. Hell, he even noticed Smith touched her for no other reason than it seemed an impulse.

There was something about this woman...something damn special.

Kyra picked up her wineglass, her eyes still crinkled in amusement at something Smith had said. Brock zeroed in on her pink-painted lips that wrapped around the rim of the wineglass. She took a deep swallow of her wine before she lowered the glass, then licked the moisture off her lips. "Your mother, what was she like?"

"A horrible, godforsaken bitch." Smith muttered.

It pleased Brock that she finally asked personal questions. So far, she'd been impeccably closed off. Though, regardless of the conversation topic, he also nearly groaned. His cock throbbed as his awareness to the woman next to him was nothing he'd ever experienced. Every move she made seemed like a direct assault on his control not to forget they were in a busy restaurant, bend her over the table, lift her skirt, and drive his cock...

He grabbed his beer and took a huge gulp. This dinner with her would be damn long.

Tonight, Kyra had shown up in a red skirt that looked proper enough, if he didn't know what was beneath that skirt.

Most wouldn't pay attention to the fact that she didn't wear stockings, but that told him she wore no garter and likely only had on panties.

He wanted to find out what panties she wore.

Or maybe she didn't wear any.

Her black blouse had a pink lace cami beneath it, implying modesty. To him, it only made him more eager. His cock hardened in a second flat at the sight of her long legs and her shiny black high heels.

He'd asked her to wear something sexy for their date tonight, but she didn't show it like most women did. She looked dressed appropriately as if she were going to work. The sexy came in the form of her lace cami that showed a tiny hint of cleavage, and her killer heels. Her idea of sexy paid off; she looked far sexier than a woman who chose to wear something tight and revealing.

She took another sip of her wine, then cocked her head and nibbled her lip, clearly confused at Smith's statement about their mother. Brock interjected to explain why they had such hatred for the woman who had raised them. "Our mother wasn't motherly."

Kyra frowned. "But she adopted both of you, didn't she?"

Brock leaned back in his chair and folded his arms, understanding her confusion. No one but Brock and Smith knew the truth about their dear old mom. He stayed silent as a waiter strode by the table, then said, "Marjorie was our foster mother, not adoptive."

Smith took a drink of his red wine. "A foster mother who only took us in for the checks."

Kyra placed her wineglass on the table and looked at them again, her eyebrows drawn together. "What checks?"

Brock unfolded his arms and lowered his hand to her thigh, spotting the concern in Kyra's features. A caring woman too, he liked that. "Marjorie received a monthly stipend for each eligible foster child she took in, which was why she fostered kids. It was never about loving children or wanting to provide them a home."

Kyra stared at him for a long moment before she took Brock's hand on her thigh and reached for Smith's on top of the table. "Did she feed you?"

Brock inclined his head, thinking her sympathy sweet. "That was one thing Marjorie did do. Three meals a day and one snack before bed."

Kyra looked down at Smith's hand joined with hers. "Where is Marjorie now?"

"Dead," Smith bit off.

She lifted her head, and her eyes searched Smith's. Her voice softened. "You have no other family?"

Brock shook his head, running his thumb over the silky skin near her knee. "Just each other."

Something shifted in Kyra's gaze, a tenderness he hadn't seen from her reaching the depths of her eyes. She'd been so strong, confident, and focused. Now, she looked undeniably gentle. He liked that look on her.

Kyra's sympathy for their loveless childhood shone in her expression, and maybe now she understood why they stuck together as they did—because they always had to. They'd tried living apart right out of high school when Brock moved in with his ex-girlfriend and Smith rented his own apartment: they were both miserable.

Once Brock's girlfriend dumped him for speaking of wanting a threesome, he moved in with Smith and told him the reasons behind the breakup were because Brock held an interest in a ménage relationship. Smith indicated his interest too, and one month later had been his and Smith's first ménage encounter. They'd never looked back. While they each dated separately, it wasn't what either of them wanted, so they'd both given up and stuck to sex clubs.

Sharing women just worked.

Brock didn't want the night ruined because of a past neither he nor Smith could change. He slowly moved his hand upward on her thigh and met the hem of her skirt. When she gave him a look, he paused as she said, "You want to do this *now*?"

"Yes. I want to do this *now*," Brock replied. "That conversation changed the mood. I want to lighten things." He smiled. "Watching you come will do that."

"Do I need to remind you we're in a restaurant?" Kyra looked around quickly as she held his hand, stopping his travels. "And that we're surrounded by a lot of people."

"Nope, I'm well aware." He attempted to move his hand up her thigh, but she pinned his hand to her leg.

Her eyes narrowed, even if the refusal on her expression looked weak. "What if I say I don't want you to?"

Smith lowered his voice. "Kyra, we all know you won't, because you don't want him to stop. Move your hand away. Let us have some fun with you."

Only a short pause followed before Kyra released Brock's hand, allowing him to continue to move his hand up her thigh. "Tell us, Kyra, what do you do for a living? Your ad never said anything about your employment."

She shivered beneath Brock's hand. Her breath whooshed out before she sucked it back in, and once again, gave them a disapproving look. "And you want me to talk while you're doing *that*?"

Brock's hand inched higher up her sexy thigh and finally sneaked up underneath her skirt. "Open wider for me." He hesitated until she opened her legs for him, then continued. "Yes, that's right, nice and wide." She spread her legs wider, giving him access to her panties, which he was pleased to discover were lace. "As to your question, yes, Kyra, we'd like to learn more about you."

He tickled her inner thigh, close to the edge of her panties, and she inhaled a sharp breath. "I work in management for Silverholt."

Brock glanced at Smith to see his eyebrows arching before Smith asked, "The PR agency?"

"Yes," she exhaled.

Now, Brock understood the level of confidence she had exuded. Kyra had worked among and dealt with many CEOs and other high-profile clients. "What do you do for the company?"

He tucked his finger under the hem of her panties and moved them aside, exposing her pussy. Her cheeks now flushed brighter, and her pupils dilated as she whispered, "Manager of public relations."

Brock slid his finger over her swollen clit, and when he lowered his touch, he wasn't at all surprised to find her hot and wet. "How long have you worked for Silverholt?"

Her eyes rolled back into her head and closed for only a second before she snapped them open to him again, all heated and very sexy. "I've worked there since I graduated from school, and I'll always work there."

Smith gave Brock a curious look, and Brock also didn't understand her reply. He turned to Kyra as he continued to rub her lower lips, drawing her arousal up to her clit and swirling the bud. "Why are you so sure you won't leave?"

"My father owns the company." She licked those plump lips, and her voice became raspy. "Or I should say he *owned* the company."

Brock withdrew his hand from her slick heat and settled it on her inner thigh. "We had looked into Silverholt as a possible PR agency when we moved to Baltimore, but chose to go with Oldbank instead."

Her cheeks were still flushed, yet the hazy arousal in her eyes had faded. "I know. I remember when HighDot merged with MDR Software, and we heard we lost the account." She smiled, giving them a nonchalant wave. "Business is business."

Brock studied her, now realizing Kyra had pain in her past too. "We chose Oldbank merely because your father had passed away around the time we moved to Baltimore. We thought the company might be in for big changes and would be unstable because of that."

She laughed. "Don't worry about it. It's business, not personal. I never mix the two. And you're right—big changes did take place after his death."

Smith's head tilted, his eyebrows drawn together. "If your father owned Silverholt, why don't you run the company?"

She slid her fingers around the rim of her glass. "Because I don't want to. Never did." She gave a halfhearted shrug. "I love my job and didn't want to move up the corporate ladder, so to speak."

Smith exchanged a long look with Brock. Now, it made sense why Kyra wasn't impressed by their wealth. She was wealthy herself. In fact, Brock suspected incredibly wealthy. Most people who came from old money didn't flaunt it, and Kyra didn't exude the air of a rich woman.

He liked that about her.

More so, something else impressed him. Kyra clearly knew what she wanted in her life, and she went for it. That made Brock relate to her. "You stayed in your position at Silverholt because you love your job?"

She gave him quite the cute look and even sweeter smile. "I went to university for my job, of course I love it. My father knew I didn't want to run the company. After he was diagnosed with lung cancer, he arranged it all so I didn't have to deal with the company's ins and outs when he died."

Smith regarded her while he rubbed his jaw. "You seem pretty adamant that you wouldn't ever change your mind about taking over at Silverholt. You're young, Kyra, how do you know you won't want that position in the future?"

She gave them both a hard look. "Important jobs, like your jobs, mean long working hours. I've seen it with my father. He worked day and night, and it destroyed his marriage to my mother. *That* life never interested me."

Brock wanted to disagree with her, because deep down he thought if he loved a woman enough, he could make time for her. But he also saw truth in what she said. If a woman didn't understand what running a business entailed, no relationship could last.

In fact, it's why they'd joined the Castle Dolce Vita, and why Smith had been riding his ass to hire new employees. They didn't have the time to locate women for casual encounters. The castle gave them access to what they needed and desired, and in the short free time they had daily.

Glancing away from Kyra to Smith, Brock noticed Smith's clenched jaw. Brock understood—the conversation had once again turned serious. As he'd done before, he set to lightening the mood by sliding his fingers to the junction between her thighs.

The moment he reached wet, hot flesh, Kyra gasped. Brock gathered her wetness up to her clit, where he rubbed the bud beneath his fingertips. He stared at Kyra, who now gripped the table as she looked out at the busy restaurant. Each time he slid his fingers lower, he noticed her more wet than the time before.

Kitten liked being naughty.

Hell, he loved it too.

Smith leaned back in his chair and sipped at his wine, watching her. That curve of his mouth he always had when he enjoyed something erotic appeared on his face. Brock couldn't restrain his half grin too. Beneath his hand, he sensed Kyra's rising climax in the tremble of her thigh.

He moved faster and rubbed harder against the swollen bud, taking a quick look at the others sitting at their tables in the restaurant. No one paid any attention to them, nor did they notice that right at this moment Kyra erupted into orgasm, causing her to bang her knee on the table, rattling the glasses on top.

Not even the waiter had any clue when he appeared at the table with a tray in hand, all because Kyra had stayed perfectly silent. Brock had done his best to move only his hand, not his arm. No one but the three of them knew what had taken place.

Their dirty little secret.

Brock wanted more.

The waiter placed their orders of Brock's steak dinner, Smith's chicken and rice, and Kyra's pasta on the table. The server turned to Kyra. "Do you need anything else, miss?"

"No." She exhaled, raising her head with a beaming smile. "I've got all I need, thank you."

CHAPTER SIX

The two-story Tuscan-style mansion with its rustic features was a no-brainer when Smith saw it as a possible home to purchase. From the stenciled ceiling beams to the large chandelier over the foyer to the lanterns hanging down the hallway, it all made this house feel like home.

After he unlocked the thick hardwood front door, he waved Kyra in as Brock stayed out on the porch with him. Inviting her into the house was unusual. Their sexual encounters happened either at work, a hotel, or at Castle Dolce Vita, never at their home.

Maybe because of the hardships Brock and Smith had suffered as children, the personal space and the thoughts of home were something they protected. But Kyra had been the first woman invited into their house.

Smith wouldn't pretend that didn't mean something. It had been unspoken between him and Brock, just a simple nod, that had Smith asking Kyra to come back with them tonight. He wanted to know more about her, he wanted to enjoy her. More than anything, he wanted Kyra to know them.

He watched her as she stepped into the foyer with its large wooden staircase in front of her. She scanned the high ceilings, hardwood floors, and arched doorways before she smiled back at them. "Your home is beautiful. It reminds me of Italy."

Smith followed Brock into the house, shut the door behind him. "In Italy, Brock and I vacationed at a home that looked similar. It's one of the reasons we purchased the house."

She looked at them, surprise widening her eyes. "Oh, you both live here, like roommates?"

Smith chuckled, understanding why she found that fact so interesting. It was odd for two grown men who were in their early thirties and were as wealthy as they were to live in the same house. "We're used to sticking together. Why change something that works?"

Brock kicked off his shoes, shrugging at her. "Exactly, and it's comfortable." He gave Kyra a once-over, then grinned. "Sadly, I need to go and make a business call." He turned and headed through the curved doorway toward his office.

Kyra followed Brock with her gaze, but Smith knew well enough how to command her attention. He leaned against the door, folded his arms. "Take off your clothes."

She jerked her head to him, her eyes huge. "Pardon me?"

He never stepped toward her, or made any move, and simply repeated, "Take off your clothes. Leave the heels on."

Kyra stared at him, possibly wondering if he was serious, which he damn well was. He'd been undeniably hot and hard when Brock got her off at the dinner table. Now he wanted her with a burn he wouldn't dare attempt to control.

Whatever she saw in his expression must've indicated he was dead serious, since she reached for her black silk blouse. He loved that even if something made her nervous, she still acted on it. That he understood completely. He was the same way and had always been—it's what made his business thrive. She slowly unbuttoned, and Smith watched her every move as she exposed her lace cami.

Her shirt finally fell off her shoulders, and she dropped it to the floor, as well as her cami. Then she reached for her skirt, and soon it pooled at her feet. She hesitated, her cheeks a beautiful rosy color as she studied Smith.

He waited, silent, and stared into her beautiful eyes. She reached back and unclipped her bra, letting the straps fall gingerly down her arms. Hooking her fingers into the edge of her panties, she pushed them down over her hips.

Smith pulled his tie loose. He yanked it over his head, kept it in his hand, and removed his shirt. Kyra, after depositing her panties on the floor, stood stark naked in the foyer in only her high-heeled shoes.

Ravishing.

The spotlights above beamed down on her rosy nipples, which stood out against her creamy flesh. Smith had the urge to trace all those beautiful curves of her body with his tongue. He wanted to discover every single inch of Kyra. Too bad his rock-hard cock had other ideas.

Once he dropped his dress shirt onto the table, he approached. "I know you've stated your dislike of BDSM, but this isn't about the lifestyle. This is about having fun, not a power exchange and pushing limits." He held up the tie. "I want to blindfold you, will you let me?"

She looked at the tie, and then her heated stare lifted. "Yes."

He smiled, enjoying that she liked to do wicked things, because he certainly loved it. Though he suspected the role of submissive upset Kyra, he assumed she wouldn't mind the blindfold. She had signed up to join a sex club, meaning she leaned toward the naughtier side of sex.

After he slid the tie over her face, he settled it into place over her eyes, then tied it around her head. He ensured her vision was blocked before he tugged her toward the staircase. Once there, he raised her hands and placed them up against it. "Hold on to the bars. Don't let go."

She complied, wrapping her fingers around them. He stepped back to admire the view, and he liked how she looked waiting there, unable to see anything around her. He also loved her in only her black heels.

Her beauty astounded him. Her caring soul he'd seen at dinner tonight captivated him. Her drive and love of her job impressed him. Sliding his fingers down her side in a slow sweep, he murmured, "Spread your legs, nice and wide." She moved her feet outward. "You look stunning, Kyra." He continued to stroke her warm flesh, feeling her twitching and moving her body with the path of his finger. "So, so beautiful."

She shivered, giving him a nice moan as he trailed his hand down her stomach to the junction between her thighs. He groaned. "Soaking wet already?" He rubbed her clit, and she gave him another moan. "Seems you like my tie."

He suspected the whole event turned her on, from Brock's attention at the dinner table, to Smith's order to strip, and even the blindfold. Perhaps she'd never had kinky sex before, and maybe she'd fantasized about it for a long time. Or maybe it was him touching her. Whatever the reasons she became so aroused, he approved, because it aroused him too.

Watching her strip and be so bold, and her allowing him to blindfold her, was all-powerful fuel to erotic pleasures. Smith pressed against her bare bottom and tangled his fingers into her hair, then pulled her head back. "I'm going to take you hard."

"Yes," she rasped, angling her head farther to whisper, "Take me."

Smith didn't need her to say another word. He wanted to be deep inside her. His cock throbbed in his pants and was uncomfortably hard. He reached for his wallet in his pocket, grabbed a condom, then rid himself of the rest of his clothing within one breath.

Using his teeth, he ripped the foil open, and in quick time, he sheathed his cock. With her legs still spread wide, he stepped behind her. He rested his cock against her slit right before he thrust forward.

Kyra arched her back, screaming a sound rich with pleasure. Smith wanted to hear more. He gripped her hips, and, with no sense of care for his own muscles, pounded against her. His pelvis smacked her sexy ass, and his groans mirrored Kyra's screams of ecstasy when only minutes later, her pussy clamped against him.

Knowing that Brock had already made her come once tonight at the restaurant, he could only even the score tonight with their ongoing bet. He hadn't forgotten the bet hadn't been settled, but tonight it would remain that way. He needed to make her come twice. The first, he'd let her build on her own. The second, he'd force right out of her.

With the full intent of making her see stars, he slammed against her with hard lunges. His sac caressed her clit with every thrust forward, and he angled his cock at just the right spot to call to her climax.

His tie wrapped around her head was a damn spectacular sight, and it fueled his power. Right now, she could only feel, and only be in the moment. There was no visual to distract her. And that's why it didn't surprise him she came with only a few more strokes.

Her tight heat convulsed around him with such hard contractions that he had to grit his teeth to offset his pleasure. The scent of her arousal rushed through his nostrils, causing him to breathe even heavier through his mouth to fight off his rising climax. The sound of her screams echoing in the large foyer made him proud. And the act of his cock being drenched in her increasing moisture tensed his muscles.

When her shouts of satisfaction turned into quiet whimpers, her pussy massaged his cock through her climax, and he slowed his thrusts. Sweat dripped off his nose and onto her back as she trembled beneath him. He waited her out, gave her the time to relish her blissful state, and continued to bite his lip to focus away from his hunger.

Only a few seconds passed before she wiggled her hips and pushed against him, offering more. He ran his hand up her spine, then over her ribs and reached for her breast. He played with her nipples, tweaked them until they tightened into firmer buds.

The feel of her breast heavy in his hand, and the way it seemed undeniably right to touch her, even how she squirmed into him, and how beautiful she looked, once again made his cock ache to blow. Her pussy seemed permanently clamped on his cock. Each thrust seemed more forced than the last.

Pulling out of her, even if he cursed doing it, he positioned himself next to her. He ran his hand down her ass until he reached her slit. The tightness of her pussy when he inserted a finger indicated she was ripe and ready for another orgasm, just sitting there and waiting for him to gift it.

He slid another finger inside her hot wetness and angled both against her G-spot. Her inner muscles squeezed at his fingers, and she gave a low moan as he rubbed against the sensitive area.

When she whimpered in a near beg, he enjoyed the sound, almost as if she knew he could give her another orgasm. He liked that she thought he was capable, because in this regard, he was. Some men didn't understand the G-spot, but luckily for Kyra, both of them excelled in everything they did. With his free hand firmly pressed against her bottom, he slid his fingers inside her hard and fast, in up and down movements. After two strokes, Kyra attempted to move away from him, but Smith wrapped an arm around her waist and pinned her to him.

He continued pumping them inside of her, and Kyra screamed so loud that Smith's cock throbbed in acknowledgment of the sexy sound. Wetness spread over his fingers and dripped down onto his palm. But he didn't stop his determined thrusts until her voice had gone quiet.

As he yanked his fingers out, she wobbled and whimpered, and he preferred seeing her that way. Blindfolded with his tie, unable to stand properly, cheeks flushed, and satisfied. Though he wasn't nearly finished with her.

He turned her to him, pushed her back against the staircase, and hooked one of her legs over his arm. He stared at her parted lips just under the blindfold and positioned his cock against her slick heat. Then he unleashed the strength behind his muscles onto her body.

Right now, he didn't care about her pleasure. He only cared about his. He fucked her how he wanted to—raw and dirty. Fast strokes slamming against her repeatedly, which sent all that lovely wetness of hers spreading out between them.

He inhaled her feminine scent mixed with the rich musk of her arousal, and that's all it took to send him over the edge. Heat rushed down his spine, carried into his sac, then coursed like flickers of flames into his groin. With a loud roar and a final thrust forward, his cum shot from his cock, leaving him jerking and bucking.

By the time his mind returned to a state of coherent thought, he discovered he rested his forehead against hers and her deep pants sent warm breaths over his chin. Yet, the sound of a door closing brought his focus. He lowered her leg from his arm and backed away from her. "Stand there. Don't remove the blindfold."

She straightened, her lips pressed into a firm line. "You're not leaving me, right?"

He smiled, wiping the sweat off his forehead. "Sweetheart, leaving you is the last thing on my mind."

WITHIN THE DARKNESS, Kyra heard footsteps, but she couldn't tell if they were Smith's leaving or Brock's returning. She could only stand near what she knew was the staircase as the warm air caressed her naked flesh. Her entire body shook from the inside out. Even her muscles were weak, and her body hummed in happiness from two impressive orgasms. The inability to see left her somehow excited and frightened.

Thrilling...

Part of her wanted to remove the blindfold to see the view around her, the other—naughtier—part didn't. She'd always wanted someone to blindfold her, but none of her ex-boyfriends had ever asked. Smith had asked her permission, yet he'd also held the tie in his hand as if he'd planned to persuade her if she refused. Somehow, that confidence he had exuded mixed with the naughtiness excited her.

The footsteps drew closer, and Kyra tilted her head, trying to identity who approached. Then she heard someone walking around her and her heart hammering in her ears, and that was about it. The warm air brushed over her skin as the person settled in front, and then the blindfold tightened with her smile as she recognized the *who* by her now.

Brock.

She hadn't expected to know the difference, but even with the blindfold, she discovered she could tell the men apart. It surprised her how connected she felt to them, how comfortable she was standing there naked for them. When a finger slid over her shoulder and down her arm, she knew Brock stood with her.

Smith's hands were gentle, yet determined. Brock's touches were teasing, but confident. Maybe some wouldn't notice the subtle difference. It seemed she did. The light tickling touch drew a shudder from her that had her inhaling, and she realized even their smells were different. Smith smelled like lemon mixed with sandalwood. Brock smelled like citrus and musky tones.

The latter was all that consumed her.

A low chuckle sent a hot wave of heat pooling low in her belly. "Damn, kitten, you've proved me wrong."

She shivered under his playful touch along her spine. "Wrong?"

Brock's minty breath caressed over her face. "I didn't think you could possibly get me any harder, but..." He rested his erection against her thigh. "Do you feel how hard I am?"

"Very hard," she rasped.

"Indeed," he murmured.

What interested her more was that his erection wasn't covered by his pants. Brock was naked and had already put on a condom. Tonight, the men weren't playing around, nor were they letting her own the show. They controlled the moment, and right now, she liked that.

In fact, she wanted more.

Could this night possibly sate her?

Doubtful.

Brock wrapped his hands around her shoulders, then eased her forward. Within only a few steps, he pulled her to a stop, and whispered in her ear, "There's a chair in front of you. Reach down and grab the armrests."

Kyra leaned forward, and with Brock's help, wrapped her fingers around the armrests. Then Brock's cock nudged her entrance and only another second after that—without saying a word—he shoved his cock into the depths of her.

She was ready for him. In fact, she'd never been so wet.

Kyra wondered if her orgasm at the table had revved the men up, because both Smith and Brock appeared to show no patience. Then she wondered if it was her, blindfolded, and naked in the foyer, which caused their primal advances.

Whatever the reason, she liked the rewards.

She liked being the center of their attention.

A slap against her bottom drew her out of her thoughts and into Brock's control. He gripped her ass cheeks and squeezed them tightly as he thrust in and out. The force as well as the speed with which he pumped into her indicated he intended for this lovemaking to be quick and hard.

Brock's deep grunts only increased the rise of her pleasure. She loved his manly sounds and the wet sucking noises around them. The feel of him driving into her, the erotic smells drifting through the air, and the primal nature of how he took her all set her aflame.

One of his hands left her bottom, and then there was a tug on her hair, right before he removed her blindfold. "Watch yourself while I fuck you." His voice deepened. "See what I see."

The moment the darkness cleared to clarity, she caught sight of herself in the large mirror above the chair she held on to, and her breath caught in her throat. She'd never looked at herself during sex before. Now she looked all mussed.

Brock's thrusts increased in speed and force. He gripped her bottom and spread her cheeks apart. "Do you see your face, kitten? Do you see your flushed cheeks? How your lips are parted, drawing in deep breaths? The way your eyes are begging me to take you harder?"

Yes, she could see all those things.

Instead of answering him, she looked into the mirror, and behind her, Brock's piercing eyes bore into hers with an intensity that made her burn. Then she caught sight of Smith, who leaned against the staircase. He had re-dressed in his black pants but had remained shirtless.

Brock withdrew his cock, drawing her attention to him. He thrust forward with punishing strength. "This is what I see when I fuck you, Kyra." He leaned down, pressing the full weight of his body against her sweaty back, and whispered in her ear, "It drives me crazy."

Perhaps it was that velvety voice, or maybe even that both men watched her now, but that's all it took to blast her into orgasm. She trembled, screamed, and gripped the armrests as pleasure surged into every molecule of her body. Brock thrust against her until he shouted against his own climax, and behind her, his body jerked and bucked.

Not until a finger trailed her spine did her thoughts return. Kyra tried to catch her breath, feeling boneless. Brock withdrew from her, sliding his hand over her bottom. She straightened. "God, no."

A well-deserved arrogant smirk filled Brock's face. "Had enough for now?"

"Yes," she said, breathless. "I cannot possibly survive another orgasm." Even if that was only half the reason she wanted him to stop.

With a low, sexy chuckle, which had her rethinking her decision to tell him to stop, Brock removed his hand. A loud snort came across the room, and she looked over Brock's shoulder to Smith.

The side of his mouth curved. "You are a clever woman."

Brock's brow furrowed as he watched Smith, and then his eyes narrowed on Kyra. "Let me take a guess, Smith made you come twice tonight, didn't he?"

"Yes. Why?" She batted her lashes. "Is that a problem?"

Brock frowned. "I do remember Smith telling you that we take our bets seriously. Are you ever going to let one of us win?"

She hesitated, then smiled. "Not tonight."

Smith barked a laugh, approaching her. "The bathroom is down the hallway—third door on your right. Brock ran you a bath before he joined us."

Her belly fluttered at how neither of them rejected the thought of another night with her. She damn well wanted more too. Hearing their story, learning of their difficult past, and even that they were so close they lived together, it all intrigued her. She wanted to know what made them tick, the lives behind the millionaires. Then she took in what Smith said and frowned. "You're not joining me in the bath?"

Brock tucked her hair behind her ear and smiled gently. "We have to spend a little time working tonight. Once you're done, we'll likely be finished."

Her chest constricted as the sudden familiarity of his words sent a wave of discomfort to steal her happiness. "Okay," she managed through her tight throat.

Brock gave her bottom a hard smack and her a quick peck on the lips before he turned away to fetch his clothes. After Smith mirrored the light kiss, they strode down the hallway and entered the office.

Kyra stared at the empty hallway as a memory rushed into her mind.

A young Kyra skipped down the hallway, then leaped into her father's arms. "Daddy, it's my birthday."

"Happy birthday, baby." Her father smiled, pieces of his dark gelled hair broke free and hung over his forehead. "Seven years old, you're such a big girl."

Kyra pushed out of her father's arms as he lowered her to the hardwood floor. "Mommy said we're leaving soon for my pizza party."

"I know." Her father cupped her cheek. *"But, darling, I'm sorry to say I can't make it."*

A slow disappointment slid over her, making her chin quiver. *"Why?"*

Her father's brown eyes were shadowed, his brows drawn together, and his lips pressed into a thin line. *"An important meeting has come up at work. You know Daddy can't miss these things."*

Tears welled in her eyes. *"But it's my birthday."*

"I'll make it up to you. Next year I won't miss it." Her father smiled. *"I promise, Kyra."*

Kyra blinked out of the memory, staring at the office door Smith and Brock had entered, a cold shiver sliding through her.

Her father never kept his promise.

CHAPTER SEVEN

O ne month had passed in a blur of exciting nights of hot sex. Thirty long days went by with Kyra daydreaming about those erotic adventures during her workday. The passing weeks had left her body happy and her smile genuine.

The hum of the limousine's engine slowing drew Kyra away from the memory of her wicked nights spent between two delicious men. She looked out her window, noticing the driver stopping in front of the Hotel Monaco Baltimore.

Only a moment later, her door whisked open, and she stepped out into a warm, dry night. The driver shut the door behind her, and tipped his hat. "Have a wonderful evening, miss."

"Thank you." She smiled.

It'd been a while since she'd been driven anywhere in a limousine. Her father had enjoyed the luxury of such things, but Kyra preferred a car she could drive herself. Furthermore, no matter how nice the limo was, it would've been nicer if Brock and Smith were in the car as they had planned.

She'd seen the empty seats and experienced the slow slide of disappointment before she'd received the phone call from Smith. He told her that they would have to meet her at the charity event tonight because a meeting held them up.

In the month she'd spent with them, she couldn't even count on two hands how many times they were late or had to rearrange a dinner date because of work. The tension in her chest that had developed the first night she'd slept at their place hadn't left her. In fact, it'd become worse.

With a heavy feeling forming in her stomach, she pushed the thoughts from her mind, knowing tonight wasn't about her.

Standing on the sidewalk, she inhaled the scents of stale air mixed with car exhaust.

The hotel, which was located in the Ohio Railroad headquarters of Baltimore, had been the annual spot for the charity gala hosted by both MDR Software and the hotel, which benefited Baltimore's foster families. The silent and live auctions, as well as the three-hundred-a-plate dinners, helped foster kids attend camp and join sports teams, and some even received scholarships to go to college.

Kyra noted that carved into the stone was *1906* indicating the hotel's age. She'd been in this hotel before, and it was five stars all the way.

The greeter standing at the revolving door with the earpiece and clipboard in his hand told her enough that tonight the hotel was completely off-limits to the public and had been rented out for the evening. She approached, and when she reached the young man, he said, "Name, please."

"Kyra Garner," she replied.

Holding a piece of paper in his hands, he read for only a split second, indicating Smith and Brock put her name at the top of the list. "Enjoy your night, Ms. Garner."

She entered and stepped into the three-story lobby with its original marble floor and Tiffany stained-glass windows. Kyra thought the hotel looked modern and slick, yet somehow timeless too.

Striding down the hallway lined with crystal chandeliers, she passed other attendees and smiled when she caught people watching her. No doubt, the Valentino dress Brock and Smith had delivered yesterday drew some attention.

The floor-length dress was backless, and the black lace on the gown was gorgeous. It surprised her how attentive the men were to her size. The dress fit her like a second skin and appeared designed for her body.

Bella had demanded Kyra go to the spa, and she listened. She had her hair done in a romantic braid updo, had a manicure and pedicure, plus her makeup applied too. Bella had said, every time Kyra objected to being spoiled, that a dress this nice needed to have a woman in it who looked equally as beautiful. While Kyra had felt fussed over, she happened to think the final look was all worth it.

Tonight, she did feel beautiful.

Kyra entered the main ballroom, and her breath instantly became trapped in her throat. Brock and Smith had clearly spared no expense for the event. She strode forward passing people enjoying cocktail hour. Luxurious and historical, the ballroom stunned her with its gorgeous gold chair covers and large centerpieces of fresh flowers.

The venue, however, didn't hold her attention long. The two men standing near the bar straight ahead made her heart race.

Brock and Smith were both dressed in tuxedos, and they were gorgeous. As if they sensed her arrival, they turned to her. The space between them became charged with sexual heat.

Needing to touch them, she forced her feet to move.

As she drew closer, she spotted raw desire in the depths of their eyes, causing a shiver to tickle low in her belly. Those intoxicating looks had held her captive these past weeks. She liked how they looked at her as if no other woman could possibly compare to her. It's what kept her seeing past the dinner cancellations and the always being late. When she reached the men, Brock and Smith took a step forward, their gazes doing a full sweep of her body. Under their stares, her nipples puckered, which of course made Brock smirk.

"My God, Kyra," Smith murmured. "You look ravishing."

"All thanks to the both of you. You have amazing taste." She smiled at Smith, then at Brock. "Thank you for the dress."

"You're welcome." Brock raised his finger and did a circular movement. "Let's have a look at it all."

Kyra complied, spun on her heels, and the men groaned behind her. Then as two warm, hard bodies rested against her, the air thickened. Smith's lips pressed against her shoulder, as Brock's slid over her cheek. Her eyes shut of their own accord as awareness of the two men consumed her. Smith's hand tightened around her hips while Brock's finger gently slid over her spine.

Heat flooded between her thighs and she squeezed her legs together, relishing in the ache there. The mood flowing around her was charged with sexual electricity, and she wanted to turn up the voltage.

As her nipples puckered tighter, she opened her eyes to see a distinguished man watching her. That's all it took for her to blink into focus as she remembered they weren't alone. Quickly scanning the room, she noticed the man hadn't been the only one looking. There happened to be quite a few people watching their exchange. With a blush to her cheeks, she took a step back, making Brock and Smith narrow their eyes.

She pulled herself together and slid into professional mode. "Would you like a drink? Some wine? A beer?"

Smith shook his head. "Nothing for me."

Brock gave his classically light smile, even if his eyes were guarded. "I'm good for now, kitten."

Kyra understood they had their business faces on tonight, and she doubted they'd be drinking much. Her father's professional attitude was so different from the father she remembered. Fun, sensitive, and goofy, no one in the PR world saw him like that. And at the sudden reminder of him, her heart clenched. Her father had loved donating, and attending charity events...just like this one.

Smith took a step forward, his eyes searching hers. "Are you all right?"

She forced the memory away. "Of course."

In truth, this was her first charity event since her dad had died. Perhaps with her being on edge with the men, feeling emotional wasn't all that shocking. "Let me grab myself a glass of wine."

She turned, exhaled a long breath, so glad neither Brock nor Smith had stopped her. Glancing around the room, she noticed many people giving her curious looks. No doubt they wondered *who* she was and why she had two men touching her at the same time.

To her right, she spotted a few employees from Oldbank—the PR company Brock and Smith had chosen over Silverholt—and embarrassment washed through her. She experienced the weight of all their judgmental stares on her as if they could read into her soul and knew she'd joined the Castle Dolce Vita.

She looked at the marble floor, sensing every pair of eyes on her. When she arrived at the bar, she caught sight of men and women all watching her, but she quickly put up mental blinders and stared at the bartender. "Chardonnay, please." She didn't look away from the young barkeep as he fetched her drink. Yet, a warm arm brushed against hers, and after another obvious nudge, Kyra begrudgingly glanced sideways.

A woman—in her early seventies, Kyra thought—dressed in a peacock-blue dress scanned Kyra from head-to-toe. "My dear, you have every set of eyes on you. Tell me, I must know, which one are you dating?"

Kyra bristled at the question. "Dating?"

The woman smiled, her pale blue eyes twinkling. "Which one of the MDR men are you dating? I saw you talking to them and was curious who has captured the heart of such a beautiful young lady."

Kyra's mind stuttered under the direct assault of such a blatant question. In all her preparations for tonight, she hadn't considered having to answer *that* question. Perhaps she'd been in a whirlwind with Brock and Smith, which seemed like one big fantasy where people wouldn't be asking about their affiliation.

A fantasy where a ménage relationship was perfectly normal and accepted. Where no one would judge what they were doing. Kyra realized she had no idea how to answer. Besides, she wasn't dating them. She was having the best sex of her life with them.

After a quick second, she said the only thing she thought appropriate. "I'm actually not dating either of them. We're close friends."

The woman laughed. In a much quieter voice, she said, "I might be old, but I'm not blind. Those two men are in love with you."

In love...

No, the woman had it wrong. In fact, they weren't sharing an emotional relationship. Kyra hadn't even invited them out with her best friends. Of course, she did have dinner dates with Brock and Smith and had seen a couple of movies with them. Her mind raced, making her realize that for the past two weekends she'd never left their sides. Sure, they'd had to work during that time. Other than that, they'd been inseparable.

Oh, fuck!

Her heart hammered, but she ignored the swell of discomfort. "Like I said, we're close, just not in the way you're thinking."

The woman snorted. "I've been married five times. I know what love looks like, m'dear. Both of those men are lovesick." The woman winked, nudging Kyra's arm. "And I saw it in your eyes too."

Another bartender brought the woman her wine, and she tipped her glass at Kyra. "Best you choose quickly, dear. They have a business to run, and if you leave it much longer, you'll have them sparring over you."

Without another word or piece of unwanted advice, the woman strode off. Kyra scanned the room, and her throat tightened. If people knew she wasn't only dating one of them, but she'd been sharing a bed with both of them, and at the same time, they'd be horrified.

Though what made the room spin around Kyra was the realization the woman hadn't been wrong. Kyra couldn't deny she cared about Brock and Smith, and she could only blame herself for that. She knew getting involved with them was dangerous for her after she'd talked to Kole and Bella, and she'd known she could become attached.

She'd allowed it to happen anyway.

What had she done?

The bartender returned with her wine, and Kyra didn't even look at him. She downed the drink in a few big gulps. When she lowered the wineglass to the bar and had the strength to glance up, the barkeep gave her a quizzical look.

Did he know what she'd been doing?

Sweat coated her skin, and the air in the room seemed thick. The event no longer mattered. She had to get out of there...and fast.

Leaving everyone behind and hearing nothing but her racing heartbeat, she rushed to leave the ballroom. She hurried down the hallway and headed out to the foyer. When she reached the doorway, she heard someone call her name, but she didn't stop.

She ran.

Kyra passed the greeter at the door, and he wished her a good night. Again, she heard someone yell her name behind her. That's when she realized both Smith and Brock called out to her. She couldn't stop. She needed air. She needed to breathe. Had she fallen for two men at the same time? And if so, could they somehow make this work between them?

She'd been so wrapped up in the fantasy she had longed to live and had been living for the past month, but how could this relationship work? She had allowed her emotions to entwine with what was meant to be casual sex.

Stupid, Kyra!

Once on the sidewalk again, she jogged as well as she could in her heels. She needed to think this out. Even if she slept with them individually it wouldn't put her in the best light, but that woman had seen her affection for them.

What did that make her look like?

A tease, leading two men on, she thought.

Reaching the corner of the street, a breeze swept over her skin, fluttering the loose strands of hair around her face. She didn't even know where she was going, only that she needed to get away.

She passed under the streetlamp, about to cross the street, when a hand wrapped around her arm. She turned, catching sight of Smith's wide, worried eyes. "Kyra, did you not hear us calling you?"

"I..." She closed her mouth, not even knowing what to say.

"Oh, shit, she heard us all right." Brock breathed heavily. Apparently, they'd been a good distance behind her and had run to catch up. "Why would you take off?"

She stared at both men as they stood under the streetlight, so aware of why she cared for them. Smith was the strong, unwavering dependable rock who seemed to read right into her soul. Brock was the playful, lighthearted one who held a charming confidence.

Together they made up *her* perfect man. The one she'd always wanted and dreamed of, and the idea of ending this with them shattered her heart.

With her throat closing and stomach tightening, she whispered, "What are we doing?"

Smith hesitated. "Attending a charity function."

"No." She shook her head, a sudden coldness coursing through her veins. "This...with us...what are we doing?"

Brock exchanged a long look with Smith, then arched a brow. "Dating."

The breeze that had been warm before now seemed freezing, and the night even darker. She wrapped her arms around herself, rubbing the chill out of her skin. "We can't date."

Smith took off his tuxedo jacket and reached out to her. Kyra stepped away from his touch, and he frowned. "Are you unhappy with us?"

Though her first instinct was to say no, that wasn't entirely true. Their life, how busy they were with their business, she'd sworn to herself she'd never be *that* woman. She'd never be like her mother who never saw her husband.

While that made a rock form in her stomach, even how Smith talked seemed upward of ridiculous. "See, like that, you're talking like we're all together." Kyra looked at them as the light above beamed down on their heads. "You honestly think this could work out?" To Brock, she asked, "The three of us in a relationship?"

"Why not?" He shrugged, leaning up against the lamp. "We've been doing fine so far."

"How can you say that? It's..." She almost said weird, but nothing about being sandwiched between these two men was *weird*. No, it was so right it terrified her. "How would we live?"

Both men regarded her before slow smiles filled their faces, which was not the reaction she'd expected. Smith moved in close and under the assault of his warm eyes, Kyra froze. He brushed his fingers over her cheek. "Ah, I see the problem. You're in love with us, aren't you?"

A hot shiver raced alongside the coldness in her body. "I..."

Brock settled in next to her, unleashing his charming smile. "And that frightens you, kitten."

Her eyes fluttered as Brock's smooth voice melted across her, matched with the burn from Smith's touch. She stepped back to get some breathing room, not allowing herself to go there again. When her back hit the brick wall of the building behind her, she snapped her eyes open. "I'm not scared. I'm..."

"Scared," Smith and Brock stated in unison.

She fought to find a comeback. "Someone asked me tonight which one of you I'm dating."

Brock nodded. "We saw you talking to Mrs. Hampton, who happens to be the nosiest woman alive."

Smith's eyes softened. "Ah, so that's why you ran. You didn't know what to say, and you panicked." He leaned against the wall next to her. "All right, Kyra, what did you say to the meddlesome Mrs. Hampton?"

"That we were close friends," she replied.

"Good answer." Brock gave a crisp nod. "Even though I would've been fine if you told the lady to take her questions and fuck off."

"You can't be serious?" Kyra gasped. "I was your guest tonight, and you two have to be on your best behavior." Didn't she know that well from her father? "A scandal like this could destroy your business."

"*Business* is the word here, Kyra," Smith interjected in a hard voice. "These people have no reason to dig into our personal life." He took her hand, tugging her forward. "Yes, we'll have to have discretion, but we did tonight, didn't we? I kissed your shoulder. Brock kissed your cheek. You don't need to tell anyone anything."

"What if they ask?" she countered.

Smith snorted. "You say what you said. We are close. Why is it anyone's concern what we do in the bedroom?"

Okay, so he had a point, but... "They were all looking at me, judging me."

"Of course they were watching you, kitten. You're drop-dead gorgeous." Brock gave an unamused laugh. "The women were probably envious. The men..." His jaw clenched, nostrils flared. "I think it's best we don't find out what they were thinking."

Kyra's lips parted, but Smith interjected, "Brock's right— people in that room are so straight arrowed they wouldn't even consider us to be in a ménage relationship. They might be curious if you were dating one of us, but, Kyra, why does it matter what they think?"

Even if what they said made sense, the panicked part of her mind told her to keep running. A relationship between them could never work out. How could she date two men? How could they share one woman?

She'd done this to herself. She put herself in this situation. But she could take herself out of it too.

Realizing how wrong she'd been to allow herself to go this deep with them, she also realized she'd broken her one rule she swore she never would. "Tonight made me realize how blinded I've been. How wrapped up we've all been." She looked at them, an awful ache filling her chest. "I'm sorry, I have to end this."

Not only did she break rules about how much time she'd spent with them, but she'd broken her biggest rule of all. She spent time with men who put their work before their home life.

Smith eyes blazed. "Kyra—"

"Besides the obvious reason of why this needs to end." She cut him off before he could try and change her mind. "Work is too important to both of you. I get it. Really, I do." She moved away from the wall. "I told you on our first date, I saw my mother go down that road, and it destroyed her. They told me she died of a heart attack, but I still think she died from a broken heart. Depression killed her."

When both men took a step forward, she matched their move by taking a step back and pressed against the wall again. "Maybe I was too consumed with the fantasy to care about all the cancellations, showing up late for dinners, or phone call interruptions, but I'm sorry, I refuse to accept that as my life."

"Kitten," Brock said softly, stepping fully away from the streetlamp. "We own a large company that depends on us. You can't punish us for something we can't control."

Smith inclined his head. "I apologize if our business hours have upset you. In fact, I'm aware why it does. You have good reason to be annoyed." Again, he stepped forward, as did Brock. Smith added, "But that isn't a strong enough reason to end things between us. We need to compromise, that's all. And we can cut down our work hours by hiring new employees."

She stepped away from the wall, nearly reaching the curb, and she stared at the pain and anger in their eyes. Even if they could explain away the ménage relationship and somehow make it work, she needed to walk away now. She would not be her mother. "No compromising. I told you that. I can't live that life."

Her lip trembled and her eyes welled, but she swallowed her raw emotions. To Brock, she said, "This was supposed to be fun, no-strings attached, and a bet between the two of you, remember?" Turning to Smith, she added, "That's all it ever can be. Don't follow me. Don't call me again." She turned and strode off down the street, tears trailing her cheeks.

Surprising her, what made her cry harder, was that neither of them stopped her.

CHAPTER EIGHT

Reggie's, a pub-style restaurant, where sports games showed on the handful of widescreen televisions and peanut shells littered the floor, had been a Friday-night tradition for Kyra and her best friends. Now with Bella and Marley attached, both Kole and Reed had joined in on the weekly ritual too.

Sitting on the bench side of the table, Kyra scanned the pub to her right, watching a couple sitting at the table burst into a fit of laughter. She heaved a sigh, needing this night out more than ever.

It'd been two weeks since she'd left Brock and Smith standing on the dark street, and the image of them haunted her dreams. She had returned the dress they'd bought her days after the charity event, and she'd wondered if that would stir a text or a phone call. She hadn't heard a peep out of either man.

By all appearances, they respected her wishes to stay away.

Of course, now she regretted ever saying, *"Don't follow me. Don't call me again,"* and she wished she could take those damn words back.

Bella's laughter snapped Kyra's attention into the present, and she looked out in front of her, while she all but sat alone. Kole was a good foot away near the end of the bench. On the other side of her, Sadie had left a bigger space between them while Marley, Bella, and Reed sat across the table all snuggled close together.

Folding her arms, Kyra muttered to no one in particular, "Do I stink?"

Sadie giggled, her blue eyes twinkled, and her strawberry blonde curls bounced on her shoulders. "Of course not, silly."

Kyra glared at every single one of her best friends, including the two doms at the table. "Then why is no one sitting with me?"

Sadie smirked, scooting closer. "There, is that better?"

"Much," Kyra grumbled.

Desperation made her ache from head-to-toe. She'd never been so needy of her best friends. Since ending things with Brock and Smith, she had become clingy. She'd even slept in each of her best friends' rooms for their comforting presence, at least once.

As she'd done for days now, Kyra drowned her sorrows. She picked up her wineglass and took a huge gulp, cringing at the dry, bitter taste. Ignoring the nasty afterbite, she took another long sip. The days without the men had been the worst of her life. The dark bags under her eyes only proved it. She hadn't slept well, she wasn't eating well, and there was no denying it: she was officially a mess.

Drunk!

She needed to get rip-roaring smashed so she could pass out and finally sleep well again. It would also fix the problem that every time she closed her eyes, she saw two men staring at her and she'd stop craving their heated touches.

Determined to get shitfaced, Kyra knocked back the remainder of her wine. The second she swallowed the warm liquid, she shuddered in complete horror at the acrid taste. And that's when she noticed Kole standing from the bench.

Leaning over the table to Bella, he whispered something in her ear that had Bella flashing Kyra a smile. Full of suspicion, Kyra lowered the wineglass to the table. And Sadie slid out of the bench seat, practically bouncing on the spot in classic Sadie excitement.

"What's with you?" Kyra asked.

As soon as the words passed her lips, her heart stopped beating, or at least skipped a few beats. Behind Sadie's shoulder were two sets of eyes bringing forth heat and pooling a wicked warmth low in her body.

She couldn't stop her eyes from widening as unleashed power in the form of two gorgeous men strode through the pub toward her. With stares that could melt ice, Smith and Brock were all business tonight. Their fierce expressions were something Kyra suspected their business associates faced often. Determined. Focused. Confident. Only now, apparently, she was the focus of their attention.

Brock slid into Sadie's spot on the bench seat, moving in close next to Kyra. Smith strode around the table and took Kole's seat. The men didn't put distance between them as her friends had. Both closed in on her tight, the heat of their bodies engulfing her.

After a long pause, Kyra remembered she needed air to live. She sucked in a harsh breath, so aware of the men next to her. Intense energy came off them in waves rushing across her flesh, sending flickers of flames through her veins.

Brock grinned, yet this smile wasn't one of proper etiquette. It was dirty and pure sex. "Hello, kitten."

Smith swiped at the hair curtaining him from her view, brushing it over her shoulder and trailing a finger along her skin. "You look tired. Are you not sleeping well?"

Kyra shivered, his touch burning across her already scorching flesh. The slow flame descended her body, and she blinked, staring at Marley in front of her.

Marley's green eyes sparkled as she twirled her finger through her dark curls, appearing all too relaxed. In fact, Marley looked too at ease. She'd never met Brock and Smith, and by all appearances, she knew exactly who they were.

Kyra scanned her friends' faces, and all of them, including Kole, were smiling at her. Even Reed's deep blue eyes twinkled, while he ran a hand through his dirty-blond hair. No one looked surprised by Brock and Smith's sudden appearances. With that awareness, it all made sense.

Tonight, she'd been played.

Narrowing her eyes, she pinned all five of her so-called friends with a hard stare. "What have you done?"

"Call it an intervention." Marley smiled.

"Don't be mad," Sadie interjected in her sweet voice. "You've been so..."

"Damn depressed," Bella muttered.

Before Kyra could decide if she loved her friends for the intervention or hated them for it, a finger caught her jaw. She turned and discovered Smith's eyes were warm, yet troubled. "Answer me, Kyra."

His powerful stare captivated her, and the strength shown in his features eased her. When he looked at her that way, her world settled. To be touched by him, looked at by him, it eased the coldness that'd been flowing through her veins. For the first time in two weeks, she lost herself in the sensation of rightness. "What was the question again?"

"Why do you look so tired?" Smith's eyebrows drew together with his frown, his eyes appearing nearly black. "You don't look well."

"I..." She gulped.

"Miss us," Brock stated.

His voice was classically light, and Kyra had missed the contradictions between the two. In the exact moment and dealing with the same situation, Smith was serious where Brock was lighthearted. It comforted her. Where Smith could make the mood overly tense, Brock knew how to soften it to the right amount to ensure things stayed under control.

Though she realized Brock had made a statement. One everyone at this table knew was true. Her lips parted to give some response, but all that came out was a whisper of air.

Smith captured her chin again, commanding her gaze. "Why are you punishing yourself like this?"

Kyra experienced the weight of his study right down to the center of her soul. She hated the clench of her chest. More so, she cursed the moisture welling in her eyes. Smith was right—it had been torture. She'd never been this weak, this lonely.

Each night had seemed harder than the one before. The desire to be in their arms tugged at her heart. She'd grown used to hearing their voices or going to sleep close to them. She didn't even feel like herself anymore. Where had strong, focused, depend-on-no-one Kyra vanished to?

Through all this awareness, making her realize her attachment to the men went far deeper than she'd been willing to admit, two hard truths remained. The reasons she had ended it with them hung over her like a dark cloud.

Nothing had changed.

She might love them, but she wouldn't live the life her parents had. She wouldn't repeat their mistakes. She wanted a man—or two of them—who worked nine-to-five, came home, and left work at work.

As much as her body told her to stay right there with them, she needed to stick to her reasons for ending it. She was stronger than this, no matter that her heart wept for their return and her body begged for their touch. "You know why this can't work. It's hard now," she admitted, looking at them. "Okay, yes, this has been hell for me. But I'll get over this. I'll move on, and so will the both of you."

Smith's lips pursed, and his voice became hard. "No, Kyra. I won't get over this and move on."

Brock frowned, then shook his head in frustration. "Let's be clear. You have two concerns. The first, this relationship can't work out between us because of how others will perceive us?"

Smith added, "As in, you can't imagine how we will look in the public eye?"

"Well, yes." She gave the bar a quick once-over. No one else would hear their conversation, but she lowered her voice anyway. "In public, how would I explain such a relationship?"

Kole snorted. "Kyra, didn't we already talk about this?"

She didn't need Kole coming down on her too. Just because she'd fallen for these men didn't mean they could make this work. "You weren't being questioned at the charity function. I was," she snapped. "I know what it felt like having all those people watching me. Having no idea what to say. Do you think I want to live like that forever? Having to be careful and not tell people that I'm in love with two men."

Awkward silence cut through the air.

Kole's smirk was indication enough that Kyra had put her foot in her mouth. She looked at the table, not wanting to admit again or comment on the fact that she had declared her feelings for Brock and Smith.

Another finger tapped against her chin. Not so easily this time, her head turned in Brock's direction. His full-blown smile only confirmed they'd all heard it. "All right," he said in a soft voice. "Your next concern is our business hours. Correct?"

It seemed as if the bar had vanished away and only these two men and their strong presence remained around her. Here, with them, her sadness went away. "Yes, that's the biggest issue. I don't want to be *that* woman who never sees her boyfriend...or boyfriends." Though, even now, she discovered her excuse was weak.

In truth, she wondered if being *that* woman was better than being nothing at all.

Brock leaned in, his piercing eyes drawing her into him, and his half smile seemed all too wise. "Other than those two concerns, you have no other objections to dating us?"

Before she could think up an answer or identify if she had any other hesitations, Brock slid his nose against her jawline. Inhaling deeply, he trailed along her neck, as if he had all the time in the world.

Heat raced through her veins, sending a spark of fire sizzling up her spine. Her gaze locked on Marley in front of her, before she spotted Bella, who smiled, and Kyra even noticed that Sadie watched with a sweet grin.

By the time Brock slid his nose up her neck, Kyra had become a trembling mess of arousal. She could hardly believe this was happening with all her friends present, but now she found herself so consumed in Brock she didn't care.

She forced her eyes to remain open when Brock pressed his lips against her jaw. When his tongue laved a wicked path along her flesh, she failed miserably, and her eyes fluttered closed. An ache as needy as it was desperate erupted between her thighs, and wetness dampened her panties.

"Answer him," Smith demanded, sliding a finger up the other side of her neck. "Are those your only objections?"

Kyra hesitated, her voice trapped in her throat.

Beneath the table, Smith brushed his other hand over her thigh and squeezed her knee, garnering her attention. Her breath whooshed from her lungs. "Yes, that's all."

"Good." A slow smile spread across Smith's face, his eyes positively glowing. "The other issue about how to handle a relationship between us we can deal with tomorrow." He tangled his fingers into her hair and stole a kiss right out of her mouth.

It wasn't gentle—it was hard and raw, showing every single part of his pain from their separation. He didn't only kiss her, he branded his passion all over her lips. When he broke the kiss, he left Kyra breathless, and he added, "For now, we'll clear up one immediately."

Brock slammed his hand down on the table, and Kyra gasped, realizing he wasn't nibbling her neck anymore. On the table and under his hand, she caught sight of a piece of paper. Then her gaze left the table as Brock kissed her swiftly.

The kiss was tender and more yearning than Smith's, breaking her heart. They'd been hurting as much as she had. Brock travelled his mouth over to her ear and whispered, "Your excuses to avoid us have run out, kitten."

Her breath seemed lost in her body and her only focus remained on the flood of heat between her thighs, as Smith said in her other ear, "Meet us at the castle tomorrow night at seven."

The intensity in Smith's features only increased when he stood, staring down at her. "Know this," he said with a low, harsh voice. "If you don't show up, I'll come and get you." He leaned down but didn't come into her personal space. "Tomorrow is not a night to play games with us."

Kyra's mind raced to catch up with what had taken place in the last minutes. Stunned, she could only gape at Smith and Brock as they strode off, making their way through the pub and toward the door.

Across from Kyra, Sadie exclaimed, "Dang, Kyra, that was freaking hot!"

Kyra agreed, their quick appearance, sexy touches, and smoldering looks were hot as hell. Also explaining why her body hummed with desire, her pussy throbbed, and panties were wet.

"So..." Sadie added. "What is that?"

Kyra blinked, dragging her attention away from the door Brock and Smith had exited. "What?"

Sadie laughed, pointing to the table. "The piece of paper, what is it?"

Glancing down, Kyra noticed the paper that had been beneath Brock's hand was actually a newspaper. Once she grabbed it, she flipped the paper over, and as she scanned it, her mouth dropped open.

Bella snickered. "Something big, obviously."

"Read it," Marley said.

Kyra stared at the page and processed the meaning behind what she read. Now she understood a question presented to her. Brock and Smith weren't successful for only being business savvy, they were incredibly smart men. No wonder they made their company into a multimillion dollar venture; when they wanted something, they didn't take no for an answer and they went in for the kill.

She lifted her head. "It says, MDR Software announces the addition of John Haggard and Samantha Madison to join MDR Software, reporting to CEOs Smith McDermott and Brock Robertson."

All three of her best friends smirked as the implication of what Brock and Smith had done was clear-cut. Kole, however, gave his typical smart-ass grin. "Eased up their workload, didn't they?"

Reed winked. "And they stole your biggest excuse to shut them out."

CHAPTER NINE

F resh spring air breezed through Kyra's car window as she drove down the tree-lined street, passing the colorful wooden sign welcoming visitors into the town of Bowleys Quarters. The half-hour drive from Baltimore had been uneventful, except that her mind raced through thoughts of what Brock and Smith had done.

They'd hired new employees...for *her*.

To say she looked forward to hearing what they had to say to her this evening was an understatement. They'd gone to great lengths to ensure she wouldn't shut them out. As much as she still held reservations about how they could make a ménage relationship work, warmth spread through her that they weren't going to let her walk away.

The prospect that somehow they could give this a real shot made that empty feeling she'd suffered for two weeks wash away. She breathed easier. She ate more than tiny meals today. Last night, she'd slept better than she had since she left them.

She'd already realized not dating them didn't do her any good. At this point, even if their way to fix this was weak, she suspected she'd agree. Why did she care what others thought of her? Sure, they'd have to be unobtrusive, but many couples behaved discreetly in the public eye, and no one needed to know what happened in their bedroom.

Her parents had done the whole monogamy lifestyle, and their marriage had failed. Who was to say a ménage relationship was doomed? Besides, in the month they were together, Kyra had never been happier. In the past two weeks, she'd been more miserable than she thought possible.

She decided that being *unusual* with them was better than being *typical* with anyone else.

Kyra slowed the car as the Castle Dolce Vita came into view. The castle, with its aged look and large stone facade, was a stunning sight. Even the garden around the grounds accentuated its beauty.

Turning the steering wheel, she drove up the driveway, noticing cars off to the left side in the parking lot. After she pulled into an empty spot, she turned off the car. She stared at the castle and a rush of warmth swept through her.

She'd been so worried that she'd repeat her mother's mistakes that she set up boundaries to ensure it would never happen. Brock and Smith's gesture was the sweetest thing anyone had ever done for her.

Not only did they want to be in her life, but they fought to be. Her father hadn't done that for her mother, nor had he ever done that for Kyra. He'd always put work before his family. And maybe that made Brock and Smith perfect in her eyes.

With a smile on her face, she exited the car and journeyed up the stone pathway leading to the castle's door. There, she knocked on the big wooden door, knowing from Bella and Marley that she couldn't simply walk into Castle Dolce Vita.

Before she could lower her hand, the peephole opened and a blue eye stared at her. "Kyra Garner to see Smith McDermott and Brock Robertson," she told the eyeball.

The peephole closed, and then the door swiftly opened to a man wearing black pants with a matching T-shirt that had *Castle Dolce Vita* written in bold white letters across his chest. His features were kind, as was his smile. "Mr. McDermott and Mr. Robertson have arranged to have you meet them in the Rose Room. Take the stairs, and it's the second door on your right."

She smiled, brushing past him. "Thank you."

Striding through the large foyer, Kyra glanced up at the thirty-foot-high ceilings above her before she climbed the staircase. Once she reached the wooden balcony, she scanned all the different doorways leading to all sorts of sexual fantasies.

When she finally arrived at the door with the sign ROSE on the right side, she drew in a deep breath. While she wanted to run straight into Brock and Smith's arms, she also knew she couldn't.

Yes, they'd fixed one of the problems about their being together, but there was still the issue about how this would all work.

Sure, she'd agree to just about anything with them right now. Though Kyra also knew she needed to keep her head on straight. These two men had seduced every single part of her and had claimed her heart, but Kyra wasn't only led by emotions. With her heart at risk, she needed them to prove they could, in fact, function as a threesome.

She blew out her breath slowly, then opened the door.

The small square room consisted only of a huge black leather chaise near a crackling fire in the fireplace. There were no other lights in the room, and the fire gave off a soft, romantic glow.

Though what captured her focus were the two men standing by the fireplace. Both Brock and Smith, dressed in blue jeans, had their shirts off, and the flickering flames created an orange hue highlighting their muscular bodies.

They turned to her at the exact same moment, and that was so like them. They seemed to know where each other's bodies were and what each other's next move was.

She scanned over their chests, abdomens and biceps before she forced her attention to their faces. Her mouth might've been dry, but the junction between her legs was very wet. A quick heat stormed into her as two kissable mouths curved into sexy smiles. She leaned against the doorway. "Hi."

SMITH STARED AT perfection.

"Hello Kyra," he murmured.

Tonight, she was dressed in a tight black skirt, red fuck-me heels, and a red sleeveless blouse. He'd never seen anything quite so delicious. The past two weeks had been utter hell without seeing her smile, hearing her voice, or touching her silky flesh. In fact, the distance between them tore Smith up enough that he couldn't stop from striding forward to take her hand.

When her delicate fingers twined with his, it eased the ache that had filled his chest after she walked away from them. Without a doubt he loved this woman, and he wouldn't let her go. Not now. Not ever.

He gently pulled her into the room, locked the door behind her, then tugged her toward the chaise. "Please sit. We need to talk."

She settled against the leather chaise, crossing her legs, and Smith's gaze went straight to her gorgeous thigh before he forced his eyes on her face when she said, "Interesting place to have a *talk*."

"We met because of Castle Dolce Vita," he stated, heat filling his groin and hardening his cock. "It's...*right*...to come here."

Brock gave a firm nod. "It'd be a waste not to at least enjoy the castle once before we said our good-byes to this place." He leaned against the wall near the fireplace, folding his arms. "Besides, we have the room reserved all night." A slow grin swept across his face. "I don't plan on talking long."

"Nor do I," Smith said, squatting near the chaise. He looked Kyra directly in the eye, transfixed by her. "But there are things that need to be settled."

Tonight they had a plan: removing her last objection.

Smith understood Kyra's issue with their work hours. She wanted a better life for herself than her mother had, and well, Brock and Smith did work too hard. They'd gotten used to filling an empty void in their lives, but now Kyra had taken that place.

He'd much rather spend his time with her than at the office. After Kyra walked away, Brock finally picked two people out of the pile of résumés, even if it had taken a couple of weeks to firm up.

Smith stared into her pretty eyes as her dark hair fell over her shoulder. He didn't fault her for caring about how the world perceived her. Kyra wasn't an emotional woman. She lived on logic, and in her logical mind, she couldn't see how they could have a future.

Tonight, he'd show her how. "Brock and I empathize with how you feel. We get why you can't understand how this works between us. Even how we could share you, and be okay with that."

Tucking his fingers in between the top buttons of her silk blouse, he undid one. He paused for her reaction. At her silence, he smiled, and flicked open another button. "But, Kyra, I like you with Brock." When he undid another button, he noticed the flare in her eyes. "I love the way he makes you smile and laugh."

Brock interjected in a soft voice, "And I enjoy how Smith offers you a sense of security—a solid base to always come home to, just as he does me." He pushed away from the wall, squatted beside Smith. "Do you see, we are better as two? We can give you more as two and only half of what you need as one." He brushed his fingers over her cheek. "Understand?"

Once Smith finished with the rest of the buttons on her shirt, exposing her gorgeous crimson-colored bra, she leaned forward. "Yes, I do."

Smith didn't know where this relationship would lead them, but one thing was certain, he wanted to give it a chance. He had never loved a woman like he loved Kyra. His addiction to her was relentless. In the last month, he'd never been more settled, more content, and Kyra was the reason for that.

Anything that gave him that sense of comfort, he protected and kept close to him, always. Seeing that Brock and Smith didn't have that bond with a mother when they were children, it gave them a greater need for it now. They'd finally found it with Kyra.

He brushed her shirt off her shoulders, then immediately undid her bra and tossed it aside. Her puckered nipples called for his mouth. "We've never been with a woman who we've wanted to share our life." He lifted his head. "Any serious relationships have been separate and have failed. Our ménage relationships have always been casual. Though this between us isn't something we can ignore."

Smith stood, tucked a finger under her chin, and drew up her gaze to meet his head-on. "Besides, we've already been living a ménage relationship for a month, whether you want to accept that or not. We all know what we have between us is good."

Brock grasped her wrists, tugging her to stand and pulling her close to him. He reached around her back and unzipped her skirt. A second later, the garment pooled at her feet. "We've enjoyed ménage relationships for a long time now because we like it and because we *need* it. We long ago accepted that."

Smith admired the view of Kyra standing in only red high heels and a lace thong before he closed in on the other side of her. "Is it really so odd to see that eventually it would come to this?

That possibly we could find a woman who needs us both, as much as Brock and I are more comfortable together."

She shivered as Brock trailed his fingers along her spine. Her eyes fluttered closed before she visibly forced them open. "Yes, I can see that."

Brock arched a brow, firming his voice. "So, then, we're in full agreement"—he pointed between him and Smith—"we need this, but this isn't good"—he pointed to her—"unless you are with us."

Smith brushed his fingers over her jawline, adoring how she melted into his touch. He truly loved that about her. "We love you, Kyra."

Brock slid his fingers along her neck. "Let us love you, kitten."

Tears welled in her eyes, and she cupped their faces. "I know with everything that I am that I love you both too."

Smith grabbed the rectangular black velvet gift box off the fireplace mantel and offered it to her. "For you."

Kyra stared at the box, and he witnessed her warmth vanish and her eyes narrow. "My father apologized with presents. Please don't. No gifts."

"Don't be difficult, kitten." Brock trailed his finger along her neck, and Kyra's pupils dilated, and her mouth parted. "Open it."

She looked from Brock to Smith. Her lips finally pinched as she took the box, opened it, and her mouth dropped open.

Brock chuckled, as did Smith.

No diamonds.

Nothing fancy.

But shiny and silicone.

Kyra snapped her head up, laughing. "You've given me a butt plug?"

Though Smith expected her surprise over their choice of present for her, Kyra wasn't the type of woman who'd needed fancy things, and Smith respected that about her. "Ah, I'm glad you know what it is." He winked. "That would have been an interesting conversation."

Reaching forward, Smith caressed her breast and tweaked her taut nipple. Stepping in behind her, Brock kissed her neck, and she moaned. Smith allowed the play to warm her up. Though he didn't doubt if he touched between her legs, she'd be soaking wet.

He waited for her to look at him again, then took the gift box from her hand. "Turn around. Place one foot on the chaise."

She glanced at the butt plug before a heated smile rose to her face. Turning away from him to Brock, she placed her foot atop the chaise. Smith looked at Brock as he lowered down to one knee, settling in front of Kyra. Brock hooked his fingers in her thong and exposed her pussy as Smith watched Brock skim his mouth from her knee up to her slick heat.

"Bend over," Smith murmured, placing the box on the mantel. She did as he asked. He grabbed the plug out of the box, and beneath it was a small bottle of lube. He returned to her and lubed up the plug. "Have you had anal sex before?"

"Yes," she rasped.

Smith knew the moment Brock licked her clit, because Kyra quivered beneath his hand on her bottom. With the plug in one hand, he allowed Brock to have a few minutes to get Kyra focused elsewhere.

When her moans deepened, he used his free hand to pull the back of her thong aside, and he spread her cheeks. "I'm glad you're not an anal virgin." He rested the plug against her anus and gave a steady push. "You'll take this easier."

She grunted.

He chuckled. "Or maybe not."

CHAPTER TEN

Kyra quivered against Brock's mouth as she came, and he would greedily welcome her to climax against his tongue anytime she wanted. Her sweet taste drove him mad. Once all her hard quaking turned into soft whimpers, he laved her hot slit, lapping up the evidence of her orgasm.

While Smith had stolen her moans with his kisses, Brock knew Smith couldn't wait to take her either. His tight expression was proof enough, and Brock craved with an equal fervor to be deep inside Kyra...*now*.

With that intent strong on his mind, Brock gave her hard clit a light kiss before he backed away. Looking up at Kyra, he found her staring down at him with hooded lids. He tucked his fingers under the sides of her thong and removed it.

Once he stood, he nudged Kyra's thigh so she lowered her foot to the ground. Then, without pause and acting on total need, he pressed his mouth against hers. Kyra's lips were heaven. Her smell perfection. Her taste addictive.

Unfamiliar warmth filled his chest that Kyra came back to them. These past weeks had left Brock miserable. Kyra gone from their lives was nothing he could tolerate, and something he wouldn't endure.

He vowed tonight, and every night onward, that he would continue to show her why she needed to stay. He needed her, Smith needed her, and they wanted her to need them back. He poured his love for her—mixed with the heat and primal desire to keep her—into his kiss. He gripped her hair tight in his fingers, and she melted beautifully under his touch.

When she leaned farther into Brock's hold, molding herself against him, Brock heard Smith's jeans hit the floor. He also recognized the sound of a wrapper tearing, indicating Smith was applying a condom.

Kyra's warm breath through her nose became harsher against his face, and Brock smiled against her mouth, knowing that Smith stepped in closer to her. Breaking off the kiss, Brock backed away. She looked to Smith with wide, glossy eyes, her mouth puffy from Brock's kiss. Reaching down, Brock unbuttoned the top of his jeans and lowered his fly.

Smith took her hand, then lay down on the chaise.

Brock turned to the fireplace, grabbed the condom waiting for him and looked at Kyra. Smith had settled his hips off the end of the chaise, and she straddled him with her feet flat on the floor.

Dropping his hands to her hips, Smith grunted low and deep, and Kyra mirrored the sound as she took Smith's cock inside. Brock hurried to rid himself of his jeans and sheathed himself in the condom.

Listening to Smith moaning and watching Kyra ride him, Brock settled in next to her. Smith pounded Kyra from underneath, and Brock watched her eyes widen as he tweaked her nipple. Her mouth dropped open, and her cheeks flushed pink, until suddenly her eyes screwed shut. She drew in a sharp breath before her eyes snapped open and her screams echoed against the stone walls.

Brock glanced down between her and Smith, and he smiled when he spotted the glistening wetness coating Smith's pelvis. He also noted the strain along Smith's pursed lips as he clearly fought off his orgasm. Brock was equally impatient—he wanted to love her and be as close to her as he could get.

He released Kyra's nipple and grabbed his jeans off the floor. After he reached into his pocket, he took out the small plastic bag. He gathered the lube off the mantel and approached the chaise.

Smith shut his legs, bringing his knees close together and wrapping his arms around Kyra's back. As Smith pulled her down against his chest, Brock straddled Smith's legs, settling in behind her.

When Brock caressed her bottom, she raised her head from Smith's chest and tensed, no doubt aware of his intention. "Be calm, kitten," he murmured, grasping the plug. "I'll be gentle."

Brock caught sight of Smith's dark grin right before Smith grabbed Kyra's face, kissing her with intent to keep her busy. Brock slid his finger inside the loop of the butt plug, and, with care, pulled the plug out. Then he placed it in the plastic bag.

Once he dropped the bag to the floor, he turned to Kyra, seeing Smith continuing to kiss her nerves away while he no longer thrust against her. Using the opportunity of her being preoccupied, Brock opened the bottle of lube and added a generous amount to her bottom. He repeated the move on his condom-covered cock, giving them both a shiny coat of lube.

Spreading her cheeks with one hand, he gazed over her puckered hole, his dick aching to be right *there*. Christ, she had a pretty ass...and now it belonged to him. He placed the tip of his cock against her anus, and Kyra stiffened beneath him.

He reached around her hip, placing his finger against her hardened clit, then circled the nub. As he pushed against her anus, the tip of his cock dipped into her easily, which pleased him. The plug had done what he hoped. He didn't want to hurt her. He wanted this to be pleasurable. Though they would be all joined together tonight, of that he was sure.

Brock grasped her hips above Smith's hands and he gripped her tight, pushing his cock farther inside. Smith stayed motionless from underneath, allowing Brock to enter her. Sometimes he pushed. Other times he waited for her muscles to stretch and relax.

Once Brock settled halfway into her, he murmured, "Push against me, kitten."

She did as he asked, and it was all he needed to finish the job. He groaned as the rim of muscles tightened around his raging hard-on. He'd dreamed about this since the day he met her, being joined so intimately with both of them inside her.

Withdrawing to just the tip, he continued to work her, while Smith didn't move an inch. Each passing second became easier for Kyra, and soon Brock took her beautifully. Kyra relaxed in Smith's arms, and she moaned against each gentle thrust.

The sight of his cock vanishing into her ass, of her straddling Smith, and of her turning to look at him with a greedy, sensual gaze all made Brock grip her hips and thrust faster. His primal growl and response must've urged Smith on since he groaned just as deep, then thrust in short, fast movements from underneath.

"Oh, dear God," Kyra gasped.

Brock was thanking God too. Thanking him for this woman, who accepted him and Smith for what they needed. Most women wouldn't agree to such an arrangement, and it made him so damn happy that Kyra could break free from typical society to search for what satisfied her in life.

More than anything, Brock was thankful that they finally had a woman who simply made life better. Things had started out a bit rough for them as children. Now they had more than they could ever have asked for. They had a woman who loved them for them, who gave them everything they needed, and who wanted them not as a single, but as a pair.

She was *theirs*.

The wet sucking sounds of Smith drilling into her from underneath filled Brock's ears, hardening his cock further as Kyra's ass squeezed him tight. Her sweet cunt was hot to fuck. Her ass blew his mind.

While Brock thrust much slower than Smith, every thrust Smith made only tightened Kyra's ass around him. Brock clenched his jaw, continuing to shift into her and hoping to hell she reached her climax soon.

He glanced down at her ass and immediately regretted it. Seeing his cock surrounded by her tight rosette was nearly his undoing. She was beautiful, every sexy, tight inch of her. He looked at Smith, whose expression tensed, indicating his climax was close.

Intent on making them all explode into pleasure, Brock increased his speed, yet remained gentle with his strokes. Kyra gasped, and every soft thing about her became taut with tension. Her ass tightened with her climax, and her screams of pleasure washed over him in the sweetest embrace, drawing his balls up tight. Then he roared and bucked against her with such force he could feel the speed of his cum shoot from his cock. Smith's loud shouts of release echoed almost simultaneously.

The final spurt of cum escaped from him, and Brock collapsed onto Kyra's back as she rested her head against Smith's chest. He stayed that way, unable to move, unable to think, trembling in the aftereffects of his release. Kyra's tight rim of muscles continued to convulse around his spent cock, drawing out his groans long after.

After he caught his breath, he slid off her back, dropping down on the floor beside Kyra and Smith on the chaise. She looked at him with clear eyes and bright red cheeks. She was slightly breathless, but grinning in an utterly satisfied way.

He understood not only was this a happy moment for them all, he suspected Kyra had finally fulfilled her ultimate fantasy. Sure, she wanted two men and had that with them their first night together and every night thereafter, but they'd never penetrated her together.

That they had saved for the right moment and perhaps even refrained from a double penetration until they claimed her as theirs. But what they'd done tonight, no one would forget anytime soon. In fact, he hoped they'd repeat it...*often.*

He reminisced how things began for them. To him, it all seemed destined. Fate intervened with a pact between friends that allowed them to meet. Now he knew they'd never let her go; she was home to them.

Brock even thought back to the first bet Smith and he had made. If Kyra hadn't outsmarted them and kept them on their toes, he wondered if they would've chased her as they had. And with that thought in his mind, he realized something else still wasn't settled.

He trailed his fingers along her sweaty back. "You know, at some point we have to keep track of your orgasms."

Smith exchanged a long look with Brock before he smirked at Kyra. "That's right—our original bet is still outstanding." He gave her a firm look, even if Smith's eyes remained playful. "I did tell you, Kyra, we take our bets seriously."

She laughed, shaking her head. "I never said I'd be a part of the bet, I said I'd join in on the bet." She looked from Brock to Smith, and cupped their faces. "So, sorry to break it to you, but that first night we were together, you both lost." A sexy smile curved her lips. "I won."

The End

STACEY KENNEDY

Stacey Kennedy is an urban fantasy lover at heart, but she also enjoys losing herself in dark and sensual worlds. Growing up, Stacey's mind wandered the path less traveled and that path most often led to love. She has always broken rules and she continues to feed off emotion, staying true to her heart. Those traits are now the bones of her stories.

She lives in southwestern Ontario with her husband, who puts any of the heroes in her books to shame, and their two young children. If she's not on mom duty or plugging away at a new story, you'll find Stacey camping in the summer, hibernating in the winter and obsessing over *Penny Dreadful*, *Game of Thrones*, and *Sons of Anarchy*.

Find Stacey at http://www.staceykennedy.com, on Facebook at https://www.facebook.com/authorstaceykennedy, and on Twitter at https://twitter.com/@Stacey_Kennedy.

Loose Id® Titles by Stacey Kennedy

Available in digital format at http://www.loose-id.com
or your favorite online retailer

The PACT OF SEDUCTION Series

Bind Me
Beg for It
Bet on Ecstasy

In addition to digital format, the following title
is also available in print at your favorite bookseller:

Pact of Seduction
Includes *Bind Me, Beg for It,* and *Bet on Ecstasy*

CPSIA information can be obtained at www.ICGtesting.com
Printed in the USA
LVOW07s0610170316

479376LV00001B/1/P